FOUL LINE

THE BALLERS OF ROCKPORT HIGH

BOOK TWO

By

E. M. MOORE

This book is a work of fiction. Names, characters, places, and incidents are the product of the author's imagination or are used fictitiously. Any resemblance to actual events, or persons, living or dead, is coincidental.

Manufactured in the United States of America
First Edition June 2019

Cover by 2nd Life Designs

Also By E. M. Moore

The Heights Crew Series

Uppercut Princess

Arm Candy Warrior

The Ballers of Rockport High Series

Game On

Foul Line

At the Buzzer

Rockstars of Hollywood Hill

Rock On

Spring Hill Blue Series

Free Fall

Catch Me

Ravana Clan Vampires Series

Chosen By Darkness

Into the Darkness

Falling For Darkness

Surrender To Darkness

Ravana Clan Legacy Series

A New Genesis

Tracking Fate

Cursed Gift

Veiled History

Fractured Vision

Chosen Destiny

Order of the Akasha Series

Stripped (Prequel)

Summoned By Magic

Tempted By Magic

Ravished By Magic

Indulged By Magic

Enraged By Magic

Her Alien Scouts Series

Kain Encounters

Kain Seduction

Rise of the Morphlings Series

Of Blood and Twisted Roots

Safe Haven Academy Series

A Sky So Dark

A Dawn So Quiet

Chronicles of Cas Series

Reawakened

Hidden

Power

Severed

Rogue

The Adams' Witch Series

Bound In Blood

Cursed In Love

Witchy Librarian Cozy Mystery Series

Wicked Witchcraft

One Wicked Sister

Wicked Cool

Wicked Wiccans

1

Bigger. Badder. Better. That's my motto.

The wind whips my ponytail as I dribble the ball between my legs. Surprisingly enough, the fresh summer heat is held at bay for the moment. I dribble twice more, stop, then jump. Pulling up for the shot in my backyard, I imagine the scene from the Championship game, except instead of Ryan Linc running down the court to score the winning shot, it's me. I'm the one who has the ball with a couple of seconds left. I pull up way outside the three-point line, arc the ball beautifully through the air, and watch as it swishes through the net.

I win the game.

Bigger. Badder. Better. I'm taking them out. Right where it hurts.

The last book we read in English before school let out was *The Count of Monte Cristo*. That entire book is about this guy enacting revenge on the people who wronged him. I smiled my way through the pages of that book from beginning to end, word after word. I went to Alec's regular season baseball games, sat my ass just outside the Baller box without even being asked, and dreamed of camp. I made a vow to myself at the Championship game that their asses would be mine, and I meant it. I'm playing during Championships my senior year. They'll be hiking *me* on their shoulders, they'll be screaming *my* name.

I just have to figure out how to get from here to there.

Camp is my shot. They're still the Ballers there, but no one gives a shit that they're the kings of Rockport High. No one thinks we're special because we wear blue and gold. Everyone else has pride in their school too. At camp, it won't be the entire school—including the Baller Bitches—against me. The playing field is even.

It's my chance.

I grab the rebound and place it back on the basketball rack. Under the basket, my phone chirps, alerting me of an incoming text. Pulling my shirt up to wipe away the sweat dotting my forehead, I head toward it.

Smiling, I read the text Dawn just sent. **I can't believe you're spending your last night before camp with Ryan Linc instead of me. Me! Your friend! Your only friend, I might add.**

Dawn thinks I'm crazy for even wanting to go to camp this year, which makes me think she doesn't completely understand the whole basketball thing. Don't get me wrong, she's as pissed as she should be. Every time we pass the Ballers in school, she gives them shit. They give it right back to her, but Dawn isn't one to back down. If they so much as look at me, she gets in their faces. To be honest, she's the ideal best friend. Hanging out with her makes me wonder why the hell I was even friends with Tiff to begin with.

Before I can even respond, another text comes through. **Wear something slutty. Make him pay.**

I'm not sure what that would be making him pay for. Sure, he told me he actually did like me all those years ago. Even recently, I might have felt like there was something there. But the minute they turned their backs on me that day at Ryan's house, they made their feelings clear. Nothing comes between the Ballers and basketball, and nothing comes between the Ballers themselves. Dawn thinks the best way to exact my revenge is to systematically work my way back into their lives and destroy them, much like the Count did.

I tap out a response. She knows I'd much rather be spending tonight with her...or my mom, but Dad's insistent on me showing up for dinner at the Linc house. He wants me to play nice with his new family. I know he's grasping at straws since I haven't contacted him much after the night I found out he secured the WNBA scout to show up to my game. I don't want favors from him. I don't care that he was looking out for me, I thought we had the unspoken rule that he would never use his influence to get something for me. Especially something like that. It doesn't matter that I deserved the start, it's forever tainted now.

I want my actions to speak for themselves. Hence my motto: *Bigger. Badder. Better.*

I drag the basketball rack into the garage, then go out the front, letting the garage bay door close behind me. A figure at the mouth of the driveway grabs my attention, and I stop. I know who it is, I just don't know why. Ever since school ended, Hayes "Ice Man" Irving has had a love affair with my driveway. He never comes up to the house. He certainly doesn't say anything. If I happen to be leaving or coming home, he doesn't even look at me. He just stands there, his bike parked next to the big TD hanging from the stone pillar that frames the blacktop.

Oddly enough, I don't find it stalkerish at all. As far as I'm concerned, Hayes has the least to atone for. I've briefly thought about using him to get back at the other Ballers, but that's as far as my ruminations go. How to go about doing that is another step all together. Today, though, I'm curious. With as much as the Ballers talk, he must know I'm going to Ryan's house tonight. Is there a reason he's here today of all days? It's been two weeks since I've seen any Baller but him. Two weeks of bully-less bliss. No one calling me a Baller Skank. No one sneering at me in the halls. If I said I wasn't nervous about tonight, I'd be lying my ass off. Ryan Linc...in close quarters...with our parents. It's a recipe for disaster.

With a deep breath, I take off for the driveway, my heart thumping wildly in my chest. Hayes sees me coming and leans against the stone, his back hitting the big, carved TD for Timothy Dale. I asked my mom to get it removed, but she told me to think of it as saying Tessa Dale and left it at that. I think she's having a hard time believing Dad isn't coming back. The first thing I would do if I was her is get rid of his stamp on the house.

"Hey," I say, once I get to the mouth of the driveway. When I look at him, I realize I've been hoping all this time that he's an ally. That's why I haven't seen him as a stalker or asked him to leave because he wasn't wanted. No, I've *liked* him here, which sends a solid brick of cement to the bottom of my stomach. It's not supposed to be like this.

He looks over at me slowly, taking in my cropped tank top and basketball shorts that I roll at the waist. He nods, then stares across the street to the valley below. The roads up here switchback up the mountain, so all we can see for miles and miles is the tops of other people's houses that level out into the small town of Rockport.

I lean against the stone pillar on the other side of the driveway, but angle toward him. His chest rises and lowers evenly under a Nike shirt. He's wearing a pair of plain black athletic shorts, basketball sneakers and cropped socks. He's a poster child for high school jocks. He's got the long legs, the height, and the looks. Even though he towers over most people, he's not clumsy or all limbs either. He's a force. The fact that he barely talks doesn't take away from his presence. When Hayes is around, you know it.

I bite my lip. I don't know what I expected to happen after I tried to talk to him, but words never come easily for Hayes. Was it Sloan who told me

Hayes had a thing for me? How could anyone tell? He's impenetrable, like a towering stone fortress. Ice Man is an apt nickname for him. "You've been here a lot," I say, watching my words slide over him. Despite that I know he's heard me, he doesn't react. I tilt my head back against the stone and let my thoughts spill out like Hayes cares. "I'm going to Ryan's tonight. My dad wants to have this stupid dinner with him and his mom before camp. Almost like a farewell dinner, I guess. Apparently, it was Ryan's mother's idea. I'm not sure why I'm being dragged into it. I'll see my dad while at camp like usual. He was pretty insistent on me coming though."

Not expecting him to respond, I start as his deep voice coaxes out of him. "You think it's because things are getting serious between them?"

Lowering my gaze, I catch him side-eyeing me, so I look away, back up to the cloudless sky. I've thought about this a lot. One of the reasons I'm nervous about the dinner is that I hope they don't make this big proclamation of love for one another while I'm there. I hope it's just that Dad feels guilty we haven't seen each other in a while. "I don't know," I tell Hayes honestly. "Is it wrong to hope they're not?"

"No," he says immediately.

I glance back over at him again. He's still not

looking at me. The wind is catching his dirty blond hair the color of caramel and tracking it over his forehead. My lips buzz with the need to ask him what he's doing out here, what he's been doing out here since school ended, but something holds me back. Maybe I just like the fact that I can make up my own reasons in my head. I'm going with the fact that he feels like he's helping. Maybe he doesn't want me to be alone. Maybe he feels better being close to me. I push away the idea that the Ballers are asking him to do this. It's a valid reason for him being here, but I just don't think so. I'm going to see them all tomorrow. I haven't had any Warrior basketball responsibilities since school ended. There's no reason for him to be standing out here unless he wants to be.

And I don't know how to feel about him wanting to be.

"I'm going to be leaving soon," I tell him.

"I know." His gaze tracks over the landscape before us like he's perfectly content.

"Are you going to still be here?"

He shakes his head.

"But I'll see you tomorrow?"

He turns toward me then, his lips a thin line, his gorgeous blue eyes zeroing in on me. "Camp," he says. His eyes are troubled, a swirling myriad of blue. "I don't think Lake's done with you. You should be careful."

The mention of that fucker's name makes me want to slam my fist into the stone pillar at my back. He ruined *everything* for me.

I take a deep breath instead. It's easy for me to say he ruined everything for me, but I also know that the rest of the Ballers need to take responsibility for their actions too. But fucking Lake. I was—and am—still willing to gleefully ignore him for the rest of my life. He didn't need to intercede. He didn't need to pull an ultimatum on his friends like that. "I'm not scared of Lake O'Brien," I tell Hayes through clenched teeth.

He nods like he expected me to say as much. "River's going to be there, too. Lake and River together are..."

I swallow, remembering their hands on me, holding me down. Sure, it wasn't as if they were about to sexually assault me or anything, but they held me against my will. They overpowered me, never reacting to my struggle against them.

Lake and River together are evil.

Hayes doesn't even need to finish his sentence. I get it. I knew this was coming ever since my father sent me the camp list a couple of weeks after the state playoffs. I don't know how I even forgot that Landon

Meyer, the other shooting guard that's been coming to camp with us the last several years, graduated. River is his replacement.

"Well, I'm not scared of River either." I've never seen the kid play, but he can't be better than Lake, and I'm going to make it my mission to make sure everyone at camp knows who the top shooting guard is. By the time we leave, I'll be back on top, hopefully with the backing of the rest of the Ballers, one way or another.

"I just want you to watch out for yourself."

His words spike goosebumps over my arms. I rub at them absentmindedly, watching Hayes's profile. That's why he's here, isn't it? He's protecting me. He has to be.

2

Just as Hayes said, he's not there when I drive away from the house a little while later. His bike is gone, and I don't see any sign of him on my trek down the mountain. It's such a crazy road to bike up and down that I wish I could tell him he didn't have to. If he is checking on me like I suspect, it's nice but unnecessary. I'm not glass. I won't break. If I were, I'd already have broken by now.

By the time I get down into the town, my stomach is twisted into knots that make me queasy. I haven't had very good luck in Ryan's house. First, finding out that my dad was fucking his mother. Then, it was getting my heart crushed, splintered into tiny pieces. Hopefully this time, there aren't any more secrets or asshole boys named Lake around. I don't know if I'll be able to hold back my nut kick reflex around the asshole if he is there. I've only been dreaming about it for months.

When I pull up to the house, I take a deep breath and just stare at the unassuming house. Dad's huge SUV is in the driveway just outside the closed one-door garage. Somewhere inside those walls sits Ryan Linc. I wonder if he's been thinking about this moment for as long as I have or if he even thinks about me at all. After all, he did warn me. He told me if my involvement with the Ballers messed with basketball, it'd be over. He kept true to that promise, although I disagree with him. It wasn't messing with basketball; it was messing with Lake.

I sigh. "This fucking sucks," but I shove the door open and get out anyway. I plaster a smile on my face and walk right up to the door without hesitating. If I'm going to live my new motto, there's no room for second guessing.

After I knock, it only takes a minute for someone to open the door. My smile turns genuine when I see it's my dad, halfway relieved that it isn't Ryan standing framed in the doorway. This means I get to steel myself a few moments longer before I see the guy who's completely turned my life upside down several times. If I close my eyes, I can still feel the hot sting of my cheeks when he told everyone at camp that he didn't like me, that it was all just a show. That transforms into the shower water dripping off me when he rushed into the girls' locker room, his fists bleeding because he'd punched Chase. The shivers chasing up and down my arm as he made his declaration that he'd been lying before, that I was theirs and only theirs now. My body turns to ice when I remember the look in his eyes after he told me to get out of his house. He'd sided with Lake.

"Tess!" my dad says. He's got a happy smile on his face as he pushes the screen door open. "You're here."

He steps back, and I move forward. He pulls me into a hug right there in the doorway, then keeps his hand around my back as he leads me right into the living room. This is not the same living room that I ran away from a few months ago. The carpet is new. There's a fresh coat of muted paint on the walls and a huge sectional now taking up the living room with a large—also new—TV as the centerpiece of the room.

My mind fixates on all this in moments, but then I hear Ryan's mom as she comes out from the kitchen. "Tessa, it's so nice to see you."

It kills me that she's pretty. She's not prettier than my own mother, but she's good looking in a different way. I can see Ryan in her features, but her face is much less angular than his. Hers is soft while he got all the hard planes. "Thank you for inviting me. It's nice to see you, too."

She leans down to hug me. Again, I don't hesitate. Her grip is strong and supportive. It feels like she wants to hug me, and I'll try. If this is going to be my dad's new partner, I will try, but right now, it's not about that. This is about me pretending I'm fine. No, I'm not wearing something slutty like Dawn suggested, but I'm on top of the world. At least, that's the vibe I'm going to give off in front of everyone. Success is the best revenge and all that.

"It looks really nice in here, Mrs. Linc," I tell her. I have to practically bite my tongue off in order to keep from saying something about my dad probably paying for all this, but regardless, I sound genuine.

"Thank you. We did a little refreshing." She looks around the room, a smile on her face, but then her hands smooth down the apron she has on. "I just have a few little things to get done. Take a seat. Enjoy yourself. Make yourself at home."

I wince. This will *never* be my home. I don't care if my dad moves in here permanently with Ryan's mom and Ryan ends up being my stepbrother, this will never be anything but the place where my dad lives. Instead of saying all that, I screw my face back into a smile. "Thank you."

Dad heads over to the couch, which is probably exactly where he was when I knocked on the door. Track and field is playing on the TV, so I sit down opposite him and watch. Despite the fact that we're not at our house, this feels familiar. Dad and I watching TV, discussing fitness levels and training regimens. Dad whistles. "Tess, have you seen this guy run yet? He is fast." He draws the word out, his stare fixated on the TV.

I glance that way, watch as a runner stretches out his calves before settling into the blocks. He's a sprinter. The commentator basically reiterates everything my dad just said. "Olympic hopeful?" I ask.

"You bet. They're comparing him to Usain Bolt."

I make my own noise of appreciation. "Good for him."

My dad inches forward on the couch, the remote in one hand, and leans toward the TV screen. The gun goes off, and the runners jump out of the blocks. They lean forward at first, then one after the other, they move into a straight up and down gait as they sprint toward the finish line. It's already apparent that the guy they all predicted to win is going to do so by a long-shot. It is impressive. *He's* impressive.

I'm blown away by athletes time and time again. The thing is, I know it takes a hell of a lot of work to get this far. People seem to think athletes like this guy just get up one day and they're suddenly running as fast as Usain Bolt. Wrong. It takes fitness. It takes dedication. This guy literally eats and breathes running. If he didn't, they'd never be saying these things to him.

"Alright," my dad says as the guy crosses the finish line first. The runner holds his hands in the air while he slows down on his own time, the victory of the race clear on his face.

I turn toward my dad. "I got my fifty-yard time down." This was something him and I have been working on for a while.

He beams at me. "That's great, Pumpkin. You practicing at the track?"

I nod, a little taken aback that he seems surprised I'm still working out at the track. Just because he left didn't mean I stopped our routine. "Thought I'd see you out there sometime, but I guess you're getting a little too old for that."

He laughs. "I'll meet you out there, Miss Thing. It'll have to be after camp, but I've got to see this new time."

I keep smiling for him, but inside, my heart is breaking a little. We used to go to the track on our own.

It was our schedule. All that is gone since he moved out. I don't even know if he's even been playing ball anymore, to be honest. I have to think he is. It's not like Timothy Dale to give up shooting baskets, even if it's for fun. Basketball is his first love.

"Tim," Ryan's mom calls out from the kitchen.

His head snaps up. "Yeah?"

"Can I get your help setting the table? And Tessa, would you mind getting Ryan?"

My heart freefalls into my stomach. My dad glances over at me, his expression intense as he studies me. I get right to my feet even though they wobble a little. "Of course. Where is he?"

My dad stands up much slower. He points down the only hallway in the house. "First door on the left." He's scrutinizing me now. I have no doubt I can convince my father that I'm okay. He doesn't even know who I am anymore. He was there for me through the basketball season. We exchanged words about the WNBA scout, about the panty crown, about riding the bench, but basketball is the only way my father knows how to be a father. He doesn't know how to ask me if seeing Ryan Linc right now is going to fuck me up. He doesn't know how to make sure I can handle seeing the guy who put the final nail in my coffin a few months ago. No Ballers. No basketball. No life.

It's okay that he doesn't know because I won't let the truth show anyway.

My heart thumps in my chest. I follow the new carpet right into the hallway, past the kitchen, and to the very first door. It's so dark in the hallway, I can only make out a few other doors besides Ryan's. He has a Lakers poster covering most of it, the star player dunking the ball. I met the guy once at one of Dad's basketball functions. He was kind of a douche. But everyone has a bad day now and then, so it's impossible to tell if he really is a douche or if he was just having one of those days. It goes to show you that one moment can solidify people's opinions of you.

The door is slightly ajar, so I knock a couple times and then push it open like I belong there. Ryan immediately looks up, his eyes widening. He has a pair of Beats on, huge blue ones that cover his ears. His gaze narrows as he pulls them down. I smile. "Hey. Your mom wanted me to come get you for dinner."

"How long have you been here?"

I shrug, the pulse at my wrist feathering. I'm putting on a brave face but seeing Ryan like this is affecting me. "Not long. Watched a little TV with my dad."

He sits up and swings his feet to the floor. He pulls the Beats all the way off and sets them on his nightstand. The new carpet is in here, too. While he doesn't say anything, I look around. Even though I've been in Ryan's house three times now, I've never been anywhere except for the kitchen and the dining room/living room. There's more basketball memorabilia in here, trophies and awards. There's even a picture of all five Ballers tucked into the mirror above his dresser.

This makes my false bravado snag a little. I hadn't prepared myself to see Alec and Sloan today, even if only in a picture. From the looks of it, it can't be that old. In fact, I think it's from this year's championship game.

I make myself look away and right into Ryan's gray eyes. He's staring at me, his eyes traveling down the length of my body. Suddenly, I wish I had worn something more than just a plain tank top and shorts. Maybe a push-up bra with a shirt that showed my cleavage. *Why, though? Do I* want *to tempt him?*

I think on that for a second as he continues his perusal. I don't think I want to tempt him. I just want to know if he's tempted. His face is so stoic, it's hard to get a read on him. The moment in the shower returns. Me, freaking naked. Him, dripping blood down his knuckles from attacking Chase for me. I shouldn't say for me. It wasn't for me. They did it for themselves.

They did it because they wanted complete control over me, and they got it.

Nonchalantly, I lean against his door frame and push the other thoughts aside. "You ready for camp?" I noticed an open gym bag in the corner when I checked his room out earlier. Since camp is the reason why we're all here, I might as well bring it up now.

His eyes flare with something I can't quite put my finger on before he turns away, his gaze stopping on the same bag. "Yep. Just need to throw the last-minute things in tomorrow morning."

I open my mouth to say something else, but Ryan's mom calls out, "Hey, you two. Dinner's on the table." Both he and I stare at one another again. I don't like the sound of 'hey, you two'. I have no idea why Ryan's face suddenly turned pissy, but maybe that's it for him as well.

He stands from the bed, and I quickly step out of his room and into the hall. Once I'm out of his line of sight, I feel like I can actually breathe. It feels as if I faced down a dragon and got to see the other side. I'm lucky.

Camp won't be so bad now. I saw Ryan and the world didn't implode, so I can see the rest of them tomorrow morning. I can go through camp with them again just like I've been doing since I was in middle school. The position I'm in right now isn't new to me. The Ballers never liked me, so this is already ventured territory. No big deal.

The big deal only comes when I sit across from Ryan at the dinner table. It comes when everything seems so normal and the conversation flows so easily that I almost forget that I'm just pretending, and that for all I know, he is too.

We don't want you, he'd said. I swallow hard as the swarm of hurt hits me in the chest once again.

I'm pretty sure that means he also doesn't want me eating dinner with him and his mom, which only makes me try harder. I ask so many questions about the Linc's and about Ryan when he was little, that when I finally look back over at Ryan at the end of dinner, he's scowling and miserable, just the way I want him.

I give him a too innocent, too wide smile. *Screw you, Ryan,* I think. Then, I focus back on his mom for the rest of the night.

All in all, this first taste of what it will be like gives me the strength I need to get through tomorrow when it won't be just one Baller I have to deal with, it'll be all of them. They won't get the better of me again. That much I can promise.

3

I drag my last bag down to the foyer, then turn toward the kitchen. I can already smell the breakfast my mom made for me. She's yawning, one hand over her mouth, the other clutching a spatula. When she sees me, she shakes her head until the yawn ends and then smiles over at me.

"I told you you didn't have to wake up with me," I chastise. Don't get me wrong, I'm thrilled she did, especially since I feel like I abandoned her last night in favor of Dad. Hell, I'm abandoning her for weeks and probably at the time when she needs me the most.

She gives me a look but accepts my hug when I wrap my arms tight around her. "Come on, Tess. You know I always see you two—" She clears her throat and rubs my shoulder. "You know I always see you off the morning of camp."

Pulling away from her, I take a seat at the breakfast nook and pretend I didn't hear her slip about adding Dad into the equation. This year, I'm driving to camp by myself. I'm excited about having my car there since those of us who are going into our senior years are allowed to leave camp on the weekends as long as we have parental permission. All the other years, I didn't have my car because I rode up with Dad, and I was also too scared to sneak out with the rest of the guys, being Dale's daughter and all.

She finishes making the eggs and scrapes them into a serving dish before putting them on the table. There's already a plate in front of me along with a dish of bacon, so I help myself to it all. Camp food isn't bad, but it's not homemade either.

Mom sits down opposite me in the circular seating area and shovels a small handful of eggs on her plate and then grabs two slices of bacon. We eat in silence until she places her fork down on the table and wipes her face with a napkin. "I want you to be careful at camp this year, Tessa."

I take a drink of the orange juice she had waiting for me, swallowing it down forcefully like there's a blockage in my throat. "I will, Mom."

"I mean it," she says. "I don't like all this going on. This playing on the boys' team has affected you and not for the better. Those boys..." She trails off. I have a suspicion she knows more than she's letting on, or maybe it's just a gut feeling she has about the boys. She asked me about the panties that were thrown onto the court last year. She knows they were actually mine, and even though I told her it was none of the guys' fault, she doesn't believe me. Even if I had told her Lake was most certainly behind it all, there's nothing she could have done. It would have just caused more trouble for me. Another excuse people could use for girls not being allowed to play on the guys' team.

"Nothing like that is going to happen," I promise her. There will be no other girls around. Just me, the Ballers, and a handful of other guys who are into basketball just as much as we are. We don't have time for petty Baller Bitch shit at camp. No keyed cars, no jeering. Ryan, Sloan, Alec, Hayes, and Lake aren't the Rock Ballers of Rockport High at Camp Holly. Everyone there is as good as they are. Well, almost. They are pretty damn good.

She reaches over the table and covers my hand with hers. I push my plate away and finally give her my full attention. She starts off with a small smile. "I know you want this so badly. I can see it in your eyes. I just don't know if it's worth suffering through all this."

"I'm not suffering through anything, Mom," I try to tell her.

She isn't buying it. She pierces me with another look. "You mean that wasn't you crying your eyes out the night Rockport won the state championship game?"

My jaw snaps shut. "I just really wanted to play," I tell her. It's the truth. Despair, disappointment, all those feelings come rushing back to me. I deserved to play.

She pulls away, crossing her arms over her chest. She's got her serious face on, which makes me squirm. "I've been thinking." She breathes out. "I'm fine with you going to camp since your father will be there and you've been going there for a few years now, but while you're gone, I'm going to look into enrolling you into Springs for your senior year."

I gasp. "Mom." *This can't be happening. I don't want to go to Springs.*

"They have a girls' basketball team."

My eyes practically bug out of my head. "They're not good."

She holds her hand up. "They have a girls' basketball team that you could come right onto the team and be their best player. You can still get colleges to notice you even if you're not playing at Rockport. There's other ways to go about what you're doing."

My fingers grip the side of the table as anger sweeps through me. "Like getting a scout to come to my game?"

"You know I had nothing to do with that," she says. "But I understand why your father did it. Did you think we liked hearing what those awful girls had to say to you the whole season? I don't know how you could bear it, Tess. It's not right. At Springs—."

"It's just a game," I tell her, even though I know it's not. I know Lake's minions are terrible human beings. They wanted to hurt me. They came to every game to make sure everyone else knew what they thought of me, and I only had one chance to prove them wrong. Which I did, until they brought out the panty crown.

We never heard from the scout again, by the way. I guess my father's connections only go so far anyway.

I grind my teeth together. There's no way in hell I'm going to Springs next year. It's further away, their basketball team sucks, and besides, none of that matters because the Ballers aren't at Springs, they're at Rockport. This has become just as much about proving myself to them than it has trying to make a name for myself. I just need them to see.

Mom stands, taking her dishes with her. "We don't have to make a decision right now, but I am getting the information from them, Tess. I'll talk to the coach; I'll see what she can do for you. I'm sure they'll be thrilled to find out you're even considering going to their school. Your talent was wasted at Rockport last year."

"I'm not con—"

Mom drops her dishes into the sink. They clatter, silencing my refusal to even consider what she's offering. "I thought this was about playing basketball. You didn't even play basketball this season, Tess. *You didn't play.*"

My jaw snaps shut. I stare at my mom, her hands shaking as she holds onto the edge of the counter. I try to soften toward her reaction of all this. I know she's just worried for me, but her words cut deep. In a way, she's right. If this was just about playing basketball for the love of basketball, I'd go play on any team. I would have gone to Springs to begin with just so I could play. Girls' team, boys' team, whatever. It wouldn't matter. But it's not about that. It's about playing for a *good* team. It's about playing for *their* team. Am I wrong to think that I have to prove myself more than others because I'm a girl?

Sadly, I don't think I am.

I stand, walk over to her, and put my arm around her for the second time this morning. "I know it was hard for you to watch all that last year. Trust me, it was hard for me too. But it didn't change anything, and it won't change anything."

Mom blinks. The corners of her eyes are glassy with unshed tears. "Regardless, I'm talking to Springs while you're gone." She turns away, so I just hug her tighter. My mom's stubborn. Talking to her now won't solve anything. We'll just keep going around and around in circles, saying the same things. I just have to prove to her that next year at Rockport will be different. To do that, I have to get the Ballers on my side—and the only way to do that is to take Lake down. He's the only thing standing between me and them. Between me and the best senior year ever. I don't know how I can ever trust them in my personal life again, but I don't need that to be their teammate and nothing else.

I give Mom a kiss on the cheek. "I'll see you in a few weeks."

"Six," she says, her voice not only fired up, but sad now, too.

"I'll have my cell phone. We can video chat." It's been like this every year. Dad and I go off and leave her for most of the summer. Before, she'd take the opportunity to go on a vacation with some of her girlfriends, but she's not in the best place right now. I offer it to her anyway, hoping to change her mind. "Why don't you take off for a little while, Mom? Go on a cruise or a health retreat or something."

She shrugs. "I've thought about it."

I nudge her. "Think harder. I'm sure you can get a few of the girls to go with you." I step away from her and grab an apple from the fruit bowl on the counter and bite into it. "Just don't go anywhere I want to go."

"Just for that, I'm going to go everywhere you want to go."

My mouth drops in mock horror. In all honesty, I'd love for her to take a trip for herself...mainly because I'd rather her do that instead of trying to plan my transfer to Springs next year because it's not happening. "You wouldn't."

She smiles. "Have fun at camp, Tess." Her demeanor changes. "I'm a phone call away, and your dad's right there. I promise you he'll be there for you. All you have to do is say the word."

"I know, Mom." After I give her a small wave, I kiss her on the cheek and then grab my bag before heading out the door. I throw my bag into the trunk along with another one and then go around the side of the car. The drive to camp is a couple of hours long. The camp itself is situated on a really beautiful piece of land, right next to a lake that even has a manmade sandy beach along with kayaks and canoes and a platform to swim and dive off of. It's one of my favorite places in the whole world.

My phone pings in my pocket. Expecting a text from Dawn, I bring it out so I can answer before I start the long drive. It's not from Dawn though. It's a text from Ryan Linc. *The hell?* I click on it and then have to suppress a smile. The freaking balls on this guy. What the actual fuck? **Sloan's Jeep won't start. We need a ride.**

I slide into the front seat, a smile on my face as I start the car. With the phone still in my hand, it pings again. **Your dad already left.**

I know he already left. He always leaves early because he has a ton of shit to do before the rest of us get there. I tinker with the idea of not messaging him back, just letting him wait there in oblivion, wondering if I'm going to come to their rescue or not. I'm fucking not, by the way.

Getting comfortable in the seat, I think about the perfect response. I could tell him I've already left too, but I don't want it to go down like that. I want him to know I'm telling him no. Act like a dick, get the repercussions of a dick. I type out the short message, smiling the whole time. Do they really think I'll help them? Do they really think I'd put Lake anywhere near my fucking car? Fuck them. **Um, no.**

Then, I put my phone on silent and enjoy the ride all the way to Camp Holly...by myself.

4

I step out of the car onto the stone parking lot at Camp Holly and breathe in deep. The air always seems fresher out here in the middle of the vast forest and uninterrupted sunshine. It sets me at ease, even knowing what's to come.

Past the main building and the section of cabins closest to me, I see glimpses of the glistening lake water below. The sun plays across the surface until it's shining like diamonds, a myriad of sparks in the beautiful landscape before me. Orange buoys connected with rope bob in and out of the water, signifying the only swimming area. To my left is the outdoor basketball courts. They've always been here, but my dad also put some money into the camp, building an indoor court as well as a weight room for our use while we're here. That building is further into the woods, only accessible by a trail lined with woodchips.

Coming to camp after the incident with Ryan used to make me uneasy. Now, though, there aren't as many players here that remember that year. We're the seniors, so all the upperclassmen who teased me unmercifully about it are away at college, and therefore, ineligible to attend camp. Timothy Dale Camp is strictly for high school and younger kids only. Also, invitation only. The best three players for each position in the whole state are invited. For shooting guards this year, it's me, Lake, and River. I have no doubt River is good. My dad scouts the players himself, except for me. For me, he has other unbiased parties come in to help. As soon as I'm off to college next year, he won't need to justify his choices, which will probably be a relief to him.

Leaving my bags in the trunk, I head toward the main building to sign in. There, I'll be given my cabin assignment and a schedule for the whole six weeks of camp. My dad works on camp specifics all year. What coaches he's going to bring in, what kids, and what he'll focus on while we're here. Whatever else he is, he's dedicated to making youths better at basketball. He wants to give those who were like him at this age a chance—a shot at making it big. I admire him for that.

The door to the biggest log cabin at the camp still opens with a creak. Despite the skylights and the many windows in this section of the main building, it always seems so dark in here with all the wood interior. Up ahead, my dad is standing with another gentleman. When I get closer, my dad glimpses me out of the corner of his eyes. "Pumpkin," he says, all smiles. Camp is a year's worth of work all condensed into six weeks. He's either stressed or enjoying the culmination of all his efforts. Right now, it looks like everything is going smoothly.

"Hey, Dad," I smile.

"I got you all signed in already." He heads over to the table, picks up a set of keys, and then throws them to me. "You're in Whispering Winds again."

I chuckle at that. There are perks to being my father's daughter. I get the cabin closest to the water. If questioned, my dad says it's because the cabin is a little further away from the others in our section. You know, on account of needing privacy because I'm a girl at a mainly all-boy camp, but really, I think he knows how much I enjoy being on the water.

He looks behind me. "Where's Ryan?"

I raise my eyebrows. "What do you mean?"

"He told me Sloan's Jeep wouldn't start, so I told him to call you."

I keep my voice neutral. "Oh, that," I say. "You know how small my car is. I'd never fit everyone in there with their bags and everything." I smile to take the edge off. I don't think he trusts the rest of the Ballers as much as he used to after the incident with the panties, but he does trust Ryan. He's dating his mother, after all. I don't know the extent of the conversation they had after that game, but whatever came out of it, Dad still loves Linc.

"Oh." He looks a little taken aback after that. "Alright." He reaches into his pocket, takes out his cell phone to look at the screen, then places it back where it was.

The door squeaks behind us again. Dad looks over my head, and I turn around.

Alec Christopoulos walks in. I clench my hands together, the set of keys to my cabin digging into my palm. Sometimes I just look at him and ask myself why I let him touch me so intimately. Then again, there's a good reason for that. I *liked* him. I didn't know he was going to turn on me and be a douche. So, then I just wonder how he can even stand himself after what he's done. Doing that with me and then pretending as if it didn't matter. It mattered to him. I know it did.

When he sees me, he stops. A voice whines behind him. "Alec." I look down at his feet and notice his little sister Roberta has run into the backs of his legs. "Ugh." She picks up the pillow she had in her hands that fell to the ground and then comes around the side of him. When she doesn't have the large obstruction of her brother's frame in front of her, she sees me and then she doesn't even care about the pillow anymore. She drops it to the ground and comes running forward. "Tessa!" She wraps her little arms around my legs, and I bend over to pat her back. When she pulls away, she says, "Alec's been working on free throws with me. I'm getting better. I want to show you. I keep asking him to invite you over, but he tells me you're too busy. What are you doing all the time that you're so busy?"

"Roberta," Alec says, a warning to his tone.

Just then, his mom walks in behind him. She searches the area and when she sees Roberta with me, she relaxes. "Jeez. I don't remember you being that fast, Alec. Your sister's going to give me a heart attack before I turn forty."

I crouch down next to Roberta. "That's great. I'm happy to hear that." I look past Roberta to Alec who's looking on in interest at our exchange. "And I think what your brother means is that he's too busy to invite me over..." *Because he's an asshole.* Of course, I leave that part out.

"Yeah, baseball takes a lot out of him. He talks

about it constantly. But he did specifically say that you're too busy."

I tug on her hair. "Why don't you just call me next time you want me to come over? I'll tell you if I'm too busy or not."

She beams. "Really? Okay."

I look up. Alec's walking to the folding table now. He looks at me from the corner of his eye. There's no doubt in my mind he heard everything I just said. He keeps his face neutral though.

His mom's right beside him, making small talk with my dad and signing papers. Roberta is chirping in my ear, but it's hard for me to stop looking at Alec. With his build and looks, it's difficult not to notice him or have my gaze drawn his way. The guy is perpetually in top shape because there's only a few weeks out of the year he's not playing sports or training for sports.

Roberta tugs on my jeans. "Why does my brother get mad at me when I talk about you?"

I look back down at her. "You'll have to ask him that."

"I have. He just yells at me more."

I shrug, feeling sad that she's caught in the crossfire. I lean closer to her like I'm telling her a secret. "Boys are dumb, Roberta."

She seems to take that into serious consideration.

She looks away, her eyes intent, and then she nods once, finally accepting the answer I've given her.

When I stand, Alec is staring at the both of us. There's something in his green eyes, but it's nothing for me to dwell on. All I have to do is be his teammate. Though, the harder he stares, I can't keep my body from blushing. Even with his mother and his sister here, I remember how my body responded to his confident, expert fingers. Just thinking about it makes my throat go dry.

As I make that observation, Alec turns to my dad. "Ryan, Sloan, and Hayes are going to be late. They had to make other arrangements."

Inwardly, I laugh. Outwardly, I place a pout over my lips. "That's too bad. Hopefully there's nothing serious wrong with the Jeep."

Alec's gaze cuts to mine. My frown turns into a smile. The nerve of them to even ask me to help them out. Though, I do feel badly about leaving Hayes out to dry. It's irrational, but I just keep picturing his bike parked outside my house. If he doesn't find a ride with Ryan and Sloan, how the hell is he even going to get here?

Again, the rational part of my brain jumps in. *Not your problem.* And you know what? That little voice is right. They wouldn't think twice about me if the reverse had happened. They'd laugh their way to fucking camp, and that's all I need to know.

The door squeaks again, and Lake and River O'Brien walk in with their father. I've met him a handful of times and he's just as assholish as they are. I take that as my cue to leave so I can set up my cabin for the next six weeks.

"And here's all my shooting guards," Dad announces as we pass one another.

I wave to him over my head, not bothering to even look at the O'Briens as they approach my father. "See you later, Dad."

Roberta and Alec's mom follow me out of the main building. The three of us make the trek back to the parking lot where I notice they're parked right next to me. I pull my bag out from the car as Roberta rattles along next to me. She's telling me all about how she fixed her free throws, then tells me Alec is going to work with her on her dribbling next. "Your brother's so nice," I tell her, and I can even almost get it out without feeling like I'm choking on the words. For everything else Alec is, he is a really good brother.

I drop the bag next to my feet. Alec's mom looks at it then back toward the path. "Alec," she calls out. "Why don't you help Tessa with her bags?"

"Oh no," I tell her, immediately hiking the first one

up on my shoulder. "I'm absolutely fine. I'm sure Alec has his own stuff to carry."

Alec comes around the side of the car by himself. His dark hair is a little shorter than it was during the school year. The cropped length makes his green eyes pop even more. "I can help."

I shake my head. "My cabin isn't anywhere near yours. Trust me. I got it."

Alec's mom looks between him and me. I remember the looks she used to give me after the games when the Baller Bitches made their presence known. I'd always see her talk to Alec afterward, but it doesn't matter. I'm not the Christopoulos's charity case. "Alec," she says.

Alec sighs. He turns toward me, his lips thin. "Listen, I have to help you, or my mom won't stop bugging me about it, okay?"

My jaw tightens, but his mom smiles from ear-to-ear. "That's my boy."

I'm still thinking up excuses to carry my bags myself when a voice says, "Tessa?"

I turn at the sound. It isn't a voice I thought I'd be hearing at camp. My mouth drops when I find a lacrosse clad Chase Fisher behind me. His lacrosse stick lowers as he approaches our group with a bunch of guys who are dressed just like him.

"It is you," he says.

"Hey," I finally say, feeling a rush of awkwardness swim through me when we just stand there. We're not on hugging terms, we're barely even on speaking terms. He's asked me out. I've told him no. Or, should I say the Ballers told him no for me? He's got a lot of balls approaching me with Alec in full view. If I were him, I'd be afraid the Ballers would follow through on another show of dominance to keep him away from me. Then again, he's got himself a few friends with him now. He's probably not afraid at all. "What are you doing here?"

He twirls the stick in his grip. "The guys on my lacrosse team and I decided to have a little guys' trip, sports related, obviously."

"Oh, cool. Here?"

He nods. "We rented out the cabins over there." He points toward the path through the woods that leads to another section of cabins. "But the field is over here." He looks me up and down and then at the bag by my feet. "Wait, are you staying here, too?"

"Yeah, it's my dad's basketball camp. We're here for six weeks."

Chase finally looks over. When he sees Alec, his face turns red and his gaze narrows. "I guess I know why these cabins were unavailable now."

"Wait," one of the guys he's with says. "Is this Tessa Dale?"

My face flames. I'm in that weird position where I want people to know who I am, but at the same time, when it happens, I get super nervous. Chase confirms that it is, in fact, me.

Chase introduces his teammates after that, and all I can think is what are the odds that he'd be here now?

"This is cool," one of his teammates says. I can see now that they're all wearing practice jerseys with the name Huntington College in type across their chests. And then I piece together even further that Huntington is the closest town to Holly Lake. It's not that far of a stretch to think that Chase and his lacrosse buddies would be here. It's just a coincidence that they would be here at the same time as us. "Maybe we'll get to hang out," the guy says.

"Yeah, maybe," I say, not wanting to commit to anything. I have goals for this camp, and I can't lose focus.

I bend over to pick up my bag, but Chase moves forward to intercept me. "Let me get that."

Alec, who's been quietly observing the whole time, steps close to me. "Actually, I'm helping Tessa." The way he stands, it's almost possessive. He's angled toward me and a little in front of me to stop Chase from moving forward any more.

I move away and pull my own bag up on my shoulder. "And I told you I could get it."

A few of Chase's teammates' eyes round a little. So maybe my voice came out a little more sharply than I meant it to, but seriously, what did Alec expect to happen? He deserted me. I'm not going to play nice after that. Basketball is one thing, but friends, or more, he can kiss my ass.

"Well, I've got your pillow," Roberta says. She pulls it out of my trunk before I can tell her not to. Then, she's clutching it so tightly there's really no room for me to say anything. Her demeanor, too, brooks no arguments.

A few of the guys laugh. "Is this your sister?"

"No," Alec says. "That's my sister."

Chase comes around. He slides his hand up the strap on my bag and pulls it gently away from me. "Come on, Dale. What kind of a gentleman would I be if I didn't help you with your bags?"

I peek back at Alec. His face is red and fuming.

I let Chase take the strap from me. Another one of his teammates grabs the other bag from my trunk until I just have a small canvas bag with some books, sunscreen, and a couple snack packs inside.

We're just about to turn and head toward my cabin when a car pulls into the parking lot. It looks oddly familiar, but it isn't until it passes us and Coach Bradley waves from the driver's side window that I realize why it looks familiar. He parks the car and Ryan, Sloan, and Hayes step out.

Hayes shuts the door behind him, then glares at me. He assesses the situation, taking in the lacrosse guys surrounding us. He eyes them coolly, spending a particularly long time on Chase. I know he punched Chase, too. I don't know why. I actually think they might get along if it weren't...well, if it weren't for me, apparently.

"They rode with Coach?" I ask to no one in particular.

"They didn't really have a choice," Alec bites out.

I turn to look at him. "No, I guess they didn't." Then, I spin toward my cabin with the lacrosse team—and Alec's sister—in tow.

5

I spend the rest of the afternoon getting my cabin ready. The lacrosse guys didn't stay long, which I was grateful for. I don't need another spectacle between Chase and the Ballers. One was plenty. Roberta, too, left when her mother came to retrieve her without Alec. Once I was left to myself, I rearranged the small cabin, put my sheets on the bed, and texted my mom to tell her I was safe. I'd hoped to finish with enough time to take my first swim in the lake this year, but instead, I worked right up until dinner.

With my hands on my hips, I survey the small, one-room cabin to see if anything else needs to be done. A knock sounds on the door behind me, so I turn to get it, expecting my dad. It's not him coming to remind me about dinner, though, it's Hayes. He's so tall he takes up the entire frame of the door and then some. He crouches a little to take a step inside, so I move back to let him in. "Um, hey," I say, a niggle of apprehension burrowing into my side.

He stops in the middle of the room, gaze bouncing off the small touches I put here and there. I have no idea what the boys' cabins even look like on the inside. I've only ever seen inside my own temporary living space. Without so much as a greeting, Hayes turns to stare at me. "Did you know Chase Fisher was going to be here?"

My eyebrows pull together. "No... Why would I?"

He runs a hand through his thick hair. Now that it's summer and he's been spending so much time outside my house in the full rays of the sun, there's a handsome copper glint to his hair that I can't help but notice.

He doesn't answer my question. I'm not going to let him get away with that. "Listen, Hayes, if you're going to stand outside my house and now finally talk to me, you're going to have to start giving me some answers."

His gaze locks on mine. "We don't need a repeat of what happened at Rockport, do we?" His fists clench at his sides.

I know exactly what he means. It's clear. I also

know Hayes has a reputation. Sure, he's the quiet type, but that doesn't mean he's meek. He's the exact opposite. He might not start fights, but he'll end them. He might not start arguments, but he'll end them, too. I sigh. "I wouldn't think that was a problem anymore, considering the Ballers obviously unclaimed me." I think back on the last few months of school. They barely even looked at me let alone talked to me.

"In words, maybe. You know I don't care much for words anyway."

"Yeah, well, I do. Words mean a lot. Actually, words mean everything. They can hurt, they can heal. They can—"

"Actions mean more." His blue eyes dare me to disagree with him.

I shake my head. I don't know why I thought he was any different. "Spoken like somebody who just wants to get into a fight."

"I'm not talking about that, Tessa."

I freeze at the sound of my name on his lips. I don't think he's ever said my name before. It makes my stomach squeeze and my anger slowly unravel. After a moment, I find my voice. "I didn't know Chase was going to be here. You can ask Alec. He was there when I first saw him."

Hayes looks to his feet. "Alec doesn't really like talking about you."

I roll my eyes. Of course he doesn't. He'd rather I just didn't exist, I'm sure. "Yeah, well, feeling's mutual, I guess."

Hayes takes a breath, and with that one action, it's as if he sucks all the air from the room. My gaze darts to his. His lips purse before he says, "I'm sorry about this year."

The world closes in on me. The cabin, my things, and everything else around Hayes and me disappears. I just stare at him. He looks contrite. Ashamed, too. I can tell he means what he's said, but I don't know if I can find it in me to care.

"None of us thought it was going to go down like that."

I stand there for a minute, watching him squirm in the silence filling the room. Good. He deserves it. "I guess you were right, Ice Man. Words don't really mean all that much." I walk past him, keeping my eyes intent on his face until I push my cabin door open and step out onto the porch. I wait for Hayes to walk out after me. He doesn't look back as he steps off the porch, but he does wait for me just off the side of the steps while I lock the flimsy door.

Why apologize now? And why start this whole

conversation asking about Chase like he has something to do with any of this?

When I step off the porch, he starts walking. I follow him all the way to the main building, but in a way, it's almost as if he's following me. He's aware of where I am every single step of the way. I have no doubt that if I were to veer off the path, he would stop and follow. When we get to the big log cabin, he opens the door for me, and I step through.

Immediately, I'm assaulted by the smell of hot, barbecued food. Through a door to our right is the mess hall that's set up much like RHS's cafeteria. Already, I can hear the chatter of those who've beaten us to the food. My stomach tells me I've waited too long to eat, so I head straight for the door without thinking what I'll see on the other side of it.

Heads snap around, most noticeably the Ballers. They glance over me and then behind me, surely taking note of Hayes following me inside. That's where this ends for Hayes though. He goes right over to where the rest of the Ballers are sitting and makes himself comfortable.

For the first time since school ended, I see Sloan. I have to suck in a breath at the dark circles under his eyes. He looks so tired. They make me think of the naps I took with him, of trying to take care of him, which in turn makes my heart ache. All that's washed away though. He couldn't even find it in himself to stick up for me when Lake started his shit.

Forget him.

Instead of wallowing, I move toward the other guys I recognize from previous years. I say hey to them and then introduce myself to the others. I recognize their names, and now I have the faces to go along with them.

Just as I'm about to pick a place to sit, noise from the entrance wafts in and soon, Chase and his lacrosse friends are making their way into the mess hall. He catches my eye and smiles.

Ryan stands. In the middle of everything, he's on his feet in seconds, his fists by his sides. He glares at Chase with a hatred I don't understand, but Chase just casually ignores him. I don't look directly over at the Ballers, but I can tell none of them like the idea that the Huntington College Lacrosse Team is here. It is a little different from previous years, but I honestly don't mind. I walk forward to join them in line to get food. "Dale," one of Chase's teammates says when he sees me. "You want to sit with us?"

Relief floods me. "Yeah, I think I will."

When we're finished going through the small cafeteria line, filling our plates with barbecued chicken, beans, and potato salad, I follow the lacrosse players to a table in the far corner, the exact opposite side of the room the Ballers are sitting at. I can feel my teammates' stares on the back of my head—another control method, I think. I'm sure they'd rather me sit at a table all by my myself, talking to no one. They don't want me to be happy. They don't want me to have anything, but I'm going to prove to them that I don't care what they want. I'm going to do exactly what I want, when I want, regardless of what they think.

Sitting with the lacrosse team is actually nice. They regale me with funny stories from their last season. I can tell Chase fits in so well with them. It makes me jealous to see what a team really should feel like. I know I'm a girl playing on a boys' team, but not having a dick doesn't mean I should be a freaking outcast. In fact, me being dickless doesn't seem to bother the Huntington Lacrosse Team at all.

When a few of them start talking strategy, Chase, who I'm sitting right next to, leans over. "Christie told me the end of the basketball season didn't go that well for you."

I poke at my beans with the plastic fork. "Did she now?"

"She said some major shit happened."

I can tell he wants me to open up to him about it, but I'm not going to. That's in the past, and I have so much looking forward to do. I shrug. "Nothing that shouldn't have been unexpected."

He glares over his shoulder. "I know those guys are fucking assholes. A couple of black eyes and some bruised ribs proves that."

My jaw snaps shut. I knew they all punched him, but damn. Bruised ribs? "Are you okay?"

A small smile forms on his face as he turns toward me. "You know I just basically asked you the same question, and you sidestepped it instead of answering." He places his fork down and angles toward me. "I know you don't care that I care, but I do. Don't trust them. Don't—"

A voice hovers over us. It's dark and sharp. "Tessa, a few of us are about to go outside and shoot around some." I turn to find Hayes, Ryan, and a few of the other non-Ballers behind me. "You want to come?" Hayes asks.

I swallow. It means more that Hayes is asking, but still, no. They aren't going to rule me here. "Actually, I'm not done with dinner. Thanks though," I say sweetly. I turn back around and look at Chase. He and Ryan are glaring at one another, but I poke him in the leg. "You were saying?"

Chase turns around with a cocky smirk, and for a second, I honestly fear for him. The tension thickens right around us. Hayes and Ryan are fuming, and I honestly can't say why. They made their choice. Actually, it was more like Sloan and Alec made their choice. Ryan and Hayes didn't have shit to choose over.

Sure, the little voice keeps nagging me about Ryan's declaration, but it doesn't matter, right?

The other lacrosse players turn around now. It's like everyone can feel it. "Actually, I was just saying," Chase starts. "The guys and I are going to have a bonfire tonight on the beach. You should come."

My reply is immediate. "Sounds like fun."

A few of the guys whoop in excitement. One even says, "At least we'll have one hot chick." Hayes's ice-cold gaze cuts to him, but the guy doesn't even notice. The lacrosse team has already started lamenting that the only downside of having their little lacrosse camp here is that there's no "P" for miles.

It makes me laugh.

Ryan and the others walk away, heading out the mess hall door that leads directly outside. As soon as they're out the door, I turn to Chase. "Give me a sec, okay?"

I run out after the group. Hayes and Ryan are huddled together. The others are just a few steps ahead of them, so when I make myself known, it's only Ryan and Hayes who turn.

"Don't go near Chase again," I tell them, putting on my best authoritative voice. "There's no stupid claiming in place. You guys gave that up when Lake asked you to. As far as you're concerned, we're just at the same basketball camp." Ryan's practically shaking at the mention of Chase, but I don't let it deter me. "I hope you guys brought your A game because I'm not backing down here. This is as much my turf as it is yours."

After staring at me for a while, Ryan asks, "Is that all?"

I nod, then spin on my heel and head back toward the mess hall, bumping right into Sloan as I go.

Instead of feeling some sick satisfaction for telling the guys off, the skin where Sloan and I brushed against one another heats, then travels up my arm, over my neck, and to my face, so that by the time I sit next to Chase again, he's asking me if I'm okay. Several different emotions war with one another inside my chest.

"Fine," I tell him, needing to fan my face. "About this bonfire?"

I take all the information in, ignoring the voice in my head that's telling me to go to Sloan to see if he's okay. The dark circles under his eyes were even worse up close.

6

Basketball camp actually does have a curfew and rules, however, no one's ever checked up on me. It probably has something to do with the fact that my dad runs it, and that I've never given them a reason to check on me before. Right now, as I leave the cabin at nine to head down to the beach, I'm pretty happy about that fact because I'm not worried about someone coming around my cabin at ten to see if I'm in bed by curfew.

I slip right out onto the beach from my small porch and then skirt around the water's edge toward the tree-line. I wave at a couple of the guys who are just now packing up their stuff to head back to their cabins. They're both juniors and live down state, so the only time we see one another is at this camp. At the edge of the treeline, a figure comes into view. For a second, my heart beats hard in my chest. From far away like this, the shadow looks tall and menacing, so I wonder if it's Hayes paying me another visit to try to prevent me from going to the bonfire. I'd be lying if I said I wasn't worried about the Ballers showing up. Chase asked me to come right in front of Ryan and Hayes. If they wanted to, they could be dicks and show up to ruin this for me just like they ruined everything for me last year.

When I get closer, I realize it isn't Hayes though. It's Chase. "Thought you'd like an escort."

Damn. He really is sweet. I happen to really like his sister, too. Anyone else would've gotten pissed at me when a bunch of assholes kicked the crap out of their brother because of me, but not her. She knew where to place the blame. The only people who control the Ballers is themselves.

I smile at Chase as he approaches. He's not as tall as the Ballers. He and I are almost the same height, though he does have that sporty build I like. He's also not an asshole. That should put a bunch of hash marks in the positive column, but I don't know. Chase is nice, but that's just about all there is, I think.

I follow him down the small wooded path that leads to the other beach in front of where the lacrosse players' cabins are. Camp Holly is normally a camp for younger kids, but guys like my dad and the lacrosse players can rent it out for weeks at a time. One year, a group of girl scouts had the neighboring set of cabins. I swear their favorite pastime was showing up to ogle the guys when we played on the outdoor court. Not that I blamed them, but they seemed a little too young to be checking out hot guys to me.

"My sister says hi," Chase says, his smooth voice interrupting my thoughts.

"Yeah? You told her you saw me here?"

He chuckles a little. "I don't know if you noticed, but she's shipping us hardcore. I think she has a bit of a girl crush on you herself, so she's projecting it onto me."

I run my hands through my hair, pulling it over my shoulder. I left it down today, so there's a lot of it. Mostly, I'm just trying to avoid him talking about us as anything more than friends. "It must be nice to have a sister or any sibling for that matter."

He shrugs. "I guess I never thought about it before. I don't know any other way."

We break through the trees, and immediately, I see the fire lighting up the darkness ahead. Shadowy figures surround it, some sitting right in the sand, some standing. I don't think we've ever done anything like this at basketball camp. Then again, I wouldn't be invited if they had, so for all I know, they could've enjoyed all-out parties with me sleeping in my cabin completely unaware.

I bite my lip and move forward with Chase. His shoulder bumps mine when we walk, which reminds me of the short dance we shared at homecoming. Part of me wonders why I don't like Chase. I look over at him, staring at his squared jaw, athletic build. He's good looking. He truly is. But he doesn't make my heart race like...well, like any of the Ballers. I know that's dumb and sick, but I can't control the way my body reacts.

He catches me looking at him and smiles wide. "I'm glad you decided to come. If you didn't show, I was going to drag you out of your cabin. I half expected one of those assholes to lock you inside."

I laugh out loud, but he's probably right. At least, they would have when they had the claiming order in place. Back then, I would've wanted to stay with them, too. Now, they can go fuck themselves. "Thanks for inviting me. As ridiculous as this sounds, I've never been to a bonfire on the beach."

His mouth drops. "Seriously?" His eyebrow raises. "How are you so sheltered, Tessa Dale? It doesn't make any sense."

I've often wondered the same thing myself.

Anyone else would have taken advantage of the fact their father is wealthy and connected due to being a pro basketball player. I've never felt the need, for whatever reason. I shrug in response. "Just a good girl, I guess."

By the time I answer, we're at the bonfire. Chase leads me to an open space with a log big enough for two people to sit. He lets me sit first, then joins me. Our thighs brush. Nothing. No goosebumps. No dry mouth. Other than the fact that I recognize how good looking he is, I don't feel anything from the innocent touch.

This is utter crap. I don't know how, but it's all the Ballers' fault. They've ruined me.

One of Chase's teammates starts talking to me about basketball, which turns into a conversation about our worst sports injuries. I've been pretty lucky in that department, but some of these guys...damn. I wouldn't want to be them. I find myself rubbing my knees and silently praying for them to stay strong. My dad always says that the best way to avoid injury is to eat healthy and stay moving, even during the off-season. I'm not saying I don't eat the occasional ice cream, but I do run and weight lift year-round for this exact reason.

The conversation eventually moves on, and I find myself staring into the orange and red flames, watching them flicker into the night sky. I'm enjoying myself, I realize. This time with the lacrosse players is giving me a slight reprieve before camp begins tomorrow and it starts being all about basketball all the time.

I pull my phone out and check the time. I can't be out too late because we have an early day tomorrow. After breakfast, it's straight into an early morning run with one of the coaches leading. Camp is how I got into my long-distance running habit. With Dad, we only worked on shorter distances, a mile tops. Here, I found that I liked the solitude of running more miles, listening to music, and just dreaming. It's my favorite time to think about what it'll be like in college, pro, and even the years after.

"Can I ask you a question?" Chase asks.

I blink away my thoughts and look over at him. "Sure. What's up?"

"You never really answered my question before... about going on a date. The assholes answered for you."

My stomach sinks. I rub my hands together. It would be so much easier if I just liked Chase. He's from Rockport. He's another athlete, so he would get my obsession with basketball. There's nothing there though. I give him a small smile, my gut roiling at the same time. I can't let Chase think that something might come of this. It's not fair. "I think I just need friends right now," I tell him, and it's the definite truth. I tried to be more with Alec and Sloan and look where that got me. I never thought in a million years they'd betray me like they did, but here we are.

"They really did a number on you, didn't they?"

The only people he could mean are the Ballers, but I still don't want to talk about them. The whole backstory makes me sound weak. I place my elbows on my knees and prop my head up in my palms. "It's over," I say cryptically. "We're not in Rockport anymore, so they don't have a say in what I do. They can't force me to do anything anymore."

Chase scratches his cheek, then turns toward me with a look I don't immediately recognize. "It was more than just control over basketball, Tessa. Guys don't beat up another guy just because. They knew I was there to see you, and they were jealous."

A couple of them, maybe. Alright, Ryan, too. He straight up admitted it to me. But, honestly, with him, I think it's more of a control thing than an actually like me thing. If he liked me, why didn't he ever try anything with me like Sloan and Alec? "I don't know."

He smirks. "I'm a dude, Tessa. I know jealousy when I see it, and they were all consumed by it. Trust me. I didn't realize the entire basketball team liked you."

I laugh at that. "That's not a problem anymore, if it ever was. You can trust *me* on that."

Chase places his forearms on his thighs and looks straight ahead at the fire. "You say you want a friend? Someone who will tell you the truth?" He bounces his knee off of mine in a playful gesture. "Trust me on this. I saw right through them today. The two who came to the table when you sat with us? It wasn't actually to invite you to play ball with them. It was a show for me, except you didn't let it play out the way they wanted. They expected you to follow them instead of staying with me. I mean, I thoroughly enjoyed their faces when you dismissed them. I loved seeing those assholes get put in their place. I'll gladly help you do it again." He leans over, his mouth close to my ear. "Even more so if it'll help you change your mind about just wanting to be friends."

Chase pulls away, the fire reflecting in his eyes. When he notices goosebumps on my shoulders, he shrugs out of his hoodie and places it around me. I pull it tight around my arms. "Thank you." I knock my knee off of his now. "I'm going to disagree with you on what those guys want though. Trust me, they don't want me. They've made that much clear."

Chase smirks and looks away, shaking his head the

whole time. His hand comes up to rest on my thigh. "You're just blind to it. It's cute, actually."

I go to disagree with him again, but a shadowy figure emerges from beyond the reach of the bonfire and moves within the furthest flickers of light. I squint, but I can't tell who it is yet. Just one word drops from the tall shadow before moving in closer, the firelight lighting up his deep blue eyes. "Tessa," Hayes says. His voice is part strain, part laced in thinly cloaked restraint.

Chase squeezes my thigh, then reaches down for my hand, interlacing our fingers. I look over at him, asking him with my eyes what he's doing, but he just winks at me, then looks back over at Hayes. "Hey, man. What's up?"

Hayes doesn't say a word. His gaze zeroes in on where my hand is intertwined with Chase's, and I'm sure he doesn't miss the fact that Chase's large hoodie is draped over me, too, almost swallowing me up in it.

I know what this looks like.

"You're Hayes, right?" Chase asks.

Still, Hayes doesn't speak. His lips are thin, and the flames from the bonfire make his skin even paler than normal. My stomach clenches at the sight of him like that. I don't know why Chase is testing him like this. He knows what happened before, but I also know there are six or seven lacrosse players around us that aren't going to let shit happen to their teammate. It's the perfect opportunity to, as Chase said, 'put the assholes in their place.'

"Aww, shit," one guy says, since we're suddenly the center of attention. "Fisher got the only girl in a five-mile radius."

Chase looks over at me. His eyes are gleaming. I can tell he likes this. He's trying to help me, but there's more there, too. He wants me to change my mind. He leans in closer, his lips near my ear again. "Just go with it. You want to get back at them, this is the way."

My eyes flutter closed. Dawn said something similar, but I'm still not sure this is the best course of action.

"Get the fuck away from her," Hayes finally says.

He moves forward, and I immediately stand, Chase's hoodie falling to the sand behind me. Chase is right next to me now, too, his arm possessively around my back and pulling me close to him. "Not happening."

The lacrosse guys move around us, their gazes narrowed right at Hayes, their chests inflating like there's about to be a throwdown right here. That wouldn't be good for anybody.

Hayes looks at me. His jaw ticks. He's holding it so tightly closed I wonder if he might crack a tooth.

One of the guys on Chase's team says, "It's cool, bro. Chase got her. No big deal. After camp, it's a whole other story. More girls for all of us."

The guy is just trying to diffuse the situation, but Hayes's eyes are still flaring from when he said, 'Chase got her.' There's something in "Ice Man's" look that says there is no other girl. It's just me.

Hayes doesn't look like he's going to leave. Not without me. Chase certainly isn't going to back down either. He has to love this. The Ballers aren't going to do shit to him with all these lacrosse players here. I squeeze Chase's hand, which doesn't go unnoticed to Hayes, and then move forward. "It's okay, Hayes," I tell him, ignoring the fact that everyone, including me, knows now that Hayes is jealous as fuck. I act like he's only worried about me because we're teammates. "I'll be heading back to my cabin soon. I know we have an early day tomorrow."

Hayes's eyes lock onto mine. There's an incredulous look there...and fury.

"Really," I tell him again. "I'm fine."

The lacrosse players all shift on their feet. They're noticing now, too, that this might become something more. At this point, I'm worried for Hayes.

"It's okay," I whisper again, trying to tell him just to go before this escalates.

His deep blue eyes look almost menacing with the flecks of fire reflected there. "It's not," he forces out.

I look back at Chase. He has his arms crossed over his chest. He looks so pleased. I would be too if it wasn't Hayes this was happening to. If it were Sloan, Alec, or Ryan, I'd let them wallow in it, but Hayes has tried to make amends. He apologized. He's stood guard outside my house like...like I don't know what. I still don't understand it.

I think Chase can feel my indecision. His jaw hardens, and then he moves forward, his hand coming to rest on the small of my back. "Why don't I walk you back to your cabin?"

"I can make it," I tell him, then look at Hayes, too. Neither one of them needs to follow me or escort me.

Chase lifts his fingers to run them through the hair around my ears. "I know you can, babe. That doesn't mean I don't want to make sure you're safe." He looks at Hayes pointedly, who's about to lose his shit.

My heart takes off in my chest, pumping painfully. Slyly, without making Chase look like a fool in front of his friends and teammates, I maneuver out of his grasp. "Okay. Hayes, I'll see you tomorrow, okay?" I plead with him with my eyes to not do anything brash or stupid. He has to see right through Chase, right? He knows he's just trying to get to him.

Chase waves at his friends and then he and I walk along the sand again until we hit the trees. I'm almost scared to look back, but since I don't hear anything, I allow myself to. Hayes is no longer at the bonfire. He's not following us either. I don't know where he is.

I let myself relax a little. Chase, too, lets out a breath. "That was fun. Serves that fucker right. He's got a hell of a right hook."

I almost feel sick. For whatever reason, I can't picture Hayes hitting Chase. Hayes, who barely talked to me before, punched Chase for me. I just can't reconcile it in my mind. "I'm sorry about that. The other guys must've roped him into it."

Chase shakes his head at me again. "Are you sure you're not supposed to wear glasses? I think you're the only one who can't see."

I bite down on my lip. Maybe I don't have any idea what's going on. The moment I think it's something else, my mind takes me back to what Sloan said to me before: *"Don't pretend you know what's going on here because you have no idea."*

7

Chase and I don't say much when we get to my cabin. I'm too wrapped up in my own head trying to untangle my thoughts. The Ballers gave me up when Lake asked. I don't see how the situation can be any clearer than that, so why the hell is Hayes showing up at the bonfire and demanding someone get off me? They haven't spoken to me in months. They're the reason I didn't play any minutes for the rest of the fucking basketball season. That alone should make me hate them.

But at the same time, I've always felt like me and them are the same. Cut from the same cloth. Made from the same stuff. Maybe if they weren't basketball players, I would hate them.

I honestly don't know what the fuck is wrong with me.

Chase says he'll see me tomorrow. I give him a small wave, then turn to unlock my door, except it's already unlocked. *What the hell?*

Bringing out my phone, I check the time. It's barely even ten yet—so much for being excited to break curfew. Whoever unlocked my door isn't one of the coaches looking to get people in trouble. I fling the door open to find Hayes standing in the middle of the small room, silhouetted in the dark. "Jesus Christ, Hayes," I whisper yell. "What are you doing?"

The door bangs closed behind me, and I turn on the overhead light. His expression looks so much harsher here than in the subdued light of the campfire.

"How'd you even get in here?"

Disregarding my questions, he asks, "Do you like him?"

I drop my head back. Of course he would want me to answer his question before he answers mine. "What if I did?"

"You don't."

"What if I did?"

"But you don't, do you?"

I tilt my chin in the air. "Maybe I could grow to like him."

He moves forward. I back up against the door until he's towering over me. His blue eyes are so intense, I'm suddenly caught up in a Hayes tornado of emotion. Everything he says and does seems heightened because he's quiet and still most of the time. When he moves, it's noticeable. When he speaks, it's as if his words are coming straight through a megaphone. "Tessa," he says. He grabs my hands in his. "I'm sorry. I'll keep saying it until you believe it. I'll keep trying to prove it to you. I should've told Lake to fuck off that night. I wanted to."

I swallow. "You...you like me like that?"

He presses his lower half into mine. The fact that he's turned on is apparent. A chill shoots up my spine. *Hayes...*

"But you like me?" I press. "You don't just want to..." I shake my head. "You don't just want to do things with me?"

He turns his head, his brows pulling together. I move out of his grasp and away. "You know all about Alec and Sloan. That's all they wanted." I face him again, my hands on my hips. "That's not me, Hayes. I don't let just anyone touch me. I've learned my lesson."

He closes his eyes. When he opens them again, there's a certain amount of torture there. "I wish you could see inside my head. Words have never been my thing." He points toward the closed door. "If you knew how badly I wanted to rip that fucker's arm away from you, maybe you'd understand. Or the fact that you're so pretty it hurts. Or if you knew why I hung out outside your house for two weeks straight. I've been trying to show you, Tessa. And I'm trying to tell you now. You said you wanted words. I'm trying. I'm sorry." His last proclamation is said with so much force that I suck in a breath.

I sit back on my bed, the mattress cushioning my fall. I hold my head in my hands. This camp was just supposed to be about basketball. I'm supposed to try my best. I'm supposed to kick their asses on the court. Not this. Not in a million years did I think I would be back in this position with one of the Ballers. I squeeze my eyes closed until stars appear, then relax. "I can't do this right now, Hayes. I'm fucked up in the head. I'm...I don't know. I obviously don't know anything anymore."

The floor creaks underneath him. I peek up to find him coming closer. His face is pinched and tinged in worry. "I have no right to ask you this. I don't deserve any of it, but please, Tessa, don't push me away. I'll wait right beside you. I'll keep apologizing. I'll be your friend, but don't tell me to go away. I did that once and it broke me."

I'm trembling. The power of his words, the force of my feelings. My brain is trying to combat my body, so I'm lost in the middle, not knowing what to do. All it does is shake in response. "Lake," I force out. Just that one word, and it makes my previously mush body turn to steel. I straighten my shoulders and look up into his eyes.

"I've about had it with fucking Lake," he says. He clenches his jaw, like that one sentence was so hard for him to admit. "He's one of my best friends, but that's... that's it. That's the truth. I'm beginning to see that some things run deeper than friendship."

He sits down next to me on the bed, and I scoot over. "You're confusing me."

"Good."

I shake my head. "Not good. I didn't even know you liked me like that."

"I *like* you like that, Tessa. We all do."

"Don't speak for them," I say through clenched teeth. "Just don't." If they all still like me and let Lake do that to me, I don't even know what to do with that.

"Fine. *I* like you."

"But tomorrow if Lake asks you not to, you won't."

He shakes his head. "Not again."

"I don't believe you," I say wistfully. I really wish I could believe in someone right now.

He swallows. "I know you don't. It's my fault."

I run my hands down my face and look over at him. God, his eyes. They're like stars in the night that beg to be looked at. Already, I feel ten times the emotion I've ever felt around Chase even though I know rationally that Chase is the better option. Fucking Chase Fisher doesn't do it for me though.

Fucking Hayes. What am I supposed to do with this?

As if he can tell what I'm still thinking, he says, "Don't push me out."

"Don't give me a reason to."

"Never again," he pauses between the words, imbedding the promise into me. I just hope I can believe him.

Emotion crawls up my throat. The air in here feels so heavy with unsaid words and thoughts and feelings. It's like my skin is stretched so tight trying to keep everything in. He won't look away from me now. I lift my hand and move it toward his face. His cheekbones are so defined, almost elegant. I brush my fingertips across them. He closes his eyes, staying as still as a statue even though he's so wound up he looks as if he could snap at any moment. I don't want to know what that would look like.

I retreat, pulling my hand back and just stare at

him some more. After a while, I say, "I think I should go to bed now."

He nods. "I'll leave you alone."

I nod back in answer. Words are failing me now, too. Then again, I'm not the best with words either. I'm better than Hayes, but only marginally. If I was better, I'd have told all of these guys to get the fuck out of my life a long time ago and meant it.

He stands. He's so tall he almost brushes the low ceiling. His hair definitely tangles in the rope leading from the single ceiling fan in the room, but he just moves it out of his way as he backs up, still facing me. When he gets one hand on the door, he asks, "Are you still going to play that game with Chase tomorrow?"

I guess Chase and I weren't fooling anybody. Hayes knew it was bullshit. "Maybe."

His lips thin. "He knows you don't like him like that."

I can't tell if he's asking me a question or if he's trying to reaffirm it to himself, but I just nod anyway.

"He's playing a dangerous game," Hayes muses.

Don't I know it. My jaw tightens. "Don't do anything to him."

He hides his face, looking down at the doorknob as he twists it in his hand. "Good night, Tessa."

"Good night," I choke out.

It isn't until after he's left that I realize he never said he wouldn't do anything to Chase. The rest of my mind doesn't want to dwell on that though. It wants to replay everything that just happened over and over and over again as I drift into sleep.

Hayes "Ice Man" Irving likes me.

8

The next morning at breakfast, I sit with Chase and his lacrosse teammates. I guess I really am going to push this game with him. Serves the Ballers right. Also, it's because the lacrosse players are the least threatening option right now. Hayes is still sitting with the rest of the Ballers even though he's as far away from Lake as he can get. But truly, they're friends. Best friends. They've all proven before that they would choose him over me. What makes me think they—or even Hayes, specifically—won't do it again?

"Hey, Sunshine," Chase says.

I bite my lip and sit next to him with my tray. It's becoming apparent that I'm going to be seeing the Huntington Lacrosse players at every meal. The camp personnel probably only want to serve food three times a day instead of breaking us apart and serving at different times.

I blush when he uses such a sweet nickname for me. I'm not completely immune to things like a pet name, even when it's uttered by Chase.

"Did you sleep well?"

I shrug. The truth is, the mattress sucks, but I came prepared. I brought a foam thing to roll over it this year. I swear I'm not trying to be prissy about it, but sleep is so important. "Not bad. You?"

"Would've been better with you."

His words should shock me, but they don't. I know why he's laying it on thick. Shaking my head, I smile over at him.

"You nervous about camp?"

Now this is comfortable conversation territory. "Yeah, no. I don't know if you've heard, but I'm pretty good at basketball."

The rest of the lacrosse guys hear this and laugh. It ricochets around the room and after that, I'm pretty sure I can feel the strain of at least a few pairs of eyes on me. Thank God I'm sitting facing away from them or else I'd be tempted to sneak glances at their table throughout the short meal.

Ten minutes prior to our scheduled run, I stand. I only managed to eat some eggs and drink a little bit of juice, but I really want to come out strong on this run.

"You leaving?" Chase asks, a frown forming on his face.

"We have a run," I explain.

He reaches out to place his hand on my hip, taps there a few times almost dangerously close to my ass, and says, "Go get 'em."

I can tell he's loving every second of this. His teammates are looking at him with appreciation though, so it makes me smile.

However, when I turn around, it's a whole different story. I'm almost thrown back by the amount of hostility coming from the opposite corner of the room. Hayes stares where Chase is touching me until I step away and his hand falls off naturally. Then, his gaze moves up to my eyes where they keep staring until I'm the one looking away. I told him I was probably going to do this. And if it's truly affecting him, so what? He should've thought about that before he took Lake's side.

I place my tray near the return, smile at the lady next to the dishwasher, and head back out into the main area. My dad is there talking to a few of the coaches. He waves me over and introduces me to them. We never have the same set of coaches. He switches them up every year, bringing in people that will help us in different areas, and help us in different ways, too. When we get to the last coach, my eyes go wide. *Holy shit, I recognize this guy.*

My dad laughs. "Yes, it's Jacquin Sellers."

"Wow," I say. "Nice to meet you." I reach out to shake his hand.

"Jacquin, this is my daughter, Tessa. One of the best shooting guards in our state."

"Yeah, I've heard of her," he says.

I realize then I haven't pulled my hand away from shaking his, so I do so now, my cheeks flaming. Jacquin just got drafted out of high school. He'll be playing for the Cavs next season, and he's all anyone can talk about in the basketball world right now. People are debating whether he should've gone to college first instead of straight to pro. Regardless of his decision, that's a great position to be in. I envy him.

He also looks like a scrumptious piece of milk chocolate.

With that thought, I quickly excuse myself and go outside to stretch before the run starts. My dad never runs the long distance runs with us because of his knee problems, so it'll be one of the other coaches leading us this morning. I make sure to stretch everything out, limbering up as much as possible in preparation. I don't know if they'll decide to go easy on us right out of the gate or try to test us. It could go either way.

Soon, others join me. First, it's some of the other players from around the state, but then a familiar body stands next to me. I look away, avoiding Sloan Ivy's gaze. He doesn't seem to have that problem though. "Any idea where Hayes went last night?" he asks, an almost humorous lilt to his voice.

He's got that stupid politician-like smirk on his face too. He probably fucking knows Hayes came to see me last night. Hell, Hayes probably told him all about it. When I look over at him again to give him a sarcastic answer, I notice the shadows under his eyes have lifted a little. Relief floods me, then another bout of *What the fuck? Why?!* I should feel nothing in reference to him. "I'm sure you could just ask him, and he'd tell you," I say.

"Probably. It's just funnier this way."

"Yeah, funnier than a bunch of Baller Bitches throwing panties around, claiming they're mine." Oh yeah, that still happened. They didn't have my personal panties for the rest of the season, but that didn't mean they didn't claim to.

His face turns red. *Good. Asshole.*

"You know I never told them to do that."

"Do I though? And why the fuck are you even

bothering to talk to me, Ivy? You've made your feelings crystal clear, I think." He opens his mouth to say something, but Lake just now is walking out of the main building with his brother. "Shh," I tease. "I wouldn't want you to get into trouble with your master." With that, I turn and move as far away from him as I possibly can.

Stepping out of the cabin right after Lake and River are my dad and Jacquin. He introduces him to us —like he needs an introduction. If someone here doesn't know who he is, they should probably just leave camp now because they're not taking this basketball thing seriously enough. "Sellers is going to lead your morning run," Dad announces.

Jacquin smiles and then stretches alongside us while my dad runs through how the day is going to go. I'm shaking my calves out when my dad finishes and Jacquin tells us all to follow him. I start out in the middle of the pack, but that's not good enough for me anymore. I move up to right beside Jacquin who's keeping a really good pace. He leads us out of the camp and down the side roads.

Ryan and Lake's voices sound behind us. There's even some bitching, which I can only gather is coming from Lake himself. There's no way in hell he's beating me on this run though. He can groan all he wants.

I strike up a conversation with Jacquin and learn all about how the Cavs recruited him. I'm not going to lie, it's inspiring, and I'm almost dying of jealousy.

"Hear that, Dale? That's as close as you're going to get to your own Cinderella story," Lake crows.

I hold my hand up to flip him off.

Jacquin looks behind us, taking Lake in. I don't even bother. I already know I'm going to see the most pompous face ever. Jacquin looks at me briefly before switching back to watch the road in front of us again. Instead of commenting about Lake, he says, "Your dad tells me you played for the Rockport Warriors boys' team last season."

I nod. I'm sure Jacquin has seen all the stats on the camp attendees, including mine. He's seen our playing time and numbers. I'm not going to tell him what happened at RHS, I'm going to show him during camp why it should've been different. Lake, however, says, "Did he also tell you she barely played?"

"He did, actually," Jacquin says.

Jacquin picks up the pace, and I push it alongside him. This is faster than I normally run my long runs, but I'm determined to stay in front of all the Ballers.

Jacquin looks over after another mile or so. "Nice stride, Dale."

I smile at him, but because we're going faster than

normal, I'm also breathing harder than normal and at the same time, trying not to let that show. I don't feel the others breathing down my neck anymore, so I could let off the gas if I wanted to, but I don't. Before I know it, we're at five miles as we swing back around toward camp.

"Pick it up near the end," Jacquin shouts back.

I take my chance to look around. Ryan and Sloan are the only ones close to us now. Sloan is glaring at Jacquin and me. Lake is running with River while Hayes and Alec are intermixed with the rest of the guys invited to camp.

Jacquin starts to sprint, so I kick into the next gear, too. He looks over at me. "Are you trying to prove something, Dale?"

"Yes," I push out, my breathing harsh.

"Good."

He flies across the bit of grass between the two trees near the main building that symbolizes our finish line, then slows, placing his hands behind his head. I finish right after him. Well, like five strides, but I do finish closer to him than anyone else. He winks at me right before I bend over, pulling in air as fast and even as I can. Someone's helpfully left a bucket of water bottles near us, so I grab one of those, too, gulping it down. With what's left in the bottle, I place it on the back of my neck as sweat drips down my face and onto the front of my RHS tank top. It's almost completely soaked through with sweat, but I don't care about that. I care that I smoked Lake fucking O'Brien. Douche.

Hayes runs across the imaginary finish line and immediately smiles at me. "Nice work, Tessa."

Lake glares at him while the rest of the Ballers raise their eyebrows. I don't know if it's because he talked to me, or if it's because he talked at all that surprised them the most.

"Take fifteen," Sellers says, "Then meet us out on the outdoor court."

I toss my empty water bottle into a recycle bin and bend over for a new one, but there's already one in my face. I look up to find Hayes smiling at me. I take the bottle from him and drink some more. "Thank you," I say finally after I feel like I have my breathing under some sort of control. I look around. The Ballers are still nearby. River O'Brien is staring at our exchange with narrowed slits for eyes. "You're brave," I tell him, realizing that what he's doing is pretty significant. Fraternizing with the enemy in front of his people.

"You out of everyone should know that I'm not that brave. I'm just making up for being a dick."

I chuckle. "You're going to have to try harder than this then."

I walk toward the side bathrooms. I want nothing more than to jump in the lake right now but throwing water on my face will have to do before I head out onto the court. Right when I'm about to pass by the main entrance to the building, Chase and his lacrosse team come out the door. He looks at me from head-to-toe, and something more flares in his eyes than has been there previously. He moves forward, catching me before I pass him and drops a kiss on my cheek. "Jesus, Tessa," he almost growls.

"Lucky Dick," one of his teammates says.

I laugh even though the catch in Chase's voice makes me uncomfortable. I head toward the door with the girl painted on the front, but turn when a voice says, "Looks like someone's about to get his dick sucked."

Chase is right behind me, acting like he's going to follow me into the bathroom. He stops when he hears the words. Whipping around, we both stare at River. I open my mouth to tell him off, but I don't have to. Hayes says, "Shut the fuck up, Baby O'Brien."

My eyebrows raise. I just stand there, my mouth hanging open. I guess I don't need to stick up for myself this time. Too bad for Hayes he's getting daggers from Lake. Oh well, they can fight it out for all I care. "See you later, Chase," I say, making sure he's not actually going to follow me into the bathroom.

He mumbles something back that vaguely sounds like, "Yeah, sure."

I don't even stay to watch what happens next. I have basketball to worry about.

9

The short workshops throughout the day are grueling. They're also laced with nasty quips from Lake and his tool of a brother, River. *What? Were their parents high when they named them? Do they have a sister named Sea?*

I stomp toward my cabin faster. I should be the last one to talk about names. After all, I'm named after the fact that my dad was going after his fifth championship ring when I was born. I'm ecstatic I can shorten it to Tessa, so it actually sounds like a real name. I shake my head at myself. I'm only picking on their names because I'm pissed they still picked on me today.

I didn't let them get away with it once. I may not have always came back with a retort of my own, but oftentimes, I let my actions speak louder. *Call me a bitch again, and I'll pull up for a three in front of you and smile as it hits nothing but net. Assholes.*

As soon as I get back to my room, I peel my clothes off and throw them into the hamper. I forgot how many times I have to do laundry while I'm here. My mom usually takes care of it for me back home, but eventually, I'll have to make the trek to the wash house that has a full laundromat plus extra showers and bathrooms, not that I've ever seen anyone use them before. Each of the cabins has its own bathroom, though I suppose the guys have to share more than I do. Maybe they use the extra showers. Who knows?

After I'm rid of my sweat-soaked workout clothes, I pull my bathing suit out and slip it on. I've been dreaming about taking a dip in the lake all morning and afternoon. Grabbing a towel from my bag, I throw it over my shoulder and then slip out of the small cabin. There's only a few feet of grass before I hit the sand of the manmade beach, so I don't even bother with footwear. I just drop my cabin keys and my towel right in the sand and keep walking until my feet glide into the water.

I look both ways down the beach. There's no one else in sight. Perfect.

I move in, letting the small ripples of water lap at me until I'm waist deep. The sun is hovering halfway between the horizon and the sky, its rays still on full blast. I splash some water on me, but then figure, fuck it, and dive in. It seriously feels so good. I love the natural feel of the water, the crisp, cool of it on my skin. Back home, the water smells like chlorine and somehow, it's just not as naturally refreshing as this is. I make a mental note to call my mother after I go back to my room before dinner, and then I lie back and float on my back for a while, eyes closed, and arms outstretched.

Today went well. I did everything I wanted. Played well, worked hard, and impressed the coaches. Though, that usually doesn't take much. Unfortunately, when they hear Timothy Dale's daughter is coming to camp, they automatically think I got in because he's my dad. All I have to do is make a basket and they're congratulating me. It'll take them a while to understand that I mean business. I'm not just here for looks or because my dad doesn't want to hurt my feelings. No, I deserve it.

It's kind of fucked up that guys probably never have to have this conversation with themselves. Plus, if Lake calls me Daddy's Girl one more time, I'm going to straight up murder his fucking ass.

I slip under the water and open my eyes. Everything around me is muted. The big ball of a sun is fuzzy around the edges, rays reaching out in every direction, almost refracted by the water. Beyond that, I can see the very tip of the canopy of trees that surround Holly Lake. When I was younger, I used to play around with the idea of buying this land and using it as nothing but an all-girls basketball camp. No boys allowed.

The girls wouldn't have to prove anything to the coaches. They wouldn't have to worry about telling everyone they're fine if they tripped over their feet and ended up sprawled on the ground. Everyone would already know they could take it and that they don't need to be treated like fairy princesses for Christ's sake.

By the time my lungs start to burn, I place my feet on the sandy bottom and push, letting the water glide down my face as I emerge from the surface. I've floated farther from shore, my shoulders just barely above the water line now. I pull the hair tie from my hair, put it on my wrist, and let my hair cascade down my back. Holding my head back, I let the water roll over the tresses and then pull my head back up again. It's straight as silk now.

"Never thought I'd see that," a voice says.

Startled, I turn, blinking when water runs into my eyes. Sloan Ivy is sitting next to my towel on the beach.

His shoes are off, stuffed into the sand as if he's been there for a while. He's shirtless and leaning back like he doesn't have a care in the world other than watching me swim.

There goes my moment of peace.

"What's that, Ivy? Seeing a girl swim?"

I go to walk out, but all of a sudden, I feel exposed. I'm wearing my two-piece and with the way Sloan is staring at me right now, I'm not sure I want to get out just yet. Not with him here watching. "You forget I've seen you swim, Dale. But no, that's not what I'm talking about."

My face heats under his scrutiny. He's talking about the time my dad invited all the Warriors over to my house when I made the team. All those players who were so quick to turn on me ate my food, hung out in my house, and swam in my pool. What a bunch of bastards. "I don't think I care to know what you're talking about."

He shrugs. "I'm talking about Hayes talking shit to River...over you."

"Well, someone around here has to have a set of balls."

His jaw clamps shut, and I have to stop myself from smiling and giving myself a pat on the back. I'm actually really proud of that one.

And just because I feel like being a bitch, I ask, "How are your parents, Ivy? Good?"

I swear even from here I can see the pulse on his neck feather out a crazy rhythm. "So it's going to be like that?"

"Afraid so," I tell him.

"I didn't really peg you for being petty, Dale. You just said you didn't care. I think you care too much."

"I guess you'll never know."

He chuckles and shakes his head. "That's where you're wrong. You're an open book. Always have been."

I don't say anything only because I think he's right. Somehow, they always seem to know what I'm feeling even before I do. I'm going to have to work on that.

Without thinking, I start to walk out. Once I'm in front of him, my toes in the sand, I ask, "What did you want, Sloan?"

He hands me my towel, briefly glancing at me before I can get it around my shoulders and cover myself up. When I'm hidden behind it, he looks away. I was right about the pulse in his neck and the feathering of his jaw. He looks like he's trying to stay cool, but his body is revolting against the idea.

I wipe a corner of the towel down my face. "Nice talk. Glad you came all the way out here for that."

I step away, but his hand closes around my ankle. When I look back, he lets me go and leans back in the sand again. "I just wanted to tell you I didn't think it would get that far."

I can't tell from the look on his face what exactly he's talking about. Is he talking about his friend being an asshole? Or is he talking about us...together? "What? You almost going down on me? That day in the classroom? Or...?"

His gaze drops to my mid-section. I'm completely covered, but his eyes are burning a hole right through the soft fabric of the towel. "Neither, actually. I was talking about Lake."

"Oh," I say sarcastically. "The day you let me know in no uncertain terms that I was basically just another Baller Skank to you. I mean, my car already said it, so..." I shrug. "Did you have one of the others key it there?"

"It wasn't like that and you know it."

"Could've fooled me."

"I didn't know he would pull that shit."

I roll my eyes. "Christ, Sloan, it's been months. Why do you even care? We spent day after day in basketball practice, Saturdays on a bus sometimes, and you're just now coming to me with this?"

He swallows. "I don't have an excuse, Tessa, so if you're looking for one, you won't find it here."

"I'm not looking for anything when it comes to you."

His face shadows over. I don't know what he expected, but it clearly wasn't this. For a split second, the shadows make the dark areas under his eyes more pronounced, and I feel an ounce of guilt. I'm giving him shit, but Sloan Ivy doesn't have the best life. For all outward appearances, it's great. He's a senator's son. He's wealthy. He's great at basketball. I know the truth. He'd opened up to me about what actually goes on.

"I used to wonder how you could still like us after everything we did to you. I guess that only goes so far, huh?"

My throat starts to clog. Shame washes over me. Clearly, I put my faith in the wrong people. "I guess so."

He wipes his hand down his face and then gets to his feet. His hazel eyes are the perfect myriad of colors today. It makes me ache even though I try to push the feeling down. When I still feel an inkling of remorse for him, I push it down even further. He sighs. "I guess I just wanted you to know that I've never seen Hayes do that before. Maybe he's the only one of us who deserves you."

I tip my chin in the air. "None of you deserve me."

Sloan catches my gaze for a second, but then looks away. "I think you're right about that."

He spins in the sand and walks away. I stand there, lake water still dripping off me as I watch him go. He cuts through the beach, over the lawn, and toward one of the cabins on the other side of this section. A few of the other camp attendees are outside throwing a frisbee around.

I know I need to stay strong, it's just the fact that I thought we connected over something before. I have to tamp the urge to run after him and ask—for real this time—about his parents. I know something must be going on. He's not losing sleep for no reason.

Before I can do just that, I lean over and quickly swipe my keys out of the sand and head toward my cabin. I have just enough time to throw some real clothes on and head in for dinner. Maybe tonight I'll grab a tray and eat by myself in the privacy of my own cabin. There's a lot less bullshit in here than there is in any other part of this camp.

10

I'm able to avoid any testosterone-fueled nonsense until the next day.

One of the coaches my dad got to come to camp this year isn't a basketball coach at all. He teaches about mindset, specifically the mindset of young entrepreneurs and athletes. I was actually pretty thrilled with this idea until the guy tells us he wants us to break up into partners. As he's explaining everything that he wants to happen, my blood pumps like crazy. The air-conditioned room we're in in the main building feels like it's blowing cold air right on me.

This can't be happening. It'll be just my luck if I get paired with one of the Ballers, or worse, Lake or his fucking jackoff of a brother. How is that kid only about to be a freshman? He's already a rotten human being.

"I've pre-arranged the partners," the mindset coach says. I'm glaring at him. I hope he can tell. He's supposed to be really good at youth psyche, so doesn't he know breaking us off into partners is like the worst thing ever? I thought only high school teachers did that just to get back at us students for being general pains in their asses.

He calls us up by name one-by-one. My mind is whirring, trying to figure out who's left, who I'm inevitably going to be partnered up with, when he says, "Lake and Quintessa."

All the air rushes out of me. *No. Fucking. Way.*

About four voices speak out in dissent, not one of them is mine or Lake's. The guy—Petrie, or Petrie something—glances up. Alec's voice transcends the others. "That's not a good idea, Sir."

Petrie pushes his glasses up his nose. "Excuse me?"

Lake scoffs. "Yeah, I'm not pairing up with her. Sorry. Not sorry?"

I glare at him as his brother laughs aloud. Like I want to be paired with him.

"Oh." Petrie switches his gaze to me, but I refuse to make a sound. I won't back down. If I have to work with Lake, I will, even if it is to prove a point.

"I'll work with Tessa," Alec offers.

Lake sneers. "How chivalrous of you."

When Petrie turns to make the adjustments, Alec gives Lake the bird. Only, it's not as forceful as I would have done. He smirks as he gives it until he catches my eye. Then, he turns away, accepting the packet of papers from the mindset expert.

I just know this day is going to be absolute torture.

Everyone files out of the room ahead of us. I don't even move from my seat until Alec does. "You didn't have to do that, you know," I tell him.

He gives me a look. "Yes, I did. Lake would've eaten you alive."

"Lake can kiss my fucking ass."

Alec ignores me, looking through the papers. I read over his shoulder. Petrie explained a little bit of what was going on. Mindset is so important, especially when someone is trying to play sports at a high level or be a CEO of a business. High stress, high stakes. It looks like the packet is a cross between learning to rely on others, a.k.a teamwork, and learning about other mindsets. I have a feeling this kind of class is going to help only those who take it seriously. My father attributes a lot of his success to mindset. He's read enough self-help books and has even been to a few Tony Robbins and the like seminars.

"Alright, let's find a place to go over this thing," he says. I'm about to suggest the beach, but he heads down that way anyway. The screen door slams behind us and we walk across the grass until he plops his ass in the sand facing the water. "This should be good, right?"

No one else is around. I wouldn't be surprised if some of them blow this exercise off. Alec brings the worksheets in front of us, and I lean over to read. The first question is a biggie. It wants us to tell our partner our individual goals. A goal for the next year, five years, ten, and beyond. It goes on to say that admitting one's goals is super important, blah, blah, blah, but all I can think is thank God I'm not partners with Lake right now. I don't give a shit about his goals. His one-year goal is to probably keep me off the damn basketball team.

"You go first?" Alec asks. "One-year goal."

"Easy," I tell him. "My one-year goal is to once again make the Rock basketball team, except this time, I'm actually going to play." Alec opens his mouth to say something, but I cut him off. "I'm not done. I want to play a significant number of minutes in the championship game. I want to make a difference in whether we win or lose. I want to help my team. I want to win," I say, my voice hardening with each promise I make to myself. It isn't as if what I've just said is any different than what I normally say to myself, but it seems so much bigger now that I've said it in front of Alec.

When I'm finished, his emerald eyes move to mine. His throat works. "You could've done all that," he says.

"I could have," I say back, reinforcing it. "I should have."

We just stare at one another, his eyes searching mine. I hope mine don't betray any of my inner thoughts. Right now, I'm thinking about how good looking he is. I'm thinking back to how he was the first Baller to be sweet to me. How he held me outside the baseball locker room, his fingers working inside me. I swear my face flushes, but I don't look away. He knows what we did, and he's the only one who should feel ashamed of it.

"You go," I say finally.

He tears his gaze away. "Next year, I want to continue to focus on my athletic abilities."

He looks down at the paper like he's going to move on. I put my hand over it. "That's it? Alec, that's hardly anything. You're not promising yourself anything with that kind of talk. What do you want out of this next year?"

Maybe this kind of talk is unfamiliar to Alec, but I'm used to it. Dad constantly asks me what my goals are—broad and specific. "I don't know," he says.

"You don't know? That's not an answer. Don't bullshit your way through this. It's important."

"Fine. I wish I could get my sister to stop fucking talking about you. How's that?"

"Okay," I grind out. "Don't use words like 'wish', you should be saying, 'I'll get my sister to stop talking about Tessa Dale.'"

I swear I can hear his teeth grinding. "I'll get my sister to stop talking about Tessa Dale."

"Great," I deadpan. "What else?"

"I want to start being a better person."

I scoff. I can't help it. "Good luck with that."

"I'm pretty sure as my partner you're not supposed to make fun of my goals."

I smile, my lips moving in this incredulous way like I can't believe he has the nerve to say that to me. "Anything else, Christopoulos? Do you want to shit rainbows while you're at it?"

"Fuck you."

I burst out laughing. "Fuck me? Seriously?"

"I'm trying to tell you I want to be a better fucking person and you're mocking me."

"How did you think I would react? Do you want a fucking badge of honor or something? You shouldn't have to *try* to be a better person. You just do it."

He shakes his head and looks away, muttering something incomprehensible. "Five years," he says finally, indicating the worksheets again.

"In five years, I'll be finishing up my winning college career and bartering with WNBA scouts about who's going to give me the best deal."

His gaze zeroes in on mine. It's like he's trying to see me for the first time. At least, that's what it seems like. He's quiet for too long, but eventually, he says, "In five years, I'll be finishing my winning college career and be handling offers from several different pro teams." He swallows hard. "Several different pro *baseball* teams."

My mouth unhinges. "Baseball?"

He nods slowly.

"Are you serious?"

Bringing his knees up, he rests his forearms on them as he stares out over the lake. I feel like he just dropped an atomic bomb. Sure, if it were anyone else, no one would care. But Alec is a Baller. A fucking Baller. And he's so good at basketball. Seriously.

"I'm shocked," I tell him honestly.

He shrugs. The tips of his ears are turning red.

"I didn't say there was anything wrong with it, I just thought you guys all had NBA dreams."

He scratches the side of his face. "Once upon a time, but we can change our minds, can't we?" He turns his full gaze on me. "Last year, I often looked back at you while you were riding the bench and wondered how come I was out there and you weren't. It's messed up, Tessa."

"You're the best power forward we have," I tell him, just speaking logically.

"I like being known as the best power forward for RHS, but even more, I want to be known as the best third baseman Rockport High has ever seen. Did you know my stats are out of this world amazing in baseball? No one ever talks about them. I have the highest batting average the school has ever seen."

"Jesus, Alec," I say at his revelation. I knew he liked baseball; I just didn't know he loved it.

He blinks and looks over at me. "If I could, I'd trade places with you. Right now. I wouldn't look back."

I bite down on my lip. The full force of what he's just said hits me in the chest. "I'd be a terrible power forward," I say quietly, knowing full well that isn't what he meant. "Do the guys know?"

Alec shakes his head. "I think Ryan suspects, but the others have no idea."

"What are you going to do? I hate to say this, but you should be focusing on baseball, if that's what you want. Shit, Alec, if you got hurt playing basketball..."

"I know."

"You shouldn't even be here. I'm sure there are summer baseball camps."

"I know," he says a little more tersely.

I snap my mouth shut then. Clearly, Alec has other problems with the Ballers besides not sticking up for me when he had the chance. "You could have told me," I tell him. No matter how hard I try not to, my heart hurts for him. He's stuck somewhere he doesn't want to be, too.

He smiles at that. "I wanted to. It's just that you love basketball so much, I didn't know how you would take it."

"Obviously, I think basketball is the superior sport, but Alec..." I say, all kidding aside. "You have to say something to someone. You can't just keep living a life that's not yours."

"Hence me wanting to become a better person, Dale. I feel like I'm living a lie." He looks over at me. "One after the other."

I lie down in the sand and take a deep breath. These Ballers are still fucking with my head.

"Are you dating Chase Fisher?"

I open one eye and then squint into the sunlight. Finally, I give up and close them again. "No, but I think he wants to." Chase is having fun messing with them, but just the way he's been holding me, and those words he said to me after I got back from running, he's clearly not just playing a game like I am. "You're not going to beat him up again, are you?"

"I'm not promising anything."

I tamp down on the urge to roll my eyes. "I thought you said you were trying to be a better person. You can start there."

"I don't want to waste my generosity on someone who likes the girl I like."

I let the words sit there between us, but then anger consumes me again. I sit straight up, sand falling off me. I get right to my feet as fire runs through my veins. "Well, you should've known how to fix that one, Alec. All you had to say was you weren't giving me up. Literally like five words. Five fucking words, and it would've changed all these months. Five words, and my goal wouldn't still have to be that I want to help us win Championships because I already would've accomplished that one."

He swallows. "I was wrong, Tessa. I didn't know it was going to go that far. Before I knew it, I couldn't take what happened back."

He sounds like Sloan with the whole he didn't know it was going to get that far talk. I'm not buying it. "Is Lake a mystery to you? Have you ever really looked at your best friend? He's a fucking asshole."

His mouth opens, but then he closes it again. "I don't know what to say."

I lean over and snatch the worksheets out of his hand. "I guess we don't have anything to say to one another then." I spin on my heel and head toward my cabin. I can look through the papers back in there, in the sanctity of my own room. Before I know it, though, Alec's pulling back on my arm. "What?" I growl.

He flinches. "Please don't tell anyone about the baseball thing. Okay? I'm not ready yet."

I rub the back of my neck. "Sure. Whatever."

I hit the swatch of grass in front of my cabin before I hear his voice again. "Hey, Tessa, what's your ten-year goal?"

I ignore him, letting myself into the small cabin, thinking I should add not having any more male drama in my life ten years from now while I'm also scoring the most points ever in the WNBA.

How's that for a long-term goal?

11

I make it to the weekend by keeping my head down and focusing on basketball. My mom decided to go on a short trip with one of her girlfriends, so we've been keeping each other updated over text. I'm not giving her any of the drama-filled stuff, just the normal, "I'm not injured, and I'm having fun" stuff. Dawn, however, is loving every scrap piece of info I give her. She almost broke her exclamation point button when I told her Chase Fisher was staying at the same camp. She thinks it's an excellent idea that I use him to get back at the Ballers. She's all for him cozying up to me. However, she also thinks it's nuts that I'm not at all attracted to him.

We had plans for David to drive her into town so that we could meet up and talk about things Saturday afternoon, but apparently David has to go visit his sick Grandma. **I'm sorry!!!**, she texts.

I sigh. I was really looking forward to some girl time and not having to keep my head down to avoid any and all male gazes except for the coaches and my dad. The only good thing about camp right now is that I feel like I'm doing well. Jacquin has made it a point to help me any chance he can get, throwing tips at me here and there. He's a nice guy. **It's no big deal**, I text back. **Maybe next weekend?**

I put the phone away and head toward breakfast. I've still been eating with Chase, but I've been quieter lately, concentrating on basketball and dodging their invitations for me to come hang out on their side of camp. I have a feeling that the lacrosse side of camp isn't taking this as seriously as the basketball side. It seems more like a bunch of frat guys decided to hang out with one another rather than any real skill sharpening. I'm sure it's good for teamwork though.

Just my luck, I end up right behind Ryan and Lake in the line to get breakfast. They don't notice me until I grab a tray and let it fall to the stainless-steel counter. Lake only smirks back at me but turns right away. Ryan, however, holds my gaze for a moment. Beyond him, Lake is rattling about how they're going to get away from camp.

They, of course, want to ask one of the other guys here who has a car so they can go into town. I'm glad they've learned not to ask me. I couldn't give a shit if they leave camp or not. Hell, I might not even leave camp today.

Ryan nods at him absentmindedly until they turn away with full trays of food, and it's my turn to grab some. Once I'm loaded up with eggs, toast, bacon, and a pancake, I head toward the lacrosse table. There aren't a lot of them here this morning, but Chase is. I come up behind him and set my tray down. He looks back, a full smile on his face already. "Good morning, Sunshine."

"Where is everyone?" I ask.

He chuckles. "Some of us got too inebriated last night to make it in time for breakfast."

"You should've come," one of his teammates says. "Chase was sulking."

Chase's cheeks color a little.

"I don't drink," I say. "I'd be a downer at a party like that." It's kind of true. It's not that I've never had anything to drink before, but I'm definitely not drinking during my father's basketball camp. That would be a disaster waiting to happen.

"Aww, come on, it's the weekend," his teammate says. "We're probably going to have more drinks tonight, and you can't use basketball as an excuse. Sunday is a free day, you said so yourself."

I pick my fork up. It's true I don't have plans anymore, so hanging out with them wouldn't be terrible. They're actually really nice guys. "Maybe," I tell him, not committing to anything.

The guy smirks. "Hear that, Chase? You just have to ask her nicely."

"I have been asking her nicely."

"Maybe she's just not that into you." His friend pauses, screwing his mouth into an "o" of surprise. "Oooohhh," he says like he's thrown down the gauntlet to a burn war.

Chase is embarrassed. I can tell. His shoulders stiffen, and he looks down at the table in front of us. I put my hand on his shoulder. "I'll hang out with you tonight. Promise."

Jokingly, the guy says, "Well, okay then. That escalated. Someone's getting laid tonight."

It's funny until I hear Lake's voice pierce the air behind us. Then, my blood is boiling. "Like that's something special. Ask Alec and Sloan."

That motherfucker.

I twist in my seat, grabbing the first thing that catches my eye, which happens to be my juice glass, and I throw it right at Lake's smug face. He bats it away easily, but that doesn't mean he's spared from getting a shirt full of sticky orange liquid. I'm on my feet in the next second, barreling toward him.

"Bitch!" Lake growls. He stands up next, his hands fists at his sides, juice dripping down his cheeks. He's having trouble keeping his breathing under control, but so am I. I've had enough of his bullshit.

I launch myself at him, my fist rearing back, but a body grabs me from behind. "Don't," Chase says in my ear.

I struggle against him. I've seriously had enough. Part of me is hurt by what Lake said because he's right. I shouldn't have done anything with Alec and Sloan because look what they fucking did to me. The other part of me just fucking hates the asshole standing in front of me.

He has my friends. He has my position. I loathe Lake O'fucking Brien.

"Excuse me," a woman says from inside the kitchen area. "Someone is picking that up."

Every one of us ignores her. Lake and I are having an epic stare down. The lacrosse players are behind me, flanking Chase. There's so much fucking testosterone in the room right now it's ridiculous.

River laughs. "She thinks she can take you, brother."

"She won't have to," Chase growls.

This makes Lake laugh. "Like last time, pussy?"

"I think it's more of a fair fight now. What do you think?"

Chase is trying to push me behind him, but I don't need anyone saving me, and he's not going to fight my battles for me either. Finally, I push his hands away and move closer. Lake meets me head-on. Hayes is there in an instant. "Don't you ever fucking say that about me again."

"What part of it pisses you off the most, Dale? The fact that you're a whore? Or the fact that they don't want you anymore?"

"Dude," Sloan says, his hazel eyes like fire. He seems to have gotten a few splashes of juice on him, too. In fact, the whole Baller table got caught in the crossfire, but I don't give a shit about that. "Knock that shit off."

River shrugs. "I thought it was funny."

"Get fucked," Hayes says to him. The stare he levels at the younger O'Brien makes the other shrink back. I have a feeling Hayes doesn't like River much.

Lake's gaze switches between Sloan and Hayes. Alec and Ryan are standing, too. In fact, the whole fucking cafeteria is standing. Lake puts his hands up. "Sorry, Ivy. I forgot how much you liked her...what did you call it again? Tight, little cunt."

I move quick. With two hands on his chest, I shove him with everything I have. He stumbles back a few steps, his brother's hand snatching out to help save him from tripping over. He makes a noise in the back of his throat and comes toward me, his face bright red. Chase is pushing forward, too, while Hayes is trying to get me out of harm's way.

It's a fucking mess of tangled bodies until Jacquin walks in. He pushes through the circle. "Whoa, whoa, what the fuck is going on here?" He looks at me first, but I look away. I'm so angry, I'm probably going to cry soon. Damn hormones. I'm not sad, I'm not even furious. I'm super fucking pissed, but for some reason, it comes out as crying.

When none of us say anything, Jacquin appraises the situation. He sees a couple bodies surrounding me, juice all over the table, and the Ballers. It's not hard to figure out I was involved.

"Is there something going on here, Tessa?"

I bear down on my jaw, trying to keep my emotions at bay. I glare at Lake. It doesn't matter if I say anything. It won't change who they are or anything else that will happen. "No," I tell him. "Lake's just a klutz is all. I think he dropped his juice."

The fucker in question sneers at me. Jacquin just nods his head. He knows what I've just told him is all bullshit, but I'm not going to prove him right either.

"Come on," Chase says. He grabs my forearm and tries to lead me out of the room, but Hayes takes over.

He puts his hand around my shoulders and steers me back around, taking me out the back door and straight outside. He's stiff beside me, his fingers digging into my upper arm as he takes me back toward my cabin. I don't even try to get away from him. He's so much taller than I am that it feels as if he's trying to shelter me. Right now, that's what I need. Someplace safe. He opens my cabin door and takes me right to my bed, pushing me down to sit on it. "Don't leave this room until I get back."

"What?" I snap, but Hayes has already turned and left, his face a mask of fury.

I flop back on the bed. A part of me wishes I'd punched Lake. That would have brought up a whole other round of problems, including probably getting suspended from camp. I don't think the fact that my dad runs the place would've stopped that punishment from happening either, no matter if Lake deserved it or not.

A couple minutes later, there's a knock on my door. I look up cautiously, but I see Chase standing there beyond the screen. "Come in," I tell him, my stomach dropping. How embarrassing. Now *everyone* knows I've done something with Alec and Sloan.

The door groans as he opens it. Once inside, he holds up my tray of food. "I brought this for you."

I give him a small smile. Perpetually being nice to me. I don't get it. "Thank you." I take the tray and set it on my lap before I dig around in the cold eggs. I decide not to bother with those before I tackle the bacon and the toast. At least I can get something into my empty stomach. "I'm sorry about that in there," I tell him.

"You have nothing to be sorry about," he says. "Why don't you say anything about it? The bullying? Wasn't that one of your coaches? You should've told him."

"This has been a thing between us for a long time. It's not going to get better if I tattle on him; it'll only get worse," I confess. "I prefer to fight it out with basketball, but Lake's a douche."

"He's probably scared you might actually be better than him."

I raise my eyebrows and smile. I think that's exactly what he's afraid of, but since I have a mouth full of toast, I don't say anything.

Chase runs a hand down his face. "I hate seeing them treat you like that. It's not right." He sits in the only other lone chair in the room and looks back over at me. "I'm going to ask you something, and you don't have to answer if you don't want to, but did you even do anything with Alec or Sloan? Or both of them?"

I swallow, my face turning red.

"You don't have to give me details."

"I don't have to tell you anything."

"True. That's fair." He leans forward, his elbows on his knees. "You're so much better than them, Tessa. I see the way you look at them. I know you somehow have this crazy need for them to accept you, but you're so far out of their league..." He shakes his head. "I don't know. I just don't get it."

I blow out a breath. "I don't know anything right now, Chase. I really don't." I set the tray down on the floor.

Chase uses that as an opportunity to come forward. He sits with me on the bed, turning toward me. Lifting his hand, he filters it through my hair. "I don't want to see you hurt. I want to see you with someone who will actually be nice to you. I—" He swallows. He's stopped trying to talk now. He just keeps staring at my lips. He moves closer and closer. My stomach tumbles over itself. I feel like I'm stuck in place, wanting to see what happens. What if I let him kiss me? Will I actually like him then?

"Tessa," a voice says.

I start and scramble away from Chase. Hayes is silhouetted in the door, and he looks even more furious now than when he left.

He steps inside, crossing his arms over his chest. His gaze zeroes in on mine, and my heart beats like crazy.

The "Ice Man" is showing us why that's his nickname. A shiver crawls over my spine, and I hug my hands to myself. What have I gotten myself into now?

12

I think Hayes glared Chase from the room. I'm not sure. All I know is that it's just the two of us in here now. I vaguely remember Chase saying he'd text me later, but all I can do is stare at Hayes's deep blue eyes that haven't left mine.

"Were you just going to kiss him?"

"I—I don't know," I answer honestly. I think I was going to let him kiss me.

"I punched Lake for you."

"You did?" Then, I'm suddenly pulled out of my trance. "You what?!"

His gaze turns to slits. "I punched Lake. Maybe it wasn't even for you. It was probably for me. He pissed me off."

I shake my head. "This doesn't make any sense."

Hayes moves forward. I'm startled when he drops to his knees in front of me, placing his hands in my lap. "I'm sorry for what we all did to you. I'm sorry I stood back and didn't say anything. Don't kiss that guy just because you're upset about that."

He's right. That's exactly what I was going to do.

Before I can stop the words from coming out, I say, "I'm so mad at myself. I let Lake get to me. I freaking let Alec and Sloan touch me when they obviously didn't care about me the way I thought they did."

"Don't do that to yourself," Hayes says. He grabs my hands and squeezes them in his own. "There's more that you don't know. Alec and Sloan—"

I squeeze his hands once. "Don't answer for them. All I need to know is what they've shown me, and what they've shown me is that they let someone else dictate their feelings for me. Here you are apologizing, and you're probably the last one who should be."

Hayes shakes his head. His dirty blond hair flops over his face. "I have a lot to apologize for. I could have stopped Lake before. I should have told you I liked you before instead of always standing in the background. Maybe it would have made a difference. Maybe a lot of things would have changed if I had."

Like before, I raise my hand to Hayes's cheekbones, letting my fingertips graze them. His eyes flutter closed. His hands smooth up my thigh and around to my ass before he moves me forward on the bed. I bite back a yelp at his touch. Hayes has always been so quiet. I like the person I'm beginning to know, but I don't know all that much about him. I've never seen his parents at games. Actually, I take that back. I think I remember seeing his parents at camp the year I first came. But ever since then, he rides in with one of the other Ballers' families. "There's a lot more I need to know," I tell him. Already, I feel the urge to pull him against me, but I'm not doing that again. I gave in too easily to Sloan and Alec and look what happened. I don't want to add Hayes to my whore list just so I can get made fun of again.

"I'll be completely honest with you," he says. He doesn't take his hands away from me. They're digging into my backside, sending steady pulses of heat to my core. It's like torture. Wanting something but knowing it's not right for you or if it ever will be. He glances up. "You're so beautiful."

I bite down on my lip as his words sink into me. "I need a minute."

He backs up immediately. He sits in the chair a few feet away, looking like an adult in a children's tearoom playset chair. With him over there, I can think clearly, and my head isn't so mussed with him and everything else that's going on. "I told Sloan and Alec to stay away from you until they've grown a pair of balls," he says.

I smirk at that. "It doesn't bother you that you all like me? Do you all like me? Still, I mean."

Hayes's jaw clenches. "We've shared before. Not at the same time. I think they thought it would be easy. It's not." He leans back, and the chair groans. "It's a totally different scenario, but none of us have any right to say anything to you about that. As far as I'm concerned, you can do whatever you want. I just hope I'm a part of what you want."

"Because you're not going to stand in the background anymore?"

His blue eyes flare. "No, not again."

"I'm going to need to see proof." Offhandedly, I say, "I wish I'd seen you punch Lake."

I can't help but frown a little. Hayes has to hide a small smirk. "You'll be able to tell when you see him next."

I pull my legs up and hug them to my chest. "Why does he care who you guys see?"

"He usually doesn't. I could see it was bothering him. Ryan could, too. Alec and Sloan were too caught up in you to care. I know you don't want me to answer for them, but this is probably part of the problem you're going to want to know. For a lot of us, the five of us are all we have. Sloan's family life is a mess. You know that. Ryan's mom flits from guy to guy. Alec is probably the only one of us who is semi-normal. We pick on him all the time about how he got mixed up with us. I thought he would be the one to tell Lake off first."

Except Alec has a secret, too.

I sigh. He's probably worried about losing his friends after the truth comes out about him wanting to go to college for baseball, not basketball.

"He just can't stand the fact that I play the same position as him."

"That, and that his friends all like you."

I look into my lap. "Stop saying that."

"It's true."

"It's hard to believe."

He's silent for a little while. "The problem is that he sees you as a threat. Not just on the basketball team, but in our little group, too. We've never all liked the same girl before. It's a disaster waiting to happen."

It probably is. But who am I to judge? I like all of them, don't I? Besides Lake, of course. Lake can go burn in the fiery pits of hell for all I care. "Probably," I tell him. "Ryan warned me that it would interfere with basketball."

"Ryan brings everything back around to basketball."

I can't blame him. All of us have so much riding on the fact that we have to be great at it in order to accomplish our goals. Well, I guess everyone except for Alec now. But Alec's still in the same boat, just a different sport.

My phone buzzes. I pull it out of my pocket and stare down. It's Chase telling me he hopes I still plan on coming over to the lacrosse section tonight to hang out. I screwed that up, I think. I shouldn't have let him get that close.

"If that's the lacrosse boy, I think you need to tell him you don't like him like that."

I glance up. "I already did."

"He's not getting it."

"Yeah, well, he's worried you guys are going to break me."

Hayes's jaw hardens at that. I'm still not completely sure he'll keep his hands off Chase, so I don't say anything else. Whatever is going on, this whole fucked up mess has nothing to do with Chase.

And what a mess it is.

"My mom wants to send me to Springs next year."

His eyes widen. "What?"

I nod. "She, obviously, didn't like what was happening this last year. She thinks it's too much."

"You're staying at Rockport," Hayes says, his voice even.

I chuckle. *Yeah, sounds great. Is that what I'm supposed to say to her? I can't leave Rockport because Hayes "Ice Man" Irving says I can't.*

"Things will be different next year."

"I tried to tell her."

"What about your dad?"

I glare at him. "I'm sure you've noticed that my dad is playing house with Ryan and his mom, so I'm not sure he actually gets a say."

I can tell Hayes feels sorry for me, but he's interrupted by his phone. He takes it out of his pocket, glances at the screen, and then puts it away.

He continues to look at me like nothing else happened, but I can't keep myself from asking, "What was that about?"

"It's Ryan. He wants me to come talk to Lake."

"Are you going to?"

"Eventually. But you know I don't like talking."

"If you plan on punching him again, can I come watch?"

He snickers. "I'm not going to punch him again

unless he asks for it. I just meant I'm not much for conversations in general."

He's not wrong. This is the most he's ever talked in my presence. Ever. Then again, it's just the two of us. "He is one of your friends. You should probably go talk it out."

His brows lower over his eyes. "You're a mystery."

"So I've been told."

He runs his hands through his hair. "I don't like the idea of leaving you alone."

No wonder why he used to stand outside my house. "If you're going to be with Lake, I have nothing to worry about. He'll be too preoccupied to start things with me."

"He's not the only one I'm worried about."

"River?"

He shakes his head. "Lacrosse guy." His gaze passes over me. It's half jealousy, half fear of not wanting to let me go.

"I'll be fine," I tell him. "I've gotten through seventeen years without you, I can manage."

"I have no doubt. I just don't want you to."

The way he says it sends goosebumps across my skin. I try not to let my mind go there...to the fact that I might actually have an ally in this after all. Part of me still rebels against the idea. Look what happened with Alec and Sloan, but Hayes just seems different. I told him before he had the least amount of apologizing to do, and I meant it. I just don't know if I can give in anymore. I don't want to deal with the aftermath if something bad happens again.

He stands to leave, and I watch him. It's awkward for a moment. I can tell he wants to hug me. Or more. Definitely more with the way his eyes rake over me. I'm not ready to let him in like that though, and I think he can sense it. "I'll be around," he says.

I nod while he leaves. The door creaks and then slams as he exits.

I certainly didn't think this would happen when I woke up this morning. At least I got a shot in at Lake.

13

I'm so bored I resort to calling my father. He answers, but he's at dinner in town with all the coaches, so I decide to go for a run instead. I really wish Dawn had her own car, so she could have spent the day with me today even if David couldn't come. For a moment, I even briefly consider asking my father to buy her a used one just so she can drive up here to keep me company and tell me what to do with all these guys.

I take the same running route we've been taking on the morning runs with Jacquin leading the way. I haven't let one of the Ballers beat me yet. Jacquin and I are always neck and neck, no matter if I feel like I'm going to throw up afterward or not. There's a lot of inner competition that goes on in camp, and I'm not about to let my guard down for one second. I did that once with Ryan a few years ago and look what happened. Basically, it got me into this mess with the Ballers to begin with.

While I'm running, I daydream about Hayes. I wonder what his story is, why he doesn't like to talk, and why he's apologizing the most to me. He's such an enigma. If he really did like me this past year, too, how could he sit back and let Alec and Sloan take up all my time? It seems odd, and unlike the persona he tries to portray. Quiet, and like he doesn't care.

I see a figure running in the opposite direction as me. I'm almost at camp, and I get to the mouth of the entrance before I realize it's Sloan Ivy. I want to roll my eyes. Yes, he told Lake to knock it off, but maybe it's a little too late for that. I act as if I don't even see him, turn the corner, and continue my run. Ivy's never one to let me get away with that though. Even when he's not supposed to be talking to me according to Lake. "I had to take a shower, you know."

"Finally smelled yourself?" I toss over my shoulder.

"Ha. No, I'm talking about the juice this morning."

I shrug, trying to keep my breath under control.

"Not that he didn't deserve it."

"You all deserve it."

"So you keep saying."

"Because it's the truth."

He smiles. "You're so cute when you're mad."

I stop, my sneakers sliding in the gravel a bit at the sudden motion.

Sloan passes me, then looks over his shoulder and laughs. He, too, comes to a stop, then walks back. The smile has slipped from his face though. He looks down my body, then back up to my eyes. "He was right about one thing. I do miss you."

"My cunt, you mean."

I push past him, but he grabs my hand. "You and I both know I don't have any real first-hand knowledge of that. That was just Lake being himself."

I shrug him off. "I'm not really in the mood to have this conversation with you, Ivy."

He swallows and looks away. "But you'll talk to Hayes?"

He looks so vulnerable in that moment that it takes me back to the circles under his eyes and the stories about his home life. Betrayal tries to combat the other feelings rising to the surface inside me, but they all just sit there in my stomach like a lead weight. "I talked to Hayes. Yes."

A small smile spreads over his lips. "He's not much for talking."

I find myself smiling back at him. "I guess he is with me."

He looks out toward the trees surrounding us. "I shouldn't be surprised. I knew he liked you, we don't keep secrets, but I am a little shocked he's throwing himself out there with you. He usually keeps to himself. I hope you like him back."

I don't know why this angers me, but I can feel my hands start to shake. He hopes I like Hayes back? What about himself? "Screw you."

I try to push past him again, but it's still fruitless. He maneuvers me against the wooden fence lining the road and blinks. "I realized something this morning or last night or I don't know, one of the many times I've thought about you. My family isn't known for saying I'm sorry. They just do whatever they want, damn the consequences. I swear when my parents walk through the house, it's like the foundation starts to crumble before my eyes, and I started to wonder what two little words might do for them. For them to each other, for them to me, and from me to you. What if my mom just told me she was sorry she took the vacation with her twenty-something year-old boyfriend instead of being around for my birthday? Would it matter? Would it make everything okay?"

I swallow. He's pressed against me, his fingers like a vise around my wrist.

"I thought about it and thought about it, and I don't think it will, Tessa. I don't think apologies really make a difference in the long run." His throat works. "But then I thought about what it might mean if they just attempted to tell me they were sorry, like they actually made the effort to try to make things right. Obviously, it would be better if my mother had decided not to go on the vacation in the first place, but that can't be changed now, no more than I can change what I did to you. But I'm going to pull something an Ivy has never done before." He reaches up, wraps his fingers around my ponytail and tugs a little. "I'm going to apologize. I'm sorry, Tessa. Fuck. I'm an idiot. I know it won't change what I've done. I can only hope that you see that I regret it. It's just that it's always been the five of us. Trying to maneuver around the problem that there's someone else I want to let in like that, but my best friend doesn't, I got lost. I shouldn't have let him make that decision for me, and I'm sorry."

My vision fractures before me. Heat gathers behind my eyes, and I try to blink it away. This is not the time for crying. This is the time to tell him to fuck off. The only thing is, I don't want to. I still don't trust him, but the guy I napped with in the car has to be there somewhere. The guy who invited me, the only girl ever, to his parents' house for a dinner party, he has to be there, right?

I clear my throat. "How can Lake have that much say over what you guys do?"

He lets his hand with my hair in it drop to my shoulder. My skin pricks at his touch. "It's just a crazy bond, Daddy's Girl. A crazy, crazy bond."

"I don't trust you," I tell him.

"For me, the part that hurts the most is knowing that you don't. It's also knowing that at the first chance I got, I jumped right into the usual Ivy M.O. Think about myself before others." He shakes his head. "I really wanted you to play more basketball, Tessa. You're so good."

His words and his actions don't match up. He never even bothered to look at me while I was riding the bench. "It hurt like hell to watch you guys win Championships and not even be able to say that I helped at all. I was just a seat-warmer."

"You deserved to play."

I shrug away from his touch. His hands clench at his sides as we stare at one another. "You were right about one thing, Ivy. Apologies don't always change anything."

I turn away, facing down the road to camp. I start at

a walk, then begin to run again. The need to get away keeps my feet hitting the road harder and faster. If I stay there too long, I'm afraid I'll fall right back into his arms again.

It's so hard for me to give up on the Ballers and just say they're assholes and that's that. There's so much more to them. I'm not saying what they did was right. I'm just saying maybe they were lost and confused, caught between the past and the present, and a friend and someone more.

Or maybe I'm way, way off.

Once I'm back in my cabin, I take a shower. I didn't bring many clothes with me, nothing like the closets I have back home, but I dress in one of the nicest shirts I brought before texting Chase. He told me they'd be hanging out all day, and since the more I stick around the basketball part of camp, the more likely I am to get accosted by a Baller who wants to tear me down or apologize to me, I figure the lacrosse side is a safer bet.

Once I cross over the short wooded area that separates the two beaches, I feel freer. The guys are all hanging out outside their cabins on picnic tables and even using the small grills that are situated here and there on this side of the camp. When Chase sees me, he gives me a wave and runs over. "Hey," I tell him.

He gives me a short hug. "I was worried you

wouldn't come over after this morning. The guys all think they're dicks by the way. They decided they didn't want to go back to the mess hall today, so we went out and bought some food to grill."

His teammates all say hi to me, and I think he's right. They seem to be happy to have me over here. None of them say anything specifically about what happened that morning, but they're all intent on making sure I'm fed and welcomed.

While I listen to some of their college stories, I get a text. I reach into my pocket where I'm sitting at a picnic table and pull my cell phone out. It's Hayes, and it's a text just to me, not like when I used to receive Baller-related texts with everyone on the thread. **I'm at your cabin. Where are you?**

I'm with Chase.

It takes a few seconds for another text to come through. **I'm coming over.**

I look up to find that Chase is already looking over at my screen. "Do you mind?" I ask. He looks away. "He punched Lake earlier. If that helps."

He turns back around, his eyebrows in his hair. "Yeah?"

"So I hear."

"Then yeah, I think that's fine. If he ends up being a dick though..."

“I don’t think it’s Hayes we have to worry about.” I send Hayes a text to come over even though I’m sure he probably wasn’t waiting for a confirmation from me. I was right. Not thirty seconds after I send the text, I see him breaking through the wooded area and onto the beach.

I watch him come toward us, and someone behind me asks, “Is this okay?”

Chase tells them it’s fine, so everyone goes back to talking. I try to gauge how his conversation went with Lake by the look on his face, but there’s a reason why they call him Ice Man. He leans against the picnic table right to my left but doesn’t say anything. I look back at Chase’s teammates and try to get back into the conversation. With Hayes here, though, it’s difficult. My attention keeps getting drawn back to him.

A little while later, a cooler full of drinks is brought out, and a bonfire is started by the beach. All pretenses of the guys trying to act as if they’re here for lacrosse seems to burn up alongside the wood they’ve gathered. I haven’t seen one lacrosse stick in any of their hands all day, for the past few days even. Though, I suppose they could be working on their stuff while I’m at camp doing basketball things.

Hayes even accepts a drink. Before long, he joins in on the camaraderie. He doesn’t exactly talk much, but he's there and accepted. Every now and then, I'll see Chase giving him a look. It isn't until then I remember that Hayes interrupted Chase from kissing me earlier. I don't know why I just sat there like that. I hadn't meant to, and it certainly wasn't nice of me to lead Chase on.

I stare at Chase, and it isn't long before he feels my eyes on him. He turns around. When he sees my look, he frowns. "I know," he says. "I shouldn't have tried to kiss you. You're confused right now and me doing that isn't helping."

"You're too nice, Chase," I tell him.

Damn my freaking body! Like what the hell? This guy is perfect, but I couldn't care less.

Just so it's clear, Chase is at the top of the really great human category. I'm in the middle. The Ballers are dead last.

14

Hayes slips his hand through mine as he walks me back to my cabin later that night. The crickets chirp, only drowned out by the sound of the tiny laps of the lake against the sandy shore. His thumb traces over my hand as we walk in silence. I already know I'm a complete goner when it comes to him. Holding myself back will be the hard part. "I'm glad you found me tonight," I tell him. His hand squeezes mine and suddenly, I'm thrown back to when he pinned me against the wall, pushing his hips into mine in answer as to whether he liked me or not.

I've already decided I'm not going to ask him about Lake. I don't want to go there with them—or him, I mean. Just him. I told Lake that night that we didn't have to like one another. I told him I'd stay out of his business if he stayed out of mine, and even that wasn't enough for him. I'll be fine if we never talk about Lake again.

"Why did you go there in the first place?" Hayes asks, his voice coming out of nowhere until it sweeps over me in a sweet caress. I'm still not used to hearing the sound of his voice.

I look up at him. I barely make it to his chest. His pecs are pretty much in my face, but they're damn fine pecs, so I don't mind. If we ever kiss while we're standing next to one another, I'll have to climb him like a tree. I can tell Hayes isn't happily on my same trail of thought. "That bothered you."

He nods.

I stop in the sand and stare up at him. "I don't think you understand how lonely it is for me sometimes."

He blinks. I can tell, aside from the fact that he has the best poker face ever, that I've surprised him with that answer.

"No one likes me here, Hayes." I try to smile, but I can't make myself. "No one liked me at RHS either, except for Dawn."

His tongue pushes against his teeth. I don't really want him to say anything to that confession. I have a feeling he'll just try to tell me that they do like me, but

I'm done listening to excuses on that front. You don't treat people you like like that.

"Dawn was supposed to come visit me this weekend, but her boyfriend had to visit his grandma, so she couldn't make it."

"If you're lonely, I want you to call me from now on," he says. Even in the moonlight, his blue eyes are mesmerizing.

I bite my lip. That was pretty much the perfect thing to say. If Hayes talks like that, he really should learn to talk more often. His hands slide down my hips. When they hit the back of my thighs, he hoists me in the air. My legs move around his waist, and we're finally eye-to-eye and chest-to-chest.

I suck in a breath as his arms wrap around me, holding me like I'm nothing. "When I kiss you for the first time, it's going to change me."

The world around us stops. The sounds of the night go mute. All I can hear is Hayes's breathing, and then the feel of his breath as it teases my lips. I lean forward.

Hayes pulls away slightly. "Not yet." He reaches a hand up to place a strand of my hair behind my ear. "Not until all the doubts I see in your eyes are gone."

I breathe out. "I kind of hate you right now."

"I kind of hate myself. For a lot of things." He lets

me go gently, and I slide down his body. He wants to kiss me. He wants to do more, judging by the defined bulge in his shorts. "I know what it's like to be lonely, Tessa. You can still feel lonely even if you're surrounded by people. Sometimes it takes just one person to make you feel right again."

Oh, God. This boy. "Are you sure you won't kiss me?"

The corners of his mouth pull up. "I think you should stop asking before I give in."

"I think—"

"Quintessa!"

Startled, I scramble away from Hayes. Oh, fuck. I know that angry voice. The voice only a father could have. I turn toward Hayes. "Go." His brows pull together as he looks back toward my cabin. I'm hoping it's so dark my father won't have recognized Hayes yet. "Please."

He hesitates, grabbing my hand again.

"Hayes, seriously," I say to him. "It's after curfew. Just go. There's no sense in both of us getting into trouble." Without looking back, I push away from him and keep my head down as I walk toward the cabin. I hope he's not following me. I really hope not. If my dad just happened to try my room and found me missing, he might not make a big deal. If it's two of us out after curfew, he might be forced to say something.

I pull my hair over my shoulder and sulk up the tiny porch. My heart is beating like crazy. I turn to check once and see that Hayes didn't listen. He's right behind me.

Son of a bitch. I turn back around. "Hey, Dad. I'm sorry. I—"

Dad looks behind me, his expression stern. "Leave now, Hayes."

Hayes's lips form a thin line. "Sir, I—"

"Now, Irving. I don't want to have to ask again."

Pretty sure he didn't ask, but he's got his coach-like authoritative voice on full blast. If my cabin was any closer to the others, he'd be waking everybody up.

Dad pushes the cabin door open for me, and I step inside. He glares behind me for a few seconds, longer than necessary even, but eventually, he turns toward me, so I can only imagine that Hayes wised up and left. He shouldn't have even walked up to the cabin with me. I don't know whether to be mad at him or happy that he decided to stick with me. I turn, forgetting all that to face my father. "I'm really sorry, Dad. I know I'm out past curfew, I—"

"Are you taking this seriously, Tess?" He cocks his head at me. "That's what I've been sitting here wondering while you've been out doing God knows what. It's a thought I never believed I'd have to put in the same sentence as your name. What are you thinking?"

His words smack me in the face. "Of course, I'm taking this seriously. I'm having my best camp ever so far. I—"

"Really?" he asks, eyebrows raised. "Not after tonight you're not. I got a call an hour ago, followed up with texts of pictures of you breaking curfew. What is wrong with you? Do you know how many players there are that would love to be in your position? I don't just give these spots to people, not even to my own daughter."

"I know, Dad," I grind out. I sit on my bed with my head in my hands. Shame washes over me. This is what I get for letting my guard down.

"You're goddamn lucky Lake's not going to pursue this."

I yank my head up to stare into his face. "What? Lake called you?" The blood in my veins turns to ice. That motherfucker. "Don't ever trust Lake, Dad. When it comes to me, don't ever trust him."

"I thought the same thing until I showed up where my daughter was supposed to be sleeping in her bed and she's not fucking here. Then, I see her walking back hand-in-hand with a guy."

I run both hands through my hair. "Don't get Hayes in trouble. It's not his fault. He was worried about me."

"I'm dealing with Hayes myself. I have a feeling O'Brien wants to keep this on the down low because his friend was involved."

"I can guarantee you that asshole only gives a crap about himself. He's not trying to save anyone. He wants you to get me in trouble."

"It seems like you're doing a great job of that on your own," Dad spits, his voice rising.

I stand. "Dad, Lake's destroyed my life. How can you not see that?"

He chuckles disbelievingly. "First, you're mad at Ryan because Ryan destroyed your life, now Lake O'Brien? Who else are you going to blame for your own actions, Tess? You were still out of your cabin when you weren't supposed to be. Lake just called you out on it."

I shake my head at him. "If you only knew, Dad."

"Then tell me. What don't I know? Talk to me. You haven't talked to me like we used to since I left your mom."

"Maybe because you're never around!" I scream,

my anger finally getting the better of me. "Maybe because you're off meeting Ryan's grandparents instead of hanging out with me. Maybe because you're not asking, and you're not paying attention. Why didn't I get playing time this past year, Dad? Why?" I'm so furious I'm shaking. My hands are fists at my sides.

My dad moves forward. "You understood how hard playing for RHS was going to be, right? You have barriers to break down, you have bias to break down. Why do you think I'm hard on you? Why do you think I'm so mad you were out of your cabin when you weren't supposed to be?" He takes a breath, putting his hands on my shoulders. "It's wrong, but if you want to play with the boys, you're going to have to rise above them in every way possible. You're different, so you're going to get mocked. You're going to be scrutinized. You're going to get teased. You're going to get knocked around and filleted wide open." He swallows hard. "But this was all your choice, Pumpkin." He moves his hands to clasp my cheeks as he stares down at me. "I'm behind you. I know my little girl is tough enough to do this, but you can't let your guard down, and you can't put me in a position where I have to reinforce rules I don't want to."

I let him pull me to him. My whole body sighs in

relief. It's been months since my dad hugged me. It's been months since my dad and I talked about real fucking shit instead of surface topics. The wave of emotion hits me like a tsunami. I grab the back of his shirt and let the tears fall. All these months of taking shit from the Baller Bitches comes out in hiccups. The final showdown with Lake where he pulled the rug out from under me lands on my dad's shirt with salty teardrops. The betrayal of the guys. All of it.

"I know, Pumpkin. I know," my dad says, rubbing my back. "Your mom wants to send you to Springs. She texted me last week that she talked to them. The coach is excited about having you."

I pull away, wiping at my face. "I'm not going to Springs, Dad. Please."

"Look at you, Pumpkin," my dad says, his face crumpling. "Look what's happening to you."

I wince. "Dad, I am begging you. Change Mom's mind. Be on my side about this. You know how much this means to me."

He opens his arms, and I go into them again. He keeps his hand on the back of my head. "Let's see how camp goes. You know I'm watching what's going on. I'm not blind, Pumpkin. I just want to see you come out the other side of it unscathed, and I hate to say it, but you have to do it yourself. That's the only way you'll prove it to these jackasses."

I squeeze my eyes, and hot tears land in my eyelashes. He's right. I've always known what he just said was true. "I'll win MVP, Dad. You'll see."

"And adhere to curfew? And not get into fights in the cafeteria?"

When I don't answer, he pulls me away at arm's length and raises an eyebrow. "Tess?"

"Who told you about the cafeteria? Jacquin?"

His gaze narrows. "No, the kitchen personnel. Plus, I came in and Ryan was on his hands and knees cleaning the floor. I knew something happened."

My mouth drops. "Ryan was cleaning the floor?"

Dad nods. "He's a good kid. He's had to put up with a lot in his life. He certainly hasn't had it as good as you."

Still. Ryan cleaned the juice up? I almost want to ask him if he's talking about Ryan Linc. Maybe one of the kitchen staff is named Ryan, I don't know. It just sounds like the exact opposite of what he'd do.

Dad leans over and gives me a kiss on the forehead. "You should get some sleep. I expect you out of bed early and out running to make up for your infraction tonight. I expect you to put everything you have into beating those guys the rest of the camp. Don't get sidetracked, Pumpkin."

"I am sorry about tonight, Dad."

"I know you are. Now get some sleep."

Dad leaves, and I fall back on my bed, the springs of the crap mattress squeaking underneath me. My eyes burn and now they're dry from crying. In a way, even though I got caught out of bed, I feel better about having told my dad some of the things that are on my mind.

Before I change into my pajamas, I pull my phone out and text Hayes that I'm fine. I leave out the fact that Lake turned us in. Like my dad said, I have to be better than them to beat them.

And if that's what I have to do, I'll do it.

15

The rest of the weekend goes smoothly, mostly because I stay to myself. I get up to run early on Sunday and my dad shows up. It makes me smile when I see him stretching out by the main building when the birds have barely started chirping. He's making an effort, and that makes me extremely happy. I feel closer to him than I have in months.

Chase messages me, but I tell him I got busted on curfew and that I have to toe the line for a couple days. I think this is the lacrosse team's last week here anyway and since I've told him a few times now that I'm not interested in anything with him, maybe we'll both feel more comfortable around one another if we're just friends without the possibility of anything more.

My dad takes me off camp grounds on Sunday for

dinner. Just him and I, and it feels like old times. If my mom were here with us, everything would be perfect.

Monday morning, though, I'm thrown back into it all. I show up for breakfast early. I eat by myself, and then I'm out on the grass warming up for the morning run while the rest of them walk by to grab their meals. Hayes comes up to me, looks around for my father while Lake narrows his gaze at us. I ignore him, but I do hide a smile at the black and blue shiner around his eye. "You sure you're okay?" Hayes asks.

I put Hayes off all Sunday, telling him pretty much the same thing I told Chase. I also had time to think about what he said, and he was right to stop us from kissing. I want to make sure I believe it first. If he keeps talking to me in front of Lake, that'll come sooner rather than later.

"I'm good. I'm more than good, actually." I lower my voice. "And don't worry about my dad. I think you'll be fine."

"Oh, your dad came and talked to me already."

"What?" I gasp.

One corner of his lips tip up. "Not about the curfew, though he threw that in, too. It was about you and me."

I'd had my foot in my hand, stretching out my muscles, but I drop it to the ground. "He did?"

He nods. "He asked me if I'd been a part of any of the bullying you received this year. I told him not directly, but that I also didn't do as much as I could have to stop it." There's no trace of a smile on his face now. "I don't think he likes me very much."

My eyebrows raise. I've never seen my dad not like anybody. Except maybe the media back in the day. "I doubt that's true."

"You didn't see his face, but it's okay. I deserve it."

A voice interrupts us. "Hey, Dale."

I look past Hayes to see Jacquin walking up to the main building. I give him a small wave, and then look back up at Hayes who's watching Jacquin like a hawk. Why the hell are all the Ballers possessive assholes? Next thing I know they'll be claiming me again.

Hayes turns. "Did you eat already?"

I nod, then tilt my head in the direction of the cafeteria. "You should go fuel up before the run. I've been kicking your ass all camp."

He smirks, but a spark of competition flares in his eyes. Good. Maybe I'll actually have someone to talk to during the run instead of just my motivation for wanting to beat the Ballers keeping me on my toes.

Before long, everyone else is out on the grass stretching as well until Jacquin is the last to make an appearance. Hayes is standing right next to me when we start off, but he can't keep up. I'm not too surprised. He has a lot more weight and height to carry compared to me. Jacquin, though, is pushing it even faster today. Soon, it's just the two of us out front, and I swear the closest person is Ryan who's fifty yards behind us and looks like he's really trying hard. It reminds me of the trials when he asked Matt if he liked being beaten by a girl. After that, I can't help the smug look that comes to my face and won't go away.

Jacquin sneaks a peek behind him before turning to me. "I've been meaning to get you alone, but since Irving is practically perched by your side every time I see you, I had to wait until now."

"O-kay," I say, treading carefully. "What's up?"

"What's up with you and the older O'Brien kid?"

"Oh," I say, turning to look straight ahead again. I wasn't expecting that question. "You mean other than the fact that he hates me?"

He chuckles. "Figured that one out on my own, thank you. Why does he hate you?"

I shrug. "It's not obvious? I'm a threat to him, I guess. I don't know. You're a guy, you probably have more insight than I do."

"His hate just seems excessive, even if you do play the same position for the same team back home."

"You'll have to ask him then," I tell him frankly.

Why he hates me is irrelevant now. Making him suffer for being an asshole is the only thing on my to-do list.

Jacquin takes all this in, nodding. He and I are in the same boat. I've tried to think back to when Lake started hating me, but honestly, all I can come up with is the year I was going to win Shooting Guard MVP over him. That's when he got Ryan to pretend to like me—which I guess wasn't pretend after all, even though he told everyone it was. That's the core of it as far as I know. Jealousy. Plain and simple.

"Fair enough." Jacquin's quiet for a few strides before he says, "I think you should watch your back though. Most competition is decided on the court, but Lake seems determined to get to you in other ways."

"You're not wrong," I say, meaning to sound as cryptic as possible. Jacquin, the guy who just got drafted and works for my father, does not need to hear my stories from last year.

After our short conversation, and after I'm practically panting from the exertion of running so fast, Jacquin slows us down once again. He slows so much Ryan is able to catch up with us. I can tell he's gassed, but the look on his face is full of determination. He looks over at me, then straight ahead again, so I do the same.

My body buzzes from having him so close. I try to

pass the feeling off as just wanting to beat him so badly, but I know it's not all that. Ryan was my number one Baller crush at one point in time. I've seen him be different. I've felt his strong arms and heard his sweet words. Maybe that's a side of himself he doesn't show to everyone, or maybe it's just me he doesn't want to share it with again, but I know he can be different. Or at least, I know he used to be different. I guess that's the catch. Just because someone used to behave a certain way, doesn't mean they can't change. And I don't need to forget that Ryan had two chances with me. Once, a few years ago, when he sided with Lake, and just recently when, again, he stood next to Lake instead of me.

But still, there's something here. There always has been.

In my next stride, I get too far over on my edge and my ankle starts to turn. I stumble, and Ryan's hand comes out to catch me. His fingers wrap around my forearm and hold me steady. I straighten out my stride and look up at him.

"You okay, Tessa?"

"Y-yeah. Thank you."

That could've been a disaster. I almost rolled my ankle, and as an athlete, my body is the most precious thing I have.

This is exactly why Alec needs to tell the Ballers he wants to focus on baseball. He could over-do it. He could get blindsided with an injury doing the sport he doesn't want to do, and then he'll be screwed doing the sport he wants to do.

I peek around my shoulder and find him in the middle of the pack. He's jogging easily, looking around at the tall trees along the side of the road. At some points, we can even see the lake through breaks in the branches. He's probably daydreaming about baseball, I realize.

"How long have you guys known one another?" I ask.

Ryan snaps his head toward me, his eyebrows scrunched together. I feel like I know this answer already, like it's a part of their lore as the kings, or Rock Ballers of Rockport High, but it'll be nice to hear it from one of them. "Since we started with intramural basketball together," he says. "I don't know, five years old?"

"Been with each other through a lot?" I ask.

Even Jacquin is looking over at me now like I've lost my mind.

He rolls his eyes. "Obviously."

I notice Ryan does that. He gets an attitude when

people hit too close to home. "Are you guys going to try to go to the same college together?"

He huffs. "That's been the plan since we were kids."

"But I mean, since they're your best friends, you'd be happy for them no matter what, right?"

His gray eyes cut through me. "What the hell are you trying to get at, Tessa?"

I try to shrug his comment off. "I don't know. Guess I don't know what it's like to have friends."

"You have friends," he says. "That spunky girl back home and David Russell."

Of course he would know David's name, but not Dawn's. "Her name's Dawn," I inform him, putting as much aggravation as I can in my voice. "How's Rhonda?"

He shakes his head. "You're such an idiot."

I don't even know why I try, or what I was even trying to accomplish, I guess. I got no answers, just the butt end of Ryan's terrible attitude. Again.

Jacquin kicks it back into gear once we turn down the road to camp. I follow after him, only this time, Ryan is hot on my heels. We pass the imaginary finish line at the same time. My dad's there, clapping as we come across. He looks at both Ryan and I like he's so pleased we performed well. My stomach squeezes at the thought that he'd be just as proud of Ryan as he is with me.

I grab a water and hide around the side of the building to get my breath under control. In the background, I can hear my dad talking to Jacquin, but that's not everything. Ryan footsteps approach as he walks right up to me. We're in the shadows of the building and like he's done before, he gets right in my face, his heaving chest brushing against my own. He squishes the water bottle that's in my hands against my ribs. "Do you remember what I said to you when you were in the shower, and you and I were alone?"

I nod. His presence throws me for a loop. He's so close that if I breathe, I'll breathe him in. No one else has finished yet, but they will soon. What will they see when they turn toward us? Two people who hate each other? Or two people who are great at pretending?

His gray eyes turn molten in front of me. "I thought you would understand you can only believe what I say when we're alone. Now...and then."

I swallow, his insinuation is clear. It's what Hayes has been trying to tell me, too. Though the guys picked Lake, that didn't mean they stopped liking me. "That's not enough."

"It's all I've got."

My jaw hardens. There's really nothing more to say to him then.

Ryan moves away, cursing. He runs his hands through his hair. Instead of turning back around, holding me against the wall like he did at the school to try to force me to bow down to him, he just walks away. He grabs a water from the cooler, and then separates himself from everyone else as the rest of the guys finally come running back in.

Ryan Fucking Linc. Each and every time.

I drop my head against the wall of the building behind me, forcing my breaths to slow. I don't know what amped me up more, finally having Ryan close to me again, or the full sprint at the end of that run.

16

Fuck me.

My stomach drops when my dad lays down what we're doing today. Hayes moves close to me. He's not even trying to be nonchalant about it. Today is position specific day. We're not going to work general skills; we're working skills for our position and for our position only. Meaning, it's all me, Lake, and River.

My fingers tingle. The thought of spending the day with the O'Brien boys makes me want to hurl. At least before, there was one other impartial player there besides me and Lake. Now, there's River. River is just Lake's clone. They both hate me.

When Dad finishes talking, Hayes looks down at me. "This isn't good."

"It's not like this is new. We knew this was going to happen."

He looks from Lake to River, seemingly having the same exact conversation with himself that I just had. It seems worse that it's going to be two against one. At least Jacquin is going to be our coach for the day. He knows Lake and I have an issue with one another, so hopefully he'll be cool about it. When I look up to find the coach in question, Ryan is next to him, their heads bent together.

My dad is waiting for Hayes while the other two Centers are already next to him. "I'll be fine," I tell him, urging him to go off with my dad and learn Center stuff. There's nothing he can do unless he wants his own training to suffer. But this is the exact reason why we come to this camp. Position specific skills. Working with the best of the best. I'll just have to remember my motto for this summer: *Bigger. Badder. Better.*

I end up having to give Hayes a shove to get him going. Once he's striding toward my dad, I walk up to Jacquin. When we're all in a tight circle that's too close for my comfort, Jacquin turns, and Lake, River, and I follow him to one of the outdoor basketball courts on the outskirts of the cabins. There's a basketball rack already waiting for us along with a cooler of sports drinks and waters.

He turns around as soon as we get onto the court, his arms crossed in front of his chest. "First thing's first, no bullshit in this training. You play hard, but you play fair. No cheap shots." He stares at Lake as he says this. "No personal shit. No smack talk." He grabs a basketball from the rack, spins, and takes a shot at the basket. He makes it. It catches the rim and follows it until it drops through the net. "We're starting off with a game of Pig."

I smile at this. My dad and I used to love to play Pig. We'd take the craziest shots and see who could make them. He used to beat me every single time when I was a kid, but as I got older, I got better.

"We're going in alphabetical order. First Lake, then River, then Tessa."

"Technically, her name's *Quin*tessa," Lake says.

I shrug and look over at Jacquin. *Does it matter?*

"Fine," Jacquin says. "Lake, Quintessa, then River."

Lake and River smile at one another. Why, I'm not sure. Lake steps up and takes the shot Jacquin just made. He sinks it. Unsurprising. Lake is good. That's why I don't understand why he needs to use his words with me—or worse, the physical shit he pulled on me from the track that night. All he has to do is beat me on the court, and then there's nothing I could say about him starting and not me.

I'm up next. I shake my hands out and then take Lake's place. I dribble twice, then bring my feet together before jumping. At the height of my jump, I arc the ball through the air. I smile as it curves and sails right through the net.

We play the game for a while. River is the first to get a letter. He's also the first to get to two letters. Jacquin is the only one of us who doesn't have a letter yet. I can see why he was drafted straight out of high school. The guy has skills, and his competitive edge comes out to play during our playful game. Because River isn't as good as the rest of us, Jacquin gets his choice of shots pretty much the entire time. He's definitely controlling the whole game.

By the time the game ends, Jacquin wins. I beat Lake only because his frustration started to take over and he let the fact that I was playing well get to him. Basically, he choked, and I was able to get the better of him. River was dead last.

Ha. Punk. I should write 'You suck' on his forehead.

Next, Jacquin runs us through some basic Shooting Guard drills. We practice passing, then pulling up short. Overall, I like the way Jacquin instructs. It's easy to tell that he's dedicated his life so far to the game. He deserves everything he's gotten. I can't pretend I'm not jealous of him. He has what I want. Although, I do think that I, personally, would like to go to college first.

It's not the same for everyone though. Pro players in the NBA make a lot of money. It's not hard to see why Jacquin would want to get pulled up already. Then, of course, there's always the threat of injury. If he decided to go to college and then got injured while there, he'd never get his chance at the professional level. There are so many factors to consider, but regardless of that, Jacquin deserves every one of them with how he plays.

In fact, I'm so enamored by his playing that at one point, I completely miss what I'm doing and run into something hard. A half growl, half cry sounds in my ear, and I turn to see Lake sprawled out on the blacktop. My shoulder burns with pain at our contact. "Shit, I'm sorry, Lake."

I reach my hand out to help him up, but he bats it away. "Watch what the fuck you're doing, Dale."

His brother basically pushes me out of the way and helps him up himself. When Lake gets up, he tests the weight on his ankle, and I see him grimace.

My cheeks flame. That really was my fault. "Are you okay?" I ask. I know he's the scum of the earth, but I hate to think that I actually hurt him, especially when

I should have been paying attention and he wasn't actually doing anything directly at the moment to deserve me hurting him.

"Shut the fuck up," Lake snaps.

Jacquin jogs over. "What did I say before we began training today? Leave it about basketball."

"I was trying to. Tessa knocked me down."

Jacquin's eyes laser through him. "Do you want me to call medical?"

Lake shakes his head.

"No? Good, then everyone can shut the fuck up. Mistakes happen."

Lake grumbles something that sounds a lot like he's insinuating I got to Jacquin, too, with my superior oral skills—only much nastier than that.

"Like you haven't done worse to me on purpose," I say to Lake, my anger finally bubbling to the surface and repressing all the 'Oops, I accidentally hit him' nonsense. His ankle seems to be fine now. He should just drop it.

Lake turns toward me. "If you can't take playing with the boys, by all means, leave."

"Have a seat, O'Brien," Jacquin says. He turns around, his face twisted in disgust.

"What?"

Jacquin spins on his heel back toward us. "I said

have a fucking seat. I don't want to hear your bullshit when it comes to Tessa or any other player you think shouldn't be here. I want players who are going to compete on the court, not with words and jibes. I warned you at the beginning."

"This is straight up bullshit," Lake says, looking around like he's searching for an ally to tell him he doesn't have to sit this out.

"Oh, is it? My court time, my rules. Take a seat."

Eyebrows raised, I watch as Lake just stands there, his face growing even redder by the second. When he finally realizes he's not going to get anywhere with Jacquin, he storms off. He kicks over the cooler filled with sports drinks and doesn't just sit on the edge of the court like Jacquin told him to, he leaves the court all together, going back toward the cabins.

River looks from Jacquin to his retreating brother. Jacquin steps up to him. "You're welcome to stay, but I won't have any bullshit in my practices. Your brother is wasting an opportunity for real skills because he has a grudge. How are you going to act?"

Surprisingly enough, River stays on the court and keeps his mouth shut. He even plays better without Lake here. Don't get me wrong, I still think he's the number one asshole in training, but when out of the clutches of his brother, he isn't so terrible. Except for when I try to give him advice on his jump shot, he stares at me like he wants nothing more than to see me shrivel up and die. When Jacquin is out of earshot, he says, "How many points did you score last season?"

I glare right back at him. "I think if you'd compare playing time to points scored, you'll find I did even better than your brother. But who's counting, right? Your brother and I are on the same team."

He shakes his head. "Not if he has anything to say about it."

I narrow my gaze at him. I wouldn't be surprised if Lake did try to do something to my position on the team. Find a way to kick me off, get me injured, or maybe even worse, make it so I don't want to join the team at all. I think that's what he tried to do this past year. He thought if I couldn't have the guys, I'd leave. But I didn't transfer to RHS for the Ballers, I transferred for the team. I transferred for basketball, period. Nothing more. Alec and Sloan, and feeling like I was on a team again, were just added bonuses. Even though I didn't have those things for very long at all, they were great while they lasted.

"Tell him to bring it, Baby O'Brien."

His nostrils flare. "You might have Hayes on your side now, but the others will be harder to get."

"There are no sides, and if your brother was smarter, he'd realize that."

"You challenged him directly. You transferred to Rockport, you signed up to try out for the team all knowing you both play the same position. That's a challenge. You don't belong there."

From behind us, Jacquin sighs, "Oh, wonderful, it's Dale's boyfriend."

I turn to find Hayes trudging up the small hill toward the outdoor courts. He's by himself, his dirty blond hair flopping over his forehead. There's a ring of sweat around his collar that ends just over his chest. It looks like my father's been working the Centers hard.

My first reaction is to tell Jacquin Hayes isn't my boyfriend, but is he? Does he want to be? He's come to my aid, he's told me he likes me, and he's freaking apologized to me multiple times. Shit, I don't know what he is right now. I don't know what any of them are to me right now. River says the others will be harder to get to my side. Do I even want to do that?

My face heats when I remember what it was like to be with Sloan and Alec. The Ballers as a whole—minus Lake, of course—have always sent my heart skittering through my chest like I'm on speed.

"I saw Lake walk back early, are you okay?"

Before I can say anything, River shakes his head in

disgust. "You're supposed to be one of his best friends. Did you ask him if he was okay?"

Hayes ignores him completely. It's as if River means nothing to him. His voice doesn't even show up as a blip on "Ice Man's" radar.

"I guess we're done for the day," Jacquin says from behind us. "If you don't mind, Irving, can I talk to Tessa alone?"

Hayes looks me over, his deep blue eyes clouded in anger as he glares at Jacquin. I walk over to him. "What's up?" I whisper.

"You played well today. This is probably going to make me sound like a dick, but I was hesitant when your dad told me his daughter played and was invited to camp. You're really good. To hell with those other guys. They obviously don't love the game enough if they're going to hate on a female player. Skill is skill."

My chest expands. *Wow. That was really nice of him to say.* "Thanks, Sellers."

He winks at me, then places the ball that was in his hand in the last spot on the basketball rack before walking back toward camp. When I turn to face Hayes, River is gone, too.

"What did he want?" Hayes asks.

"To tell me how good I am."

He peeks at him over his shoulder. "I don't like him."

"You're not a fan, 'Ice Man'?"

He turns toward me, a smirk on his face that makes me shiver. He traces his fingers around my ear, taking the flyaway hairs that escaped from my ponytail with them. "I'm only sharing you with the Ballers, Tessa."

My heart skips a beat. I stare into his eyes, and my toes curl inside my sneakers. Why does that sound like such a promise?

17

Lake and River aren't in the cafeteria for lunch, so I actually sit with the Ballers and a few of the other guys who were invited to camp. Most of them are happily talking about each of their individual sessions. Hayes doesn't talk much, but I get from the other Centers here that my dad put them through the wringer. I can't say Jacquin was that hard on us, but I think he was teaching us more than just basketball skills today. He was trying to give Lake a life lesson. I have a suspicion he knew me working with Lake and River would end up the way it did; he was just waiting for it.

Sloan and Alec keep staring at me. I'm pretty quiet throughout lunch, only because this is the first time I'm sitting with them at all, and I feel like it's only because

Lake isn't here. What if Lake were here? I'd probably be sitting by myself since the lacrosse team isn't here either. Ryan, though, asks me how our session went. I leave out the fact that I accidentally hit Lake, and he made a big freaking deal about it. I told him Jacquin was a good coach, and that he impressed me. He hasn't shown me anything new yet, but he did make a point with Lake that needed to be said.

This isn't RHS. Lake doesn't own the fucking camp like he owns the school. He needed to be taken down a notch.

Afterward, we all break, the guys groaning that they can't wait to get in the shower. Trust me, I've been in rooms with a bunch of sweaty guys before, and it's not always pleasant. Hayes, however, has this bit of sweet aroma. He doesn't smell bad at all, even though I can tell he worked hard. I wish I could have seen him practice and watch how my dad worked them. I miss being my dad's student in a lot of ways.

I run up the steps to my cabin and swing the door open. Right when I walk in, a hand closes around my arm and throws me forward, further into the room. I spin to find Lake, his muscles taut, his body practically vibrating with anger. "Don't you ever fucking do that to me again."

I swallow. He seems more on edge than I've ever

seen him. Even when he and River drew the dick on my face, he was controlled. Right now, though, it feels as if he's barely holding it together, a stretched string waiting to snap. "I said I was sorry about knocking you over. It was an accident. Get over yourself."

He stalks toward me. The back of my calves hit the bed. I teeter for a moment but stay upright. "I'm not talking about that. I'm talking about Sellers throwing me out of the session."

Lake is shaking. His knuckles are white at his sides. I take a breath and put my hand up between us to ward him off. I know Lake can be unhinged, but this is more than that. Part of me wants to say that getting kicked out of the practice was his own fucking fault. Jacquin told us he didn't want to hear any shit during practice, and he's the one who didn't listen. "I told you before we should just ignore one another."

He looks me up and down. "How can I ignore you? You're everywhere."

Bile rises up my throat. I don't like the way he's staring at me. He's like a caged tiger. I don't want to poke the beast and give him a reason to show his claws. "I think you should leave now, Lake."

His nostrils flare. "You embarrassed me in front of my little brother, and that fucking pretentious Sellers."

I lick my lips, trying to keep my own body under

control. "Lake," I say calmly. "You did it to yourself. You didn't have to start shit with me."

"I did, though, because you're always fucking around. You're always fucking in my face," he snarls. He lunges forward like he's going to grapple me. I fall back on the bed, a small scream escaping. He steps back and laughs. The sound makes goosebumps spread over my arms. He's lost it. He's completely lost it this time. "I'm sick of you always being around."

"It's my dad's camp, O'Brien. I deserve to be here because I'm good enough."

"What about Rockport? Why there?"

Even though I'm sitting on the bed and he's towering over me, I lift my chin. "I've said all this before. You think you're the only one with aspirations. You're not. If you want to be the best, you have to play with the best and against the best. That's what Rockport is to me. Nothing else."

He shakes his head, his eyes studying me the entire time. "They like you. I see it written all over their faces. They chose me then, but—" He breaks off, quickly shaking his head.

"It doesn't have to be either or, Lake. What's so bad about me playing on the team?"

"It's *my* fucking team!"

"It's *our* fucking team!"

He grabs my wrist and squeezes. I can feel the full force of his hatred for me in that grip and in the power of his eyes. He pulls me off the bed, and I struggle against him. "Get the fuck away from me."

The door behind us slams open. I jump, and Lake steps back but keeps his grip on my arm. It's Ryan who comes forward. He slams two hands into Lake, breaking the hold he has on me. "What the fuck, Lake?"

Lake steadies himself, practically growling at his friend.

"We had a deal," Ryan says.

"Well, I'm over it." Lake looks past Ryan to me, his eyes gleaming.

"I'm not," Ryan snaps, getting his friend's attention back.

My heart ricochets around my chest. I back up, watching the two of them face off with one another like I never thought I'd see before.

Ryan runs his hands through his blond hair. "The deal was you'd leave her the fuck alone if we gave her up. That was the agreement, Lake. We all settled on it."

Air punches out of my lungs. *What the...? Deal? Agreement?*

"It's not enough anymore," Lake growls. "I thought

she'd leave. I thought she'd go away, but she hasn't."

"Just what the fuck are you doing, man?" Ryan looks around the room. He sees me there, his eyes widening a little as he takes me in almost like he forgot I was even there. "You're going to hurt her."

"I don't care."

Ryan shakes his head. "That's not who you are. That's not what we do."

"You don't understand!" Lake moves forward to walk from the room, his shoulder collides with Ryan's before he stomps out of the cabin, shoving the door open so hard that one of the hinges breaks off.

Ryan moves to follow him, but I shoot my hand out to grab him by the sleeve. "Ryan."

Everything that just happened swirls around in my brain. He looks at me, then his gaze immediately goes to the floor like he can't stand to meet my eyes. "I have to go to Lake. I'm sorry."

I squeeze the fabric tighter. "Don't. Not right now. What did you just say? Is that what happened?" It's like there's an echo. My voice sounds so far away, even to my own ears. When he doesn't answer, I let out an aggravated breath. "Ryan!"

He pulls out of my grip. "Lake's not in a good place. I have to go help him."

I'm almost out of my mind now. I need to know

what's going on. Were the last few months a fucking lie? I move toward him, placing my palms on his cheeks and forcing him to look at me. His gray eyes burn into mine. "You gave me up, so he would leave me alone."

My whole body is on fire. My hands tremble against his skin, and the more he stays silent, the more I don't know what to do with myself. It's like he's grappling with some inner turmoil.

Before long, though, whatever it is breaks inside him. His hands slide around my hips. He pulls me to him, his erection straining against his basketball shorts. He strikes, his lips colliding with mine. I barely had enough time to register he was going to kiss me before his lips landed. He catches me on an exhale of surprise and then continues to steal my breath as his lips move over mine. A guttural sound makes its way up his throat. He's clinging onto my shirt, balling it into his fists at the same time he keeps trying to pull me closer and closer. It's like he's kissing the last few years into me. All the missed chances, all the time we should have had, he's trying to make up for it in this one kiss.

He's so similar to the boy I first kissed, but also so, so different. He's more skilled. He's more demanding. I'm dizzy with all of it, and I don't want it to stop. I moan, long and hard.

He breaks away. My lips buzz and feel like they've

been worked over. They're certainly plump and almost pulsing at the almost painful stroke of his desire. "Fuck," he says, dazed, like he's just awakened from a dream and can't believe he's here with me right now. "That wasn't supposed to happen." He licks his lips. "I'm so sorry, Tess. You know that, right?" There's an innocence to his gray eyes I never noticed before. Or maybe that's because it's only surfacing now. He closes his eyes and swallows. "I have to go find Lake. I'm sorry. He needs me."

My body says I need him, but the look of pure terror on his face over Lake makes me pause. I have a feeling something else is going on that I don't know anything about.

"I'll call Hayes. He'll be here as soon as he can." He squeezes my hand once, then turns and sprints from my cabin, jumping down the steps, and practically landing already in a full-out run in the direction Lake took off in.

I take a few steps back until my calves hit the bed once again. When I feel the metal structure there, I sit back, the squeak of the coils sounding. My door is only hanging on by the bottom hinge. I should call my dad or maintenance, if I can find a number, to have them fix it, but instead, my brain just keeps replaying what Ryan said. *We had a deal.*

This whole time, they had a deal. The Ballers would stop seeing me in exchange for Lake leaving me alone. I think back to what happened after that night at Ryan's house. Sure, the Baller Bitches didn't stop their nonsense, but the Ballers did. They stopped talking to me all together. I thought it was because they'd gotten everything they wanted. I wasn't playing on the team anymore. I wasn't a threat to them. *My God. This* whole *time...*

Lake's shit didn't start again until camp, until I was basically forced in his face again just like he'd told me before Ryan showed.

"Tessa!"

I glance up to find Hayes sprinting toward my cabin. He leaps the stairs in one go, briefly notices the broken door on the cabin, and then finds me on the bed. He moves forward, and all I have to do is open my arms and he comes right to them, practically tackling me on the bed. "I trust you," I say, right before my lips close over his.

Hayes stills, then a ravenous hunger takes over that has him groaning "Fuck" before he presses his whole body into mine.

Ryan had already started an inferno of need between my legs, so Hayes just stokes it.

"You liked me this whole time?" I ask, finally fully

believing it.

He kisses a trail down my neck. "More than you know."

People might think it's weird to kiss Ryan then Hayes right after without a delay, but it doesn't feel weird. It feels normal. It feels exhilarating and exciting and like I would do it over and over again, with Sloan and Alec added into the mix, too. Each of them, though they have their own struggles, faults, and personalities, they light up a piece inside me like slivers of a whole.

Hayes has his quiet dominance, which is turning out to be not so quiet right now. He's voicing his pleasure in ragged breaths and moans that pull desire from me. *I want more.*

Dropping his forehead to the bed, Hayes ceases his sensual exploration of my neck. His hot breath hits my ear, making my skin tingle and waves of pleasure roll down my body. "Hayes," I say, trying to recover my own breath.

He pushes up onto his palms, hovering over me. This puts the pressure of his erection right against me. I bite down on my lip and move until it rests where it feels best. I'm not sure because I haven't actually seen Hayes's size in the flesh yet, but there's an old saying about tall guys having huge penises. I'm willing to bet that's the truth based on what I'm feeling right now.

Hayes swallows and lifts all the way up. He places his knee on the mattress and then sits at the edge of the bed, running his hands through his hair. "I can't tell you how long I've thought about that."

I sit up and move forward to kiss the top of his arm. If he weren't so tall, I'd be able to kiss his shoulder. While my breathing starts to calm, my rational brain begins to take over again. I stare up at him. "You guys gave me up, all of you, to keep Lake away from me?"

Hayes nods. "Lake needs...help," he says. "I swear he wasn't always like this. He wanted us away from you, so we bartered with him. We thought you'd be better off."

Reaching over, he pulls me into his lap until I'm straddling him. He's still hard, but not as rock solid as he was only a minute ago. It's probably best this way. I know I was a little out of control there for a few minutes.

"None of us wanted to."

I wrap my arms around his neck and squeeze, just letting the steady rhythm of his heartbeat bring me back to earth with this new information. I can't help but think that everything will have changed from here on out.

Everything.

18

Since I'm still sweaty and gross, I kick Hayes out of my room, so I can shower. I'm also going to use this time to try to get my head on straight. As soon as I finish up in the small, rustic bathroom, I lie on my bed, stomach down, and pull out my phone to video chat with Dawn. I cross my fingers, hoping she's around and not too busy with David. I imagine, since I'm not there for a few weeks, they're spending plenty of time together. For her sake, I hope things works out between them because she is totally smitten with him.

"Girl!" I hear before Dawn's face even appears on the screen. She's mid-laugh, and I notice she's in her room, propped up against the ridiculous number of pillows she has on her bed. There are rainbows, unicorns, and sun pillows. Her whole room is bright colors, which I so wasn't expecting the first time I went over. "What's up? I miss your face!"

I smile at her, but it's short-lived. I miss her, too. Dawn was my rock after the Ballers abandoned me. She stuck by me when no one else did, and even with the short amount of time we've been friends, she's the closest one I've ever had. I groan immediately. "Dawn, I'm so fucked."

Her eyebrows pull together. "Something at camp? What's going on? Don't tell me those douches are being mean to you again."

How to even explain it to her? Yes, and no. Yes, they were, but now they're not? Well, I don't even know that, really, do I? As far as I know, they could go back to being douches again.

I don't answer quickly enough for Dawn. She widens her eyes at me. "What is it, woman? Don't keep me in suspense. Hayes isn't still stalking you, is he? Is it about your dad?"

Her theories about Hayes were over-the-top. She thought it was the creepiest thing that he would sit outside my house, even though I secretly felt safer when he was there. "Listen, I can't explain any of this." I pull my hair around my ear. "Some shit went down.

So much stuff. I don't even know where to start." I can tell she's growing even more frustrated by my vagueness, so I explain everything to her. I tell her how Hayes, and basically the rest of the Ballers, have all apologized to me. I tell her Ryan told me they dropped me last year for my safety. My face flushes when I tell her Ryan kissed me, and then Hayes.

"Wait, wait, wait, wait, wait." She holds her hands up, and then sits straighter. "You kissed Ryan *and* Hayes? You've kissed, now, four out of the five Ballers?" She puts a finger up. "One, you're a lucky bitch. Two, I think you're losing it, Tessa. What's changed other than the fact that they apologized and made up some story about doing something for your own good? Do I even need to tell you how sexist that sounds?"

I laugh at that. "They seemed to really mean it. They were worried about Lake."

"If they were worried about Lake, they would've told *him* to fuck off and not you." She shrugs when I frown. "I just don't know if I fully believe them. We know the Ballers are used to getting what they want. I'm looking out for you. Don't forget that you didn't play at all last year after shit went down with them. How could they do that to you?"

I bite my lip. She's right. That hurt a lot. That

broke me. Not just the part about them choosing Lake over me, but the fact that they basically froze me out of everything to do with basketball. Was that supposed to be for my own good, too? That was pretty much the exact opposite of my goals. I run my hands through my hair. "I don't know. See, this is why I called you."

She matches my expression, looking away from her phone screen for a second before looking back. "Let's say there's some slim chance that they really do like you, and that you could get over their massive betrayal of ruining your basketball dreams..." My stomach drops. I can already tell Dawn thinks this is all just a ridiculous story to hurt me some more. "Which one would you pick?"

"W-what?"

She raises her eyebrows. "Which Baller would you pick? I mean, you know I'd be all over Alec and then some, but if they all really like you, you'd have to choose one. Hypothetically, of course. Strictly hypothetical."

A weird twist starts in my stomach. I didn't even think about that. To me, it's never been the Ballers as individuals, even though I sort of, kind of dated Ryan briefly before he ripped my heart out the summer before Freshman year. It's usually the group of them that makes my heart stutter. They have what I always wanted: A tight-knit group of friends who understand what the others want.

Though, if I'm honest with myself, now that I know more about them, do they really have that? Alec won't even tell his best friends that he wants to play college baseball. Even at the risk of injuring himself. Hayes, too, looked out for me without telling any of his friends because he didn't want them to know. What if they're not as strong as I thought they were?

"I have no idea," I tell her honestly.

"Well, it's a good thing you probably won't ever have to make that decision," Dawn says. She moves the bright pillows behind her and then leans back again. It's like she's relaxing on a bed of happiness. "Be careful while you're there. I feel terrible that you're all alone. Even your dad doesn't get you right now."

"I didn't even tell you that part," I start, sighing as I remember the conversation I had with my father. "Lake spied on me when I was out after curfew and turned me in to my dad."

"That fucker."

I nod. She's got that right.

"Wait," she says. "Did the fact that Lake must've been out after curfew, too, ever come up? Otherwise, how could he have spotted you?"

I shake my head. "It's a big mess. He's doing everything he can to get me to go away again. I think the Ballers are sick of it this time though."

A frown line appears between her eyes. "I really wish you wouldn't trust them yet. Let's see how this all plays out. I mean, I'm not saying don't have fun with them..." She winks. "But like, don't get too attached. Or distracted."

Easy for her to say. I've been attached to the Ballers for years. Sometimes, I felt like a lost puppy following them around. Maybe that's my problem. I want them to want me. I want to believe that they actually like me, and that they wouldn't do this to me again.

They seemed so sincere... Then again, I believed Sloan and Alec last time and look what happened. For months, I thought they easily wrote me off even after the things we did with one another, and Dawn does have one sticking point that I don't think I can ever get over. They ruined my basketball season. No matter how this all plays out, there's always going to be that.

I groan inwardly. I'm grateful talked this out with Dawn because I was about ready to jump into their cabin and get cozy, but I shouldn't let them off the hook so easily. Like Hayes said, actions mean more than words. I'll have to see how this plays out. "So, how's David?" I ask with a sly grin.

"Oh. My. God." From here on out, Dawn launches

into a detailed description of their sexual antics, which makes me thoroughly uncomfortable, but puts a smile on my face anyway. Before long, she has me rolling around the bed with laughter.

After we say our goodbyes, I feel like I'm in a much better place. Instead of going for a swim like I'd originally planned, I head out toward the outside courts, stopping by the small equipment shed first to grab a basketball. When I get out there, I take the same shots we did earlier in the game of Pig, working on the ones I missed.

Strictly basketball-wise, I'm pleased with my performance earlier today. I performed well. In the back of my head, though, I think about what Dawn said, about me having to choose between the Ballers. I honestly don't know if I could. I do know that out of all of them, Hayes has done the least to me. He's comforting and strong. I can tell he cares, but shit, Ryan, Alec, and Sloan... It would be an impossible choice.

I take a deep breath, slam the ball down hard on the court, so that it soars back up through the air right in front of my face. I catch it on the way back down, asking myself what's really changed. So what if the Ballers like me and I like them? There's still basketball. That's the one constant I can always count on. It's the one thing that I believe I can change the outcome of. Call me a dreamer, but I have faith that if I play well enough, I could start for RHS next year, especially if I have the Ballers on my side...or at least if they don't hate me like they say they don't. An even playing field, that's the only thing I want right now. I just want a chance. Is that too much to ask for?

I feel like they have it so much easier than I do. They play on their own gender's team. They've all been friends for years. They're so good, they're the kings of the school. They don't even have to compete to keep their spots on the team, it's those that are coming up that have to fight and scrap and claw their way up to even be considered worthy of challenging them for a spot.

Trying out for RHS is like this game I played as a kid: King of the Hill. The kings have the better vantage from already being at the top. They can easily knock others down. They can see everything coming at them and have a heads up as to how to play defense. Those of us crawling our way up have to be a few plays ahead. We have to be strategic. Everything has to go just right in order for us to claim a spot at the top of the hill.

The part that's difficult is that I've never wanted to dethrone them. I never wanted to knock them down a peg or two. I just wanted to *join* them. Yes, even Lake.

We both want the same spot, but that doesn't mean I wanted it all for myself. I was willing to share. With everything that's happened now, I have to ask myself if sharing is good enough for me anymore. Has he crossed the point of no return? Will I be satisfied if we share starting honors?

Or maybe I won't be satisfied until he's the one fighting for every last scrap I decide to give him.

I know that he certainly deserves it that way. But, even if the Ballers like me, I doubt they would agree. That's what years of friendship gives you, a fierce protective instinct. I'm just starting to gather that now. Dawn would have to do some pretty fucked up shit in order for me to turn my back on her. She's the only reason I even made it through Junior year with my dignity—and mentality—intact while everything else went to shit around me. Mom and Dad, basketball, the Ballers... She was there. She calmed me down, she made me laugh, and she pushed me through it.

I'm not sure there's any way to repay her, but surely loyalty is one of those ways, even when someone is going through something major.

By the time I sink my last shot, I want to call Dawn again to tell her I appreciate her for everything she's done for me. I also think I might've talked myself into feeling bad for Lake. Ridiculous, I know. At the same time I think it, I want to reject it. There's got to be a fine line somewhere between someone worthy of being pulled out of the darkness, and someone who made their bed in the dark, and now just needs to lie in it—whatever the cause.

Time will tell where Lake falls in that spectrum.

19

The next morning, I don't show up at breakfast early enough to avoid everyone. I'm also not going to sit with Chase and his lacrosse teammates. I'm here at basketball camp, and it's about time I start acting as if I belong, no matter what.

I go through the line, placing some French toast slices on my plate along with a banana and a fruit cup. When I turn around, I head right for the table that has the Ballers already sitting at it. Just as I sit, Lake looks up to snarl at me. "What the fuck? You lost?"

I shake my head. "No, I don't think so." I take a bite out of my French toast as Sloan's gaze lingers on me. It makes my skin heat. "Everyone ready for this morning's run?"

Alec rolls his eyes. "I've never been a fan of running every day."

Lake glares at him, but either Alec doesn't notice because he's too busy looking at me, or he's trying not to notice the death glare sent his way. Either way, I just continue to eat my breakfast like normal. It's probably the most intense meal I've ever sat through. I thought the one with Sloan's parents at his house kept me on edge. This is worse in some ways.

Wordlessly, Hayes wraps his arm around my hips in a protective manner. It stays there the whole time while he eats his food with his opposite hand. He helps stifle the butterflies a bit, so I can listen in on what the others are talking about instead of living in my head the whole time repeating my mantra, lest I forget I'm supposed to be a badass female basketball player.

With how humid it is in this cafeteria right now, I can already tell today is going to be a scorcher. After all of today's sessions, I'm definitely taking a break to jump in that lake. "How come I never see you guys go swimming?" I ask, genuinely curious. I feel like I remember them swimming other years.

"Because the only pair of tits around here are yours," Lake says.

I shrug, looking at the other guys. I couldn't care less if Lake and his brother showed up to swim, but maybe I can get the other Ballers to hang out with me. I need friends. "I'll go with you, Daddy's Girl. All you have to do is ask," Sloan purrs. "I happen to like your—."

A throat clears behind me. Hayes's fingers press into my side while I slowly look around, just praying it isn't my dad behind us, considering there was about to be a tit comment thrown my way. It didn't sound like him, but you never know. I was too busy drooling over the words Sloan was about to speak.

It's not my dad, thank God. It's Chase. I smile up at him. "Hey, I haven't seen you in a couple of days."

He takes in Hayes's arm around my back, then slowly lifts his gaze to my eyes once more. "We decided to take the lacrosse thing a little more seriously." I laugh but am interrupted right away. "I'd still like to show you some lacrosse moves sometime."

Well, that sounded on the verge of being suggestive. Maybe it was just his smirk as he said it. Ryan must think so, too, because he rises to his feet. "Back off, Fisher."

Chase holds his hand up. "I know she doesn't like me, so fucking chill, okay?"

I'm sure my face is red and blotchy from embarrassment. "That actually sounds like fun," I say right away, trying to keep the display of testosterone to a minimum. "I'm thinking of hanging out on the beach after our sessions today. Maybe meet me there?"

"Great," he says, his smile widening. "Text me?"

"Sure."

He walks back to the lacrosse table. I wave at his teammates and then turn back around. Fewer faces are smiling at me now than were smiling at me only a minute ago. Sloan laughs darkly. "Oh, Tessa. Haven't you learned yet that we don't play well with others?"

I know I'm walking into pricker bush territory here, but I shrug anyway. "None of you seemed interested in swimming, so—."

"I'll be there," Hayes says. His arm tightens around me, and he moves me closer to him by a good few inches. My thigh is against his, and I'm almost swaddled into his side.

Ryan watches Lake's profile as if he's looking for any sign this is affecting him, but he seems disinterested for the moment. Maybe sitting here with them didn't throw him for a loop like I wanted.

Damn.

I stare at the rest of the Ballers blankly, hoping it comes across as if they can show up at the beach if they want...or not. Secretly, I'm hoping they all show up shirtless, so I can watch them from behind my sunglasses without getting caught.

I mean, it's a terrible part to have to play, but someone has to do it.

Sloan smirks at me. Alec has his gaze focused on the plate in front of him, his fork moving his food around absentmindedly. He hasn't said much this whole breakfast. Neither one of them is going to give me an inkling as to whether they're going to show up to swim with me later or not.

Forcing a casual smile to my face, I get up to put my tray away, so I can stretch, but Hayes puts his hand on my arm to stop me. He pulls the tray from my hands gently and puts it on top of his own before rising to his feet, taking them both with him to the tray return. I take the opportunity to slide down toward Alec while the rest of the Ballers get up to leave the building. "Hey," I say. He looks up at me, his green eyes overflowing with unsaid words. "What's going on?" I hedge.

He looks up at his friends who are now walking out into the main part of the building. He watches them go and doesn't relax until Hayes finally leaves us in here alone. He pinches the bridge of his nose. "My parents got a call from a college...about baseball."

My mouth drops. "You're kidding. That's amazing, Alec."

The only thing is, he doesn't look like this is great

news. "I don't know what to do, Tessa. I'm expected to go to the same college as them. We're supposed to play ball together. We've been talking about this since elementary school."

I grab Alec's hand. "But those are dreams of a young kid. You're allowed to change your mind." I lower my voice. "You found another sport that you love more, it's not like you found out you enjoy killing people, Alec. Why wouldn't they understand?"

"It's not that they won't," he says, finally releasing a breath. "I don't want to disappoint them, and I also don't know who I am without them."

I turn my head slightly. I had no idea he thought this way. I thought his reluctance to tell the Ballers what he really wanted was because he thought they'd be pissed. I run my hand down his arm, my hold tightening on him. It feels too normal to touch him like this. "You have to say something soon," I urge.

"I'm not saying anything during camp." He shakes his head. "Camp has always been a big thing for us, I'm not telling them now."

I leave it at that. I can't force him to tell the rest of the guys, even though I think it would be better if he told them sooner rather than later. "What do your parents think?"

He smiles, and the true brightness of it makes me melt inside. "They're so happy."

"Your sister?"

He laughs, the richness of it coating me like a warm blanket. "She thinks it's 'okay'," he says. "Though, she wants me to play basketball in the worst way. I think she just actually wants me to be with you."

Our gazes lock, and I bite my lip at his words. There's something so breathtaking about a boy who lets his guard down. I want to see it all with him. I want to see Alec upset and angry and happy. I want to see him with fascination in his eyes and excitement.

"They tell me you know," he says, inching closer.

I nod, assuming he means that they all cast me aside this past year to "help" me. When Dawn mentioned it, it does sound pretty sexist. I can take a lot of shit. They, of all people, should know that. "You shouldn't have done that," I tell him. I put some space between us by sliding over a little. He just feels too comfortable right now, and I don't need the temptation. "You should've let me have a say."

His mouth drops. Then, he quickly shuts it and looks away. "I did what I thought was right."

I squeeze his arm and stand. "Come on, Christopoulos, it's time for me to kick your ass on our morning run again." *We definitely don't have to discuss this right now,* I think.

He gets up slowly. I stare at him as he moves, wondering if he believed I was going to be fine with their decision because they thought they were making it for me. The truth is, they made it for themselves, too. They didn't want to rock the boat with Lake. They took the easy way out.

Alec follows me into the main building and then out the front door to the little swatch of grass where we've taken to stretching before the run. Jacquin is already out here. He and Lake are talking off to the side. I watch them intently as I come down the short set of steps. Hopefully, Jacquin is sharing with him how to be a good teammate and not an asshole, but that's probably too much to ask. Besides, Jacquin's entire job here isn't to teach Lake how to be a decent human being.

A few stretches later and we're already moving out for our run. At the turn before we take to the country roads, a body runs up next to me, and I almost trip over myself at the intrusion until I realize it's my dad. Then, I smile up at him. "Running with us today, old man?"

A few of the guys around us laugh. "Ohh, some-one's got jokes this morning," he says. "You believe this, Linc?" Dad asks.

Ryan turns around. He has a genuine smile on his face when he looks at my dad. It makes my chest squeeze a little. Is it wrong that I don't want to share my father? "She's full of it this morning, Mr. Dale."

My dad has his "Real Deal" persona on. He kicks it into gear, and soon, he and I are in front of almost everyone except Jacquin who looks impressed that the old "has been" can still keep up with us. Really, my father is an enigma for his age. He's gifted as an athlete and always has been. Ryan, too, tries his best to stick with us.

With my dad on the run this morning, I can tell that everyone else is trying harder too. There's something about him that makes people want to do better. I know it's always been that way for me.

While we're happily running along, the guys all joking instead of competing to win this morning—or maybe that was just me—Dad leans over. "Have you heard from your mom lately? I can't get ahold of her."

I turn toward him. "Well, she went on vacation."

"She told me about that. I thought she was coming home yesterday or today, but she won't pick up."

I watch my dad for a few strides. I wonder why he cares that she won't pick up. He left her. There's not much he should have to talk to her on the phone about either, because I'm older. It isn't as if I'm a little kid they need to coordinate swapping me over from one residence to another. "I can try her later," I say. "Is something going on?"

He shakes his head. "Not really. I just wanted to touch base with her about something."

"Okay... Well, if I get ahold of her, I'll tell her you want to talk to her."

For my mom's sake, I'm kind of hoping she's avoiding his calls. She doesn't need to be pulled back into the Timothy Dale stratosphere when he doesn't want her there anymore. My mom's trying to move on, but I still think she'd love nothing more than for my dad to ride back in with his expensive car and take up the other bay in the garage again. Me, personally? I don't know how she'd ever be able to trust him again.

I turn my head to look at Ryan first, then Sloan, Alec, and Hayes. It's a good question I need to ask myself, too. Once trust is taken away, can it ever come back?

20

It's been a good day. Warmth clings to my skin from the heat of the sun, and also the heat of four pairs of eyes on me.

Today, we worked on mindset again, and since we weren't broken up into partners or positions, I got to be in the same room as my Ballers for the whole day. Lunch was even brought to us, so that the fifteen basketball players in that room with dreams so big it's almost scary, wouldn't have to be interrupted.

At the end of the session about actionable planning, I'm practically buzzing with excitement. Not only did we talk about everything I've ever wanted in basketball and how to get there, but the lure of the lake with the guys is calling to me. I turn around, walking backward while I smirk at them. "What's that look for?" Sloan asks. His brown hair is flat on his head from our run earlier, but he's no less handsome than normal.

I shrug. "Nothing."

Hayes is off to the side, watching me carefully. He's got a slight tilt to his lips like he's waiting for me to do or say something amusing.

Lake and River are in the back of the pack. Before long, they break off and go toward the guys' cabins, but the rest of them are still following me. Once my feet hit the sand, I turn, peel off my shirt and run for the water. My feet splash in. When the water is thigh high, I dive forward, almost gasping as the chilled water coats me. It's a nice sort of thrill that makes me pop up out of the water with a huge gasp. The guys have followed me, tearing off their shirts at the water's edge and dropping them there. I swim backwards, moving my hands to take me further and further out.

I duck under and then come up. My basketball shorts weigh me down a bit, but I'm not taking those off. I'd only be swimming in my underwear then. At least now I have a sports bra and shorts on. The Ballers have seen me in less, but if I take my shorts off and my dad happens to show up like he did on the run this morning, I don't want him to wonder if I'm losing my mind or not.

Hayes only wades in waist deep, his fingers trickling through the surface of the water. Sloan sees me looking at him and says, "Hayes can't swim."

"No?" I ask, looking up at Hayes to find that it's true. He's blushing. I push off the sandy bottom of the lake and swim toward him until I can walk up to where he's standing, my own toes sinking into the same sand he's occupying. "You can't swim?"

He shakes his head. "My parents weren't much for vacationing."

I frown at that. Sometimes I forget that I have more than most. It's second nature for me to come home from school and just jump right in our pool. I've done it for years, winter or not. My mother used to joke that if I hadn't fallen in love with basketball like my dad, I would've been a swimmer. I take his hand and lead him further out into the waves. He's hesitant at first. "You don't have to go too far," I tell him. By the time he's chest deep in the water, I wonder why I wanted him out here at all. I've just taken away a really nice view of his chiseled abs and pecs.

Hands grab me from behind and pull me back. I hit a hard chest, and I'm suddenly encapsulated in essence de Sloan. He's intoxicating in some ways. He's so unabashed, handsome, and cocky. It wouldn't surprise me if he fell right into his father's governmental footsteps, but without all the cheating and the scandals. "I missed you," he says in my ear before he tugs on it lightly with his teeth.

"Ivy," Ryan says.

I can feel Sloan's lips curve against my cheek. He arranges both arms around me in a vise grip. "Yes?" Ryan shakes his head and looks away, which only makes Sloan laugh. "Ryan's mad, Daddy's Girl. This is the first time he doesn't want to share."

"Do you?" Ryan snaps back.

"I could live with you guys all disappearing right now," Sloan says, his hand curving around my hip, then tracing closer to my center. He's making me squirm, and I have a sneaking suspicion everyone knows what he's up to.

"Not likely," Hayes says. He says it flippantly, but in that way only Hayes can. When he talks, people listen. It's the rarity of it all, coupled with the richness of his voice. He could probably be a voice-over actor if basketball doesn't work out. Not that it wouldn't. After he's retired, he could definitely have a career in broadcasting. It's just the talking part that might get him. People do actually want to hear the announcers call the game and not just sit there looking handsome.

I put my hand over Sloan's to stop it from inching any closer to my core. Ryan's gaze locks with mine. I don't know if I should move because he's making me uncomfortable, or if I should raise an eyebrow at him and stay right where I am.

"Someone's just mad because he hasn't gotten a kiss yet."

I blink at Ryan. He just glares at Sloan without telling him the truth.

So, Ryan hasn't said anything about the kiss we shared yesterday? This is interesting. I thought the Ballers shared everything. I thought they didn't have secrets from one another, especially about girls.

Maybe I am getting to them.

Instead of speaking up, telling them we kissed, I ask, "How exactly do you guys plan on going to the same college? What if it doesn't work out?"

Alec's shoulders tense. He turns suddenly, then walks right out and sits at the edge of the water, so that his toes are in the small waves lapping at the shore. "We know where we're going," Sloan says, speaking up.

"Oh, really?" I ask. "You've already been accepted? You have scholarships?"

A tingle of fear shoots through me. Maybe I'm already late.

He smirks. "No, but we're going to State. Where else would we go? The Ballers deserve to go to the best college basketball team in the conference."

"But what if you don't? I mean, what if some of you get in, but the others don't?" It's a legit question. What are the odds that State will want all five of them? "Not only that," I say. "But, one of you might get a better scholarship offer at a different school."

Sloan lets me go. "It's not about scholarships."

"Okay, what about playing time? One of you might get more playing time at a different school. The school you end up at isn't just going to let the five of you start together. There's going to be other players, other *good* players that are already settled there."

It's silent for a while. All I hear is the gentle movement of us in the water. Ryan's looking down at the ripples his arms make as he glides them over the surface. Sloan's swimming on his back, eyes lifted toward the sky. Alec, of course, is just staring at me. Hayes's eyes are locked on me, too, though there's a slight narrowing of his like he's trying to figure out why I'm asking all this.

"Where do you want to go, Dale?" Sloan asks.

My cheeks flame. Honestly, State is on my list, too. Not only is it our home college team, but they have a really great women's team as well. There are several others I'm interested in, but instead of saying that, I tell them I'm keeping my options open.

There are a lot of factors to consider when

choosing colleges. The Ballers can keep sticking their heads in the sand, pretending that they're just going to keep coasting, but again, they're not going to be the kings of the school if they all get into State.

Even playing field.

Something like that could cause a rift between the Ballers quickly. Maybe that's why no one wants to talk about it.

Movement catches my eye. I turn toward the little stretch of woods that separates our cabins from the other section to see the lacrosse team coming toward us, lacrosse sticks in hand. I smile and wade out of the water. I shout that I'll be right back before running into my cabin to change quickly. I opt for my bikini with a pair of regular athletic shorts. Since my skin is already slicked with water, it's difficult to get changed, but I'm back out near the water's edge in record time.

The Ballers and the lacrosse guys are just staring at one another. I've pulled out all the towels I brought with me and drop them on the sand for the guys to use if they need to before walking up to Chase. He hands a stick over to me. It's not as if I've never held one of these, but it's also not something I'm used to. The other teammates hold sticks out to the Ballers, and soon, there's more going on here than just showing me how to play lacrosse. The guys—basketball and lacrosse players alike—are all talking shit. Most of it isn't serious...for now.

Two more lacrosse guys emerge from the slice of forest with collapsible goals. I arch a brow at Chase. "So, this was your goal all along?"

He smirks, not even bothering to play dumb. "I thought they could stand to be taken down a peg or two."

"You know they're just going to challenge you to basketball after this."

Chase shrugs. "It's all good."

Lacrosse is a hard game to pick up. The whole stick factor holds a different element that the Ballers and I aren't used to. In short, we kind of suck.

After the first game that the Ballers dub Big Balls vs. Small Balls, the lacrosse team takes pity on us, whether we use big balls or not, and split up the team, so skills wise, the teams are more even. Lake and River even come down and get in on a play or two. For an hour or so, things are actually blissfully peaceful until Hayes accidentally gets knocked in the mouth with a stick. His temper goes from zero to sixty in nanoseconds. He's right in the guy's face, threatening to tear it off before any of the Ballers can even run up to him. Oddly enough, it's Lake who settles him down while the lacrosse guy looks like he's going to piss his pants.

Holy shit.

"Damn," Chase says. "That was intense."

I'm looking at Hayes like he's a new person. I've never seen him like that before.

"Maybe it's time to go our separate ways," I say to Chase. When he looks at me, I continue. "We don't need anything like that happening again." I hand my stick over to him. "But thanks for showing me how to play. It was fun."

"So, you like lacrosse now?"

I smirk at him. "I wouldn't go that far. It was okay."

Most of the lacrosse players are already leaving. Hayes has turned and is walking in the opposite direction of everyone else. None of the guys follow him, which makes me think that this is just something he does. Lake and River take off until it's just Sloan, Alec, Ryan, and I with Chase giving me a last wave right before he takes off to follow his teammates.

At least everyone took Hayes's eruption rather well. There's a difference between competition and actually disliking someone. At least, that's how I've always felt. I've watched my dad go to dinners with other pro players since I was little and none of them carry animosity off the court, even if the game was a tight one amongst rival teams.

"Hey," I say, "Didn't the cafeteria signs say there

was going to be ice cream tonight?" I feel like I'm dangling a carrot in front of their faces, but ice cream does sound good to me right now. It's got to be the heat coupled with the exertion from the lacrosse games.

The Ballers just shrug, so I take off for the main building to find out. The thought of eating ice cream reminds me of when Dawn made me go to the Warriors baseball game just so we could watch Alec. When I look over at him, though, he's already veering off toward the cabins. "I have to call my parents tonight," he says, lifting his hand in the air for a semi-wave.

"Oh, okay," I say. I watch him walk away and wonder if he's pissed at me for bringing up all those questions about college earlier. It's not like I was going to say anything to the Ballers about Alec wanting to play baseball, but those are legit questions to start asking anyone. How do they think they're going to be able to go to the same college and keep things the way they are? It seems a bit nonsensical to me.

Sloan whistles low under his breath. "Well, okay then. Someone's getting something..." He trails off, his voice high and singsong like.

Ryan stops walking, so I tear my gaze off Alec and turn toward where Sloan is staring. The scene in front of us makes me stop in my tracks.

"Oh shit," Sloan says. "Is that...? Fuck. I couldn't tell from back there."

It is.

It's my dad...and *my mom* making out like teenagers against the wall of the main building. *What the hell is she doing here?*

I turn toward Ryan. His mouth has dropped open, and he looks like he's about to lose it. "Ryan, I—"

He pulls away from my attempt to grab his arm. Then, he stalks off toward the cabins. My heart is in my throat as I watch him leave.

"Shit," Sloan says.

Slowly, I turn back to glare at the two of them. I can't say that I'm not a little happy about this, but damn. Why did Ryan have to see that? Why does my dad have to be so fucking irresponsible? It's not just me my dad's screwing with, it's Ryan now, too.

I don't even bat an eye. I swivel and run after Ryan, catching his hand and making him turn toward me. "I'm sorry you had to see that."

"You're sorry?" The hatred in his eyes falters once he looks at me. He shakes his head and starts walking again. "You're probably thrilled."

"Really?" My voice rises a few octaves. "Have you forgotten I know exactly what it's like to be in your position? At least I can say I didn't know about it ahead of time."

His throat works. He stops walking and faces me. We're out of the way of the cabin, thankfully, only because another small cabin is blocking our view. "You're never going to be able to forgive me for that, are you?"

I shrug. I honestly don't know.

He steps forward until our toes touch. "I didn't think it was going to last, Dale. Nothing my mom ever does lasts. And besides, do you really think I wanted that to happen? That I want to be lying in bed thinking about you while your dad is a couple doors down screwing my mother?"

I grimace. I really didn't need that thrown in my face. "Don't be so crass."

"Or what?" His chest rises in front of him. He still doesn't have a shirt on, and it's one glorious view. "You don't want to hear how I lie in my bed thinking about you? How every time Alec and Sloan said they did something with you, I wanted to punch them square in the jaw because *I* had you first." His gaze rakes over me. "Is that too crass for you, Tessa?"

My body sparks to life. This isn't the boy I held hands and made out with a few years ago. He's so much older and more experienced. Despite the fact I'm wondering where he learned to say things like that, I'm also turned on by it more than I want to admit. "Don't change the subject," I stammer out. "You're hurt by what you just saw."

"This is just my life," Ryan says, his teeth gritting against one another. "I expect it."

I push off him. "Well, I don't." I turn away and head toward the main building.

Ryan grabs me. "What are you doing?"

"Telling my dad to get his shit together."

"What? Why? He's with your mother, isn't that what you want?"

"As far as I can tell right now, both our moms deserve better." It hurts me to say that. The pain slices through me deep. I used to look up to my father so much, but what he's been doing lately just isn't acceptable. He can't string two women along like this. What's his problem?

Ryan doesn't stop me from leaving this time. When I get to where they are, my parents aren't lip locked anymore, which is ideal. My mom sees me first. She wipes at her mouth. There are tears in her eyes. "Hi, Honey."

"Hi, Mom," I say, but I'm only glaring at my father. "What are you doing?"

My dad turns his head to look at me. I can tell he's

confused, and that my mom is upset. The whole thing just makes me sick. They're adults. They should be able to handle their shit.

"Did you know that Ryan Linc just saw all that? Did you?" I yell, pointing back toward the cabins.

My dad freezes. My mom lets out a sharp sob. "It's my fault."

I run both hands down my face. "The hell it is. Maybe if my father learned to keep his dick in his pants, we wouldn't be going through any of this."

"Quintessa," my mom exclaims, but I'm past the point of caring. I don't know whether I'm fueled more by my own hurt...or Ryan's. She moves forward. "*I* kissed him."

"From what I saw, there was kissing going on on both sides." I look up at her finally. Her face is tinged in red, more pronounced around the eyes. "Mom," I choke out. My heart is broken for her. She looks so lost.

"Tessa's right," my dad says. "I should behave better."

My mother spins. "Tim, you certainly didn't ask me to come here. I came here because I wanted to talk to you. When I saw you, I just—"

He waves her away. "If you two don't mind, I think I need to go find Ryan and tell him that even adults can fuck up."

I squeeze my eyes closed. "You should tell his mom, too. Give her more courtesy than you gave mine."

My dad winces, but there's a hell of a lot more I want to say to him. He passes by and puts his hand on my mom's shoulder. "Are you going to be okay?"

She nods, tears leaking from the corner of her eyes. When he leaves, my mom confesses the whole thing to me. She tells me she got back from her vacation missing my father more than ever, so she drove all the way here to see him. When she got here, she just couldn't help herself.

I still think he kissed her back, but I feel sorrier than ever for my mom. For Ryan. For all of us. What a fucked up situation we find ourselves in.

21

Texts to the majority of the Ballers go unanswered while Sloan sends me sarcastic updates. **Hour two of no talking. What will the third hour bring?**

They're keeping a smile on my face, but my stomach is also gnawing at itself. At least I was glad to hear that Hayes made it back to his cabin. He's one of the ones not talking, but is that really that much of a surprise?

It's Ryan that I'm curious about now. I wonder what my dad said to him. I wonder if my dad will follow my advice and actually talk to Ryan's mom to make sure she knows what happened before it just gets dropped on her like it did with my mom. Or worse, that her kid would have to tell her like I did. I honestly can't understand a fucking thing he's done since he's left my mom.

My poor mother is spending the night at a nearby hotel. My parents are supposed to talk it out, and then she's going to drive home in the morning. It's past midnight, and I should've been asleep hours ago, but all I can think about is what happened. How my heart leapt in my throat for a brief moment thinking that things were finally going to return back to normal before it came crashing down again when I realized that none of that is right anymore. Just because the past was perfect doesn't mean the same thing can work in the present anymore. My parents are two different people now. If they did find their way back to one another, there'd have to be a lot of healing and reintroducing themselves to one another.

But, honestly, I think that's a long shot. My dad wanted to go to Ryan more than he wanted to talk things out with my mom. This is just going to be another crushing case of loss for her, only this time, she brought it on herself. Not that I can blame her. I've had similar thoughts lately.

My dad even texted me, telling me he wants to talk with me tomorrow. I didn't bother responding. It's not as if I can avoid him. I'm at his camp after all.

I turn on my side. How did all of this drama follow

me to a basketball camp? It sounds like a freaking soap opera.

"Tessa," a voice whispers.

I sit up in bed until I hear the sound again. I peek toward the door that a maintenance man finally fixed and find Sloan's adorable face looking back at me. I glare at him. "It's past curfew. What are you doing?"

"It is past curfew, so hurry up and let me in."

I groan, then go to the door and unlock it. As soon as I open the door, I hear the chorusing crickets as they chirp away. I have the fan on in my room, so that the steady motor thrumming drowns most of that annoying sound out while I'm trying to sleep. "What are you doing?" I ask again. He's dressed in a wife beater and ball shorts. I love all of Sloan's different tastes. He has the 'put together Senator's son look' along with the athlete look. Then, there's this haphazard outfit probably just thrown on that still makes me swim with want.

"I was just checking in on you," he says. It's hard to tell what color his eyes are right now in the dark. But if I had to guess, they're whatever the color concern is. Maybe a little greener than normal with smudges of brown.

"I'm fine," I tell him.

He looks at me like he doesn't believe me, but he

doesn't say anything more. He moves over to my bed and sits. I stare after him, my head dropping to the side like I can't believe he'd just invite himself onto my bed like that. He pats the mattress next to him, completely unbothered by any of it. When I sit, he turns toward me, grabbing my hands in his. "Is your mom okay?"

I blink up at him. I didn't expect anyone to ask me that. "I don't know. I hope so."

"My mother's been the other woman and met the other women," he says softly. "She tries to pretend like it doesn't hurt her, but I know it does." He strokes my thumb absentmindedly. "I often wonder which one of them strayed first and how different my life would be if they weren't cheaters and adulterers. I swear my dad's like the butt of every joke in the senate."

I roll my eyes at that. "I'm sure there are plenty of others just like him sitting on their high horses."

"Apparently, my dad just sucks at keeping his shit quiet."

What a thing to bond over. My parents are just as fucked up as yours... Should we celebrate with a toast?

"I do know that they never think about us when it's happening. It took me a long time to realize that none of it was my fault," Sloan says, his lips pulling down into a frown. "Unfortunately, it doesn't make it suck any less."

"How'd you get to be so wise, Ivy?"

"Experience," he says. Then, when he realizes that one word can also be turned into a sexual suggestion, he waggles his eyebrows up and down. "Want to see?"

I laugh and push him away playfully. "I guess you can be a nice guy when you want to be."

"Don't tell anyone that. It might ruin my reputation."

"Or elevate it," I say.

He lowers his brows. "You think girls are turned on by the term 'nice guy'. You're wrong."

"I am."

He shakes his head. "No, you're not, Daddy's Girl. The fact that you're still talking to any of us is proof of that."

I stare at him head-on, a challenge in my eyes. "Maybe I just hold out hope for all of you."

He places a single finger under my chin. "I'm glad you do. Someone has to."

The way he says it makes my stomach churn. Maybe that's the recurring theme of the Ballers' lives. Everything they have is all superficial. Sure, they get the girls and the accolades, but the only thing they've ever had that's real is one another. That's why I threaten them.

Because I want in.

The shift in my thoughts comes all of a sudden. I lean up, pressing my lips to his. I've thrown him off, but only for a fraction of a second. His hands dive into my hair, bringing me close. An almost animalistic sound of hunger escapes his throat, making my pulse take off like rapid fire. His hands skim over my stomach, up around my rib cage, then finally to my breast. I inhale sharply.

"Oh fuck. You're not wearing a bra."

"I'm in my pajamas," I explain.

He kneads my breasts, which coaxes embarrassing moans out of me. He pushes me gently until I fall back on the bed. His hand slides up under my shirt, closing around my breast skin-to-skin. He leans over me, moving my shirt up until he's exposed my upper half. I feel his hot breath on me before his mouth closes around my nipple. My hips arch off the bed until his other hand catches me, forcing them back to the mattress.

"Sloan," I pant.

"God, you're so beautiful." He teases my nipple with his tongue before moving to the other. I pull him close to me, arching my body into his. "Christ, Tessa. You're killing me."

"You have months to make up for."

He groans hard. He kisses his way down the center

of my chest before hooking his fingers over the waistband of my shorts. He moves them down slowly, waiting until his kisses have caught up with my shorts that are just now moving around my hips. His mouth lingers there, swirling his tongue in delicious circles. "I've thought about this over and over again," he confesses. "I was so close last time. Just one little taste."

He pulls my shorts and panties down the rest of the way, and I help by kicking them off. He perches himself between my legs, his own excitement straining in his shorts as he lowers himself. This is so familiar, but there's no one to stop us now. No threat of Sloan's parents or party guests. The only people who can stop this now is one of us.

I place my hands on the back of his neck with gentle pressure. I swear I can hear him smirking even though that's not even a thing, but a second later, I don't even care. I feel the tease of his breath first, then his tongue as it sweeps over me. It sends a sudden jolt through me, then a long, low moan that tightens my hold on him. He kisses and swirls and teases until I'm coming apart, my hands in his hair. My fingers dig into his shoulders as I vent my release into the small cabin.

"Mmm," he murmurs, kissing his way back up my body until he lies next to me. I turn toward him, my shirt still caught up around my upper chest. He reaches out a hand to bring the hem down, then pulls the sheet up from the foot of the bed to cover my lower half. "I swear, Tessa." He locks eyes with me. "I'm going to do everything in my power to make me worthy of you again."

I want to tell him that was a nice start, but I know that's just the hormones talking. There's far more to relationships than physical connection.

"Sloan?"

"Yeah."

"I missed you, too."

His jaw hardens as he stares at me. A mixture of shame and anger comes over his face.

I prop myself up on my elbow. "What's wrong?"

"Nothing, Daddy's Girl. Nothing at all."

I look away at his nickname. Today, right now, it's bothering me. I barely want to be associated with that man at the moment.

"We all make mistakes," Sloan says.

Some more than others. "Are you going to tell the others what we just did?" I ask.

He smirks. "Hmm. It's tempting. But I think I'll keep this one to myself. I don't want you to feel like one of those other girls, Tessa. You're far more special."

He lies down, then pulls my head onto his chest. My head raises and lowers with each of his breaths. I know we shouldn't be lying here any longer. I'm so tired, it's likely I'll just fall asleep and then what will happen if we get found out in the morning?

Even after that all goes through my head, I put my arm around him. His other hand comes up to rest on my side. "Sweet dreams, Tessa."

I think I murmur the same, but I'm taken away by sleep, drifting off into a land where I only have to think about what just happened with Sloan, and not about the consequences or the aftermath.

The dream world is a nice respite from real life. It's the reason why I have so many aspirations in the first place.

22

The last thing I want to do is see my dad this morning, but he shows up right outside the main building, intercepting me as I'm about to walk into breakfast by myself. Sloan got up in the middle of the night to go back to his cabin, but not before kissing me on the forehead. Not even the memory of that can keep my lips from scowling as I follow my dad to his car parked in the lot after he tells me to take a ride with him.

I tap my fingers over my thighs as he drives us away from camp. I have no idea where he's taking me, and he's quiet for now. Things will blow up, I'm sure. This is like the calm before the storm. We drive to the smallest town closest to Camp Holly. It's basically just one intersection with a row of businesses all connected together. You know the kind, the ones that actually still have a barber, a furniture repair shop, and a candy store. It's exactly like I remember it from last year, and I'm sure the elderly people in the town can say the same thing dating back to when they were young children. It's kind of neat to see a place that's frozen in time.

He pulls over to the side of the road and tells me to wait in the car. He's going into the doughnut shop he knows I like. I look away. Watching him in there smiling and laughing with the owner just reminds me of the times when he used to do these things for me because he actually cared, not because he was trying to soften me up, so I'll forgive him.

Stepping outside with a brown paper bag, he goes around to his side of the car and gets in, placing the bag on the console between us. I can smell the sugary goodness from here. He drives back toward the small lake, but instead of going to camp, he stops at a dock slip. Putting the car in park, he picks out my doughnut and hands it to me. While we eat, we're silent. I'm watching the geese as they pad next to the shore, then of course, there's the birds that are diving into the rippling water right out in the middle of the lake trying to catch their food.

"Pumpkin," my dad says to start off what is hopefully him telling me what an asshole he's been. I shove the last of the doughnut into my mouth, and then turn toward him. He's got one hand on the steering wheel, angled toward me, his knee practically resting on the center console. My dad looks humongous in most vehicles and this isn't any different. It's always odd to see him squished in something like this. When he's outside, he doesn't look nearly as big as he does when he's surrounded by other things, including people. "I'm sorry you saw that yesterday."

I nod, waiting for him to go on. I want to ask him right away how his talk with Ryan went, but I deserve to get the same talk, so I practically bite my tongue and wait for him to get this out.

"I'm sorry *anyone* had to see it. You were right about some things. I should have told your mom about Leslie and me, and I definitely should have told you about Leslie and me. It's a sorry excuse, but I knew you had so many other things to worry about that I didn't want you to have to think about one more thing."

"I was already thinking about it, Dad. You just up and left Mom seemingly out of nowhere. I know your relationship is your relationship, but I'm your child, so I'm automatically involved." I don't want Mom to sound like a desperate woman, so I leave out all the times I heard her crying and how she walked around like she was a zombie. He doesn't need to know all the things I saw that made me more involved than he thought.

"I guess I was trying to keep you from that."

"But Ryan was going to be my teammate, didn't you think I was going to find out sooner or later?"

He sighs. "I did think of that. Ryan said he wouldn't tell you until I was ready, even though he thought it was a terrible idea. Sometimes you kids are a lot smarter than adults. I don't know."

I grit my teeth at those words. "Stop saying 'I don't know', Dad."

His gaze cuts to mine. I can see that he wants to argue with me about giving him attitude, but he doesn't. "You're right. It was wrong. I was wrong. I'm sorry. As for yesterday, I had no idea your mom was coming. I was blindsided, and I fell into an old pattern—briefly. Very briefly. And not that this part is any of your business, but I did tell Leslie, and I had a conversation with Ryan about it as well."

It saddens me that I'm hearing mostly excuses. "If you didn't want it to be anyone's business, you shouldn't have done it in public."

His fingers tighten around the steering wheel. My father and I never fight. Sloan was right about one thing. I've always been a daddy's girl, until he moved in with Leslie and Ryan anyway. "Fair enough," he says.

"Here's the thing, Dad," I say, taking a deep breath to gather my thoughts before I spew them all over him. "I know you're moving on from your old life, but that doesn't mean you should leave me out of it. Fine, be with Leslie. Move in with her. Do whatever you have to do, but you didn't have to keep it from me."

"I know," he says, shaking his head.

My anger builds and builds. "I don't think you do know, Dad, because I haven't told you. You want to know what it feels like? It feels like Ryan is your only child right now, not me. You ran after Ryan to smooth things over with him. Ryan knew about your new life, not me. You even ask him about the bullying being done to me. If you want to know something about me, ask me."

"Pumpkin," my dad says, reaching for me, his sad eyes tracing over my face. "You're my daughter, you always will be."

I sit back in the seat and cross my arms over my chest. "It hasn't felt like it."

His touch on my hand burns. He pats it a few times, then pulls away again. "I'm sorry. I know I haven't seen you as much. I've seen Ryan more, but I guess that's what happens when you live with someone."

His words stick like a dagger in my heart. "I just don't want you to forget about me, Dad."

His throat works. "I could never do that."

Like Hayes says, sometimes words are empty unless they're backed by action.

"I'll do better," he says. "I promise. I've been trying since we talked the other day." He smiles wistfully. "Your mom and I waited so long for you, baby girl. I could never forget you."

I wait for my emotions to swell up, but it never comes. He and Mom used to tell me about how long they waited for me when I was a kid, and it always made me feel special, but right now, I just feel... cautious. There's no other way to explain it.

We're silent for a few more minutes until Dad says, "Now let's talk basketball for a second. Your mom still wants you to go to Springs."

"No," I say firmly.

He holds his hands out. "I've told her I don't like the idea either because you really want to stay at RHS, but you've got to work with me here, Tessa. Talk to me about what happened last year. About the girls in the stands and the guys freezing you out after you got the start."

I shrug. "I don't really know the reasons why, Dad, but I do know Lake O'Brien hates me, and I'm pretty sure he was the reason those girls all hated me, too." I leave out the part where some of them were jealous because of Sloan and Alec, and the fact that the Ballers claimed me. There are just some things a dad doesn't need to know.

"Do you want me to do something about it?"

Though that idea is tempting, it won't work. "Honestly? Last time when you stepped in to get the scout, you just made it worse."

His jaw ticks. "Your mom's not going to let you go there if the same thing happens again, Tess. She'll pull you from the school."

"I can handle it," I tell him. "I handled it last year."

He stares at my profile, hesitating before he says his next words. "If you don't play, Tess..."

"I know," I growl out. *If I don't play, how are any of the colleges supposed to know if I'm good or not.* "I'll handle it."

He shifts back in his seat. "I'm not promising I'll stay out of it this time, Pumpkin. I get that you need to do things on your own. I know people automatically think that I just give you things. I can read it all over their faces until they actually see you play, but I will step in next year if things go too far. I made the mistake of turning a blind eye before, and I won't do it again."

I shake my head. "Dad, you'll just..."

"And I can't promise I won't support your mother if she wants to enroll you in Springs. Your mom makes a good point. If moving to RHS was supposed to be about basketball, how can you still want to go there? You didn't get the playing time, Tess. You went from playing entire games to playing one."

"But I deserved the playing time."

"You and I know that. Hell, Coach Bradley knows that, but he can't let the rest of his team go to shit for one player. I don't know how you're going to do it, but you've got to get those guys on your side."

My face heats. *Sloan was certainly on my side last night.*

Hayes is on my side, too, though something was up with him yesterday. Alec, I think, is just confused. Ryan, too. Ryan will be the hard one. He likes me, that much is obvious, but one of the reasons why he shouldn't is sitting in this car with me. How awkward will that be?

Ryan's the cornerstone of the team. I can't let Lake influence him the way he did this past year.

"I'll figure something out," I repeat.

He swings his gaze toward me, his face softening.

"I hope you do. I was proud to see you in my high school colors."

This time, a warm feeling expands in my chest. It's the first real emotion I've felt other than anger during this whole conversation. Dad puts the car in reverse. "Let me get you back to camp. Hopefully I'll have you back in time for the run. I wouldn't want the others saying you got any special treatment. Though, Jacquin tells me you've been leaving them in the dust. I think that kid might actually have a crush on you."

My dad smiles away as he maneuvers out of the parking lot. He's oblivious to the fact that my stomach has just plummeted like an anchor through still water. The last thing I need is for one more guy to like me. Camp is already confusing. It should be about basketball, and that's it. Instead, I'm in some sort of weird reality, needing to gather players on my team to overthrow the evil king or else I can kiss my basketball career goodbye.

If I were less stubborn, I'd just go to Springs like my mom wants me to. I can see that play out and end well, but I also know that the kind of colleges that will recruit me from RHS will be better than the ones that will recruit me from Springs. At RHS, I'm a novelty. I stand out. At Springs, I'll be just another good female basketball player.

A girl who wins against other girls is just good for her sex. A girl who can hang with the guys is great.

There's also the fact that the Ballers go to RHS, not Springs. Things are turning around, and I want to be with them there again.

In my head, I only see two options. Either I have to make nice with Lake or take him down. The former will be hard to do since I'm seriously addicted to his best friends. The Ballers have already shown they'll stick up for him. They care. Maybe they won't do it at the expense of me anymore, maybe they will.

The difficult part will be figuring out how to maneuver through it all.

23

My dad didn't get me back in time for the run. Instead of using the short break in between the run and the start of the camp day to wash up, I do sprints. Afterward, I run to the indoor courts where everything will take place today. The skies are heavy and dark. Right when my hand closes around the door handle to the indoor court, the first raindrop falls from the sky. The black clouds had been hovering ever since this morning. The doughnut my dad took me to get is sitting in my stomach like a lead weight as I suck in air and make my way toward the short section of bleachers where everyone else is already sitting.

Dad is standing in front of everyone. He hasn't officially started yet, so he just nods at me when I walk in.

I eye the seating possibilities before me, frowning when I see that Hayes has sat himself in the middle of Sloan and Alec. Maybe it was just my imagination before, but I thought he was purposefully sitting on the outside of the group to give me a place safe to sit. I try to catch his gaze, but he's avoiding it, choosing to stare at my father instead.

Sloan, though, has the biggest smile for me. When I sit, he bumps me with his shoulder. "Where were you this morning?"

"My dad," I tell him, nodding toward the front.

He nods knowingly. He keeps his shoulder brushed up against mine. Ryan turns, glancing over at us, and I can't help the fact that my face turns red. I feel like what Sloan and I did last night is written all over us. Sloan shouldn't be smiling that widely at me, and I shouldn't be blushing this much. I only hope my dad's not paying attention to me at the moment to figure it out.

"As you can see," my dad's voice booms through the sparse room. "We're taking things inside today. We're supposed to get some storms. I wanted to use this opportunity to remind previous attendees, and inform the new ones, that we do have the MVP awards at the end of camp. We give awards out for each position, and then an overall award. Position MVP's get one thousand-dollar scholarships from the Timothy Dale Scholarship Fund to their college of choice. The overall MVP award winner gets twenty-five hundred dollars from the TD Scholarship Fund."

My skin buzzes. Other than the bragging rights for getting the MVP awards, there's also another reason why it's so coveted, why I came into camp wanting to kick some ass. I've only won once, and that was the year the Ballers humiliated me. Instead of tearing me down like they expected, it fueled me. I've never received the overall MVP award, but Ryan's won it the past two years.

There's always been whispers about how I shouldn't win. My dad already has enough money to send me to college wherever I want to go, but if I'm good enough, I should win. In fact, last time I won, Dad and I decided to donate the money back to his fund to spend on another female player in the state. I kept the trophy though. I'm not giving that up for anything.

I'd love an overall award, but even I know that will be hard to win. Not just because everyone else here is as good or better than me, but, as my dad explained to me the first year I got invited here, I'd have to blow them all out of the water. It's a sad truth, but it is what it is. I knew going in that it was going to be harder for me because my dad is who he is.

"In order to win an MVP award, you must excel in many different areas of the game. Leadership, skills, effort, swag..."

We all laugh. I look down at Ryan. His hands are clasped in his lap, but his leg is jumping up and down. I can feel the excitement pouring off him as my dad talks about this. That year at camp, he confessed to me that getting these scholarships is a big deal to him. Winning this money helps take some of the financial strain off him and his mom.

I just hope he's prepared to lose to me this year.

My gaze rises, and I find Jacquin smiling at me. I hope what my dad said in the car isn't true. And I really hope that my dad isn't as happy about the prospect of Jacquin liking me as he seemed. Maybe he just likes the fact that he's not Hayes? He didn't seem pleased about him at all.

Don't get me wrong, Jacquin is truly gifted. I think he's hot, and I admire him for what he's been able to accomplish at such a young age, but...there's nothing there. It's like staring at Chase.

Whatever is wrong with me mentally has also transferred to my body. I only like the guys who torment me, apparently.

When Dad breaks, asking us all to line up so we can start our exercises for the day, I feel Jacquin's gaze still leveled at me. His stare follows me around the room, but I shake it off. In fact, I make a pact with myself not to worry about anything else besides basketball before we break for lunch. I can't get off track again. No more remembering what Sloan's hands felt like on me last night...or even more, his tongue.

The drills start: footwork, ball handling, and passing. All the coaches are in the room today, so it's no surprise they're looking at all of us for the MVP awards today. A few years ago, I overheard my dad talking to one of the other coaches, telling him that they like for us to settle in before they start evaluating. Especially for the new players who have never been to camp before, it's a bit overwhelming.

We just started a shootaround when the lights in the big gymnasium flicker. A crash sounds overhead. The only windows in this place are long, horizontal ones toward the ceiling. I look up to find that we can't even see outside. Rain spatter on the windows completely hides our view. Lightning lights up the sky, and it suddenly grows very dark outside. A second later, a thunderous boom shakes the gym. I admit that the crack makes me jump. The sound rattles the walls and half a second later, the lights go out completely.

This is a first.

"Let's move to the bleachers," my dad says. "The owners warned me this might happen. Let's see if the generator comes on before we continue."

My dad moves around. He and the other coaches are almost shadows in the darkened room until my eyes adjust and I make out who's who. He moves to stand with the other coaches, and they whisper about what to do. We certainly can't play in the dark. That's an injury waiting to happen.

"You okay?" a voice asks.

I tamp down a shriek that threatens to eke its way out. Whipping around, my gaze lands on Alec. "Jesus," I exhale. "Yes, I'm fine."

Finally, I get a smirk out of him. He's been so serious this whole camp, and I know I haven't been helping with my talk about baseball, but damn. He needs to do something about his dilemma soon. The more he waits to say anything, the more pissed off the other Ballers are going to be.

I move past him and stop by the cooler someone helpfully brought in for us. I twist the cap on a water and gulp it down hungrily. Another lightning strikes accompanied by a resounding growl of thunder. This building does a poor job of keeping the noise out. The rain sounds like a waterfall has let loose on the metal roof over our heads.

"Can I get one of those?" Jacquin asks, pointing at my water.

I lean over to grab him one from the cooler. When I go to hand him it, he grabs not only the bottle, but my hand, too. I glance up to find him smirking at me. "I have an idea."

"Okay." I weasel my hand out of his grip and face him.

"Something to help you and Lake out."

I chuckle. "Nothing can help Lake and me." Mainly because there is no Lake and me.

He smirks again. "I'm thinking it will," he says cryptically before walking away. My dad is summoning him.

Ignoring everything else going on, I walk up to Hayes and sit next to him. The coaches are all still talking and since we can plainly see that the lights haven't come back on and the storm hasn't let up, who knows how long we will be in here for. "Hey," I say to him.

"Hey." His word passes over me, but it's missing any of that smooth rich texture that I like so much.

I lower my voice. "What's wrong?" For a second, I'm worried that Sloan told the guys what we did last night, and that Hayes is mad. It's hard to know with him. He always seems so passive, except for when he got in the argument with that lacrosse player.

"Nothing you need to concern yourself with."

I frown at him. "Well, that's a cop out if I've ever heard one."

His lips twitch like he wants to smile, but suddenly, he's overcome with a calm sort of anger again. He drops his voice even lower. I don't think anyone else is actually listening to us, but this must be something Hayes isn't comfortable sharing with others. "There's just a lot of stuff you don't know."

"Well, I'm right here," I tell him.

Lightning lights up the room, and then a sharp, angry crack of thunder vibrates the gym again. I look over at my dad who stares up at the windows. Hayes moves closer to me. "I know," he says, practically whispering directly in my ear now. "Don't worry about me right now, okay? I promise I'm fine, and if I wasn't, I'd tell you."

I raise my eyebrows at him, letting him know I think he's full of shit.

He doesn't respond until a few beats later. "I'd send smoke signals," he says.

"You're an asshole," I grumble, trying to keep the smile off my face, but it's hard.

Sloan laughs. "That's her favorite word for us."

"It fits," I tell them. "Assholes."

Even Ryan smirks right before taking a swig of his own water bottle. *He used to be asshole number one.* Now I don't know what he is.

Dad moves forward until he's gathered all of our attention. "We're canceling for today. We don't think the storms will let up any time soon. You can go back to your cabins or stay here. We're going to run to the cafeteria to see what can be made without electricity." He checks his watch. "Let's say an hour and a half and we'll have some sort of lunch ready in the mess hall. Hopefully, the storm will have stopped by then. If things let up, we'll round everyone up again and start over."

The coaches turn to leave. A few of the other guys who aren't from RHS follow them out. When they open the door, I see the torrential downpour we're getting. There's really nothing in my cabin I need right now, especially since it's the furthest from this building. I'd be drenched by the time I got there. Plus, I don't really want to be alone in this storm. It's freaking creepy.

A few more guys get up to leave. Lake isn't far behind them. He angles a middle finger toward those of us who are left, but Ryan and the guys only laugh. I guess it could be funny if he wasn't such a jackass.

Ryan decides to follow after him, so it's just Alec, Sloan, Hayes, and me. Sloan doesn't waste any time pulling me onto his lap. It's like last year at the baseball games. When I look over at Alec, I half expect him to be in his baseball uniform. And trust me, there's nothing wrong with that. I love to see him in his baseball uniform. Even when we all weren't talking, I couldn't help but stare.

Sloan wraps his arms around me, pulling me in close. "That's hardly fair," Hayes says.

"What?"

"I know you left the cabin last night. Are you saying you didn't go to Tessa's cabin?"

"I'm saying it's none of your business," Sloan says, smiling.

"Well, I'm saying, it's someone else's turn."

Sloan's arms tighten around me. "Both of you could have done the same thing I did, but you didn't. You can't be jealous now. Maybe we should start a schedule."

I turn in his grip. "Say that again, and I'll...I'll kick you in the knee."

His eyebrows shoot up in surprise. Athletes are serious about their knees. "You're in high demand,

Daddy's Girl. I'm just trying to make it easier for everyone."

I pluck Sloan's fingers away from me and stand. I look at the three of them and then make my own choice. I sit in Hayes's lap. His arms curl naturally around me. When the next thunder claps, he tightens his grip, and I know I made the right decision. It was probably instinctual, knowing he'd be the one who could make me feel safe.

Though Sloan pouts, I don't think he's too perturbed. He makes a show of it, pretending to be affronted, but I hope they all get used to it.

They all want me, and I want all of them. There won't be any decisions in my near future. And no schedules either.

24

The storm has died down a little, so the guys decide we should move to their cabin. Hayes refuses to let me walk through the wet grass, so just before we step out into the unrelenting rain, he sweeps me off my feet and carries me with one hand hooked under my knees and the other hooked around my shoulders. I squeal in protest, but then he's moving swiftly, and somehow, someway, I'm barely even jostled.

Alec runs up ahead and opens the cabin door for us. Their cabin is bigger than mine, mostly because it's set up for more people. But just looking at it standing right there in front of me makes butterflies take flight in my stomach. This is so off-limits, right? I'll be in a small, confined space with three of the boys I'm crushing on. The only thing that would make this more nerve-wracking is if Ryan decided to join us.

When Hayes moves inside, ducking under the door frame, he sets me on my feet. I look around, my heart in my throat. Right away, I can figure out who is sleeping where. I don't even need them to move toward their separate beds to give me an inkling. A copy of Sports Illustrated sits on Alec's bed. It just so happens to have a baseball player on the cover. There are a few outfits on his bed, too, that he quickly picks up and throws into a suitcase stuffed under his bed's metal frame.

Sloan's area of the room is nice and tidy. The bed is even made, a dark blue comforter adorning it. Hayes's side is almost the most confusing. He has a book face down on his unmade sheets. There aren't any clothes strewn about, but there's a picture of a man and a woman next to his bed. None of the others have any personal pictures out. I didn't even think to bring mine with me. I can video chat my mom, and she's the only one I'd have a picture to put out of anyway because my dad is already here.

Alec props the door open with a lone chair. The wind circulates the room, almost tearing through it in a circular motion before it escapes again. When I turn, he's leaning against the door jamb, staring out at the storm. The rain is still coming down sideways. The porch of their cabin is soaked straight through, but the rain isn't coming all the way inside, even with the door open like this. Sloan moves up behind me and drops a towel around my shoulders. I pull it around my arms. Just because I didn't walk through the rain didn't mean I missed out on the wet factor.

I stay on my feet, nervous to be here with all of them when we're not playing or talking basketball. We've never hung out together like this for the purpose of hanging out. Like Sloan said in the gymnasium, it's a new kind of territory to traverse. It's something I'm going to have to get used to if my plans for next year go as I plan.

I walk up behind Alec. "It's kind of beautiful, isn't it?" Straight ahead of us, the lake is a gray sea of turbulence. It's hard to look past the onslaught of rain, and it might be the electricity in the air, but it makes goosebumps sprout over my body. Mother Nature is nothing to mess with. She can be beautiful and damaging at the same time, reminding me of the Ballers.

He smiles down at me. "I love watching the storms back home. We have a sun porch with huge windows on every side. We all sit out there during days like this."

"Roberta isn't scared?"

A smile teases his lips. "She is, but that's half the fun."

Hayes comes up behind me. He takes the towel in his hands and starts to dry me off. I close my eyes at the feeling. He works the towel into my hair at the base of my neck and then down both arms. Quickly, he squats to wipe the droplets of rain still dripping toward my shoes. "I have some clothes you can change into," he says.

"Anything you give her would fall off her," Sloan says. He's eyeing us from the corner of the room. He tilts his head. "Then again..."

Alec pushes off the side of the door and goes to his own bed. He pulls out a couple of the things he'd just stuffed under his bed and hands them to me. I take them from him and go into the small bathroom. It's about as big as mine even though there are three of them and only one of me. I change quickly, throwing my now drenched tank top and shorts over the shower door to dry.

When I step out in Alec's too big clothes, I feel like a little kid invited to the cool kid party. Alec catches me first. He holds his hand out and then sits on his bed, pulling me after him. It's a minute before anyone says anything. It's Sloan, of course, who talks first. "Tessa and I really love to play this game, a truth for a truth. We should play."

I laugh. "You like to play that game. I just humor you."

He raises his eyebrow in defiance. "Not true, Dale. I think you learned a lot of interesting information last time we played."

Alec shrugs. "It actually sounds like it could be fun. I'd love to get into your head." He needles me playfully in the side.

That's exactly what I don't want. When I say as much, they all laugh. Even Hayes.

"A game like this won't be interesting to any of you. I thought you guys told each other everything. What can you possibly learn from one another?"

"Oh, we do tell each other everything," Sloan says, a sly smile on his face. "This isn't for that, really. We're going to ask you questions."

"This sounds a lot like you guys are ganging up on me. I have to answer almost every question while I can only direct every third to one of you. Talk about unfair."

Sloan shrugs. "I guess we don't have to play. But, it's probably the only way you're ever going to get information out of us."

Well, that's tempting...

"I'll start," Sloan announces. He sits up on his bed,

his hands clasped in front of him. His rain-soaked brown hair looks even darker as he looks over at me. "Who did you miss the most when we weren't talking?"

I shake my head. "You're such a jerk. I'm not answering that."

"Well, we know it wasn't Lake," Alec says.

I glance over at him, my brow furrowing. He laughs and then pulls my feet over his lap, his fingers passing up and down my lower legs.

"Ryan," Hayes guesses. "We know it's Ryan."

I cock my head toward him. His lips are thin, and he's said it with such finality that I know he thinks he's right. Hell, he might even be right. The problem is, I haven't even thought about it. When I tell them as much, Sloan says, "Well, you've thought about it now. Who is it?"

I press my lips closed. "Can't we just watch the storm outside? That sounds like a better idea."

"Why don't we just not ask any questions where she has to pick?" Alec asks. His fingertips lightly glide over my knee, sending a tingle up my spine.

"That actually sounds like a good plan," I tell them.

Sloan grabs a package of cookies out from underneath his bed. "Fine," he grumbles. He takes a few for himself, then passes them to Hayes. All Hayes has to do is reach over from his spot on the bed. His impressive wingspan comes in handy. He doesn't even have to move to take a few out of the package. Sloan then offers them to us.

I move to the other side of the room, but before I can pick from the package, Sloan's hand shoots out and pulls me to him. I fall on the bed in a heap, practically face down in his chest. I push up and glare at him. His lips pull apart. "I know. You're going to say something about how much of an asshole I am." He leans up and whispers in my ear. "Just tell these guys you missed me the most, and I'll give you another surprise tonight."

My whole body heats, need spirals out from my core in delicious waves. I stagger away from him and right back onto Alec's bed without any cookies. Alec has to get up and grab some for us while Sloan just lays there with his hands behind his head like he just won the entire game and we haven't even started playing for real yet.

After that though, the idea of the game just kind of fades. I breathe in a sigh of relief. I feel like they're keeping too much from me right now, and as for me? I should be keeping things from them. I don't want to break up their relationship with Lake, but at the same time, I need to look out for myself. I wonder if Jacquin actually has an idea that will work.

Soon, I hear Sloan's soft snores. I'm not surprised.

We were up late last night. After that, Alec pulls his legs out from underneath me and lays down next to me on his bed. He stays semi-upright with his hand cupping his head. "You can sleep if you want to," he says, his voice a soft whisper so he doesn't wake Sloan up.

Staring at Alec takes my breath away. His emerald eyes are just stunning, and there's this fierce look in them right now that reminds me of the time outside the locker room. Alec was the first to give in to his feelings for me, and he took me right with him. "I'm okay," I tell him.

We cuddle together, staring out the still open door as the storm rages on. The time for lunch comes and goes, and I don't see anyone leaving their cabins. Maybe everyone is taking a much needed break. Tomorrow's Saturday, but eventually, the intense workout sessions would catch up to everyone. It just so happens we had a break a day earlier than expected.

Alec looks toward Hayes's bed. I follow his gaze. He whispers, "I think he's out, too."

"What was wrong with him yesterday?" I ask. I don't need a game to find things out. I want them to want to tell me things, not because a stupid game is forcing them to.

"I think he scared himself with how mad he got."

Alec's eyes cloud over. "He told us that right before the guy accidentally hit him, the guy said something to Hayes about you having a nice rack."

"Oh."

Alec finally looks down at me. "Hayes is one of those guys you really want on your side because once he's on your side, he'll never leave it."

"What about him and Lake then?"

Alec shifts uncomfortably. "I think he and Lake have come to a sort of conclusion about you." He brings his hand up and cups my cheek. "I know you think it's easy enough to say you and Lake can just ignore one another, that we can hang out with you and him, and just have everything be the same..."

I wait for him to go on because, yeah, I really do think that.

His thumb traces my bottom lip. "The thing is, Hayes, Sloan, Ryan, and I want you to be an integral part of our lives. Not just one of those girls we passed around."

He gives me an apologetic smile when my eyes narrow at him.

"Lake thinks you'll ruin everything."

"Or maybe I could make everything better." I twist toward him, placing my hand on his stomach. "I'm on your side, you know. With everything. And Sloan's, too. Whatever goes down with his parents, I'll be there for him. Whatever has Hayes upset, I can be there for that, too."

He places his hand over mine. "We're just so used to having only the five of us to go to."

"Times change. If you guys think I'll wait around to see if you choose me again, you're wrong."

The green in Alec's eyes spark to life. "Personally, I'm not going to let it get that far a second time. Lake needs to deal with his shit or he's going to drag everyone down with him."

I blink at him. "What does that mean?"

"It means I'm his friend, but he has to change if he wants to keep it that way. There's only so much help you can give someone, Tessa. If they don't want it, they don't want it."

His hand squeezes my own. The intensity in his eyes is overwhelming.

His tongue passes over his bottom lip. "What's the rule on kissing you in front of the others?"

"I don't know," I say, almost breathless. "Is there one?"

My mouth goes dry as I wait for his answer. "I guess I'm making it now." He darts forward, the eagerness in his kiss taking my breath away. He urges my mouth open, and when he succeeds, he rewards me by tangling his tongue with mine. I think it's impossible for Alec to kiss gently. Every time he kisses, it's like he's short on time or dangling from the end of a rope. He wants to reap his rewards from the onset in case he can't get any more. He nips my bottom lip, and I moan.

My eyes blink open. Maybe this was a bad idea. Sloan and Hayes are right there.

Alec senses my hesitation and pulls away. He drops his forehead to mine. "Let's play the quiet game." He maneuvers on top of me, kissing a trail down my neck. Okay, this was not what I was thinking when I worried about them waking up to us making out.

In any case, how do people keep quiet during times like this? I start to squirm as he pulls the collar of the shirt I'm wearing down. It's so big on me that it exposes the swell of my breast. He kisses me there, and I press my lips together. This is pure torture. I don't know whether to yell at him for doing this or tell him he better not stop.

Instead, I give it right back to him. I sneak my hands between us and grab him. He breaks away finally, releasing a heavy exhale. He drops his forehead back to mine. "Fuck. That's mean."

I start to stroke him. "You deserve it."

He pitches his hips forward in time with my strokes. A brief moan passes over his lips before he stops himself. Because I can, I release him briefly to move past his shorts and grab just him. The silky skin of his cock glides through my fist. Alec starts to tremble. "I don't think I've ever wanted anything as bad as I want you, Tessa. Not even baseball."

My heart constricts before locking eyes with him again.

"Oh fuck." He places his hand over mine, directing the pace. His hips move against me forcefully until he shivers with finality, hot liquid spills out over my forearm. He fights against any sort of noise, forcing his mouth shut as he trembles his release onto me. After he comes down, he takes his hand away from mine until he's caged me in on the bed. I haven't removed my hand from him, so it's still there as he glances down. "Let me get something to clean us up with."

Finally, I pull my hand away, and he quickly grabs another piece of clothing from underneath the bed, catching the evidence from dripping onto the bed from my forearm. He wipes me up, then goes to the bathroom.

While he's gone, I glance around the room and find Sloan staring at me. I swallow hard. He just smiles. "Not going to lie, that turned me the fuck on."

Oh, dear God. These Ballers are going to ruin me.

25

Bad things happen in boys' cabins. Or is that good things? It's hard to know the difference when it comes to the Ballers.

When Alec falls asleep, I carefully extract myself from him, go to the bathroom to put my now damp clothes back on, and leave. The rain has quieted down a lot, and I haven't heard any thunder in about an hour. I go straight for the cafeteria. Just eating those few cookies Sloan offered us isn't cutting it as far as meals go. When I walk in, my dad and Jacquin are in there eating. There's a hot meal in front of them and it's then that I realize that the lights are on.

"Hey," my dad says. "We were wondering if anyone was going to show up."

"I think we all conked out," I tell him, giving him a

smile and hoping it's not a smile that says I just jacked off Alec Christopoulos. Maybe not *just* jacked him off, but within the last couple of hours.

"Get something to eat and come sit down here. Jacquin and I have been talking about you."

My throat closes, but I try not to show how apprehensive that makes me. The lady in the kitchen smiles as I'm offered up barbecued chicken and macaroni and cheese. I get myself an iced tea at the fountain and then sit next to my dad at the table he and Jacquin share.

"Listen to this," my dad says. It's clear he's excited about something. "Remember when we were talking about how we were going to get you back at RHS without any of the nonsense? I think Jacquin found a way."

I flit back and forth between the two of them. How is Jacquin involved in this at all? I don't like that he seems to know a lot about my situation. "Oh yeah?"

"I think since this is basketball beef, it should be played out on the basketball floor," Jacquin says.

Funny. I've been saying the same thing.

"I say," Jacquin starts. "You and Lake make a bet."

"Not just Lake," my dad intervenes. "All of them." He starts naming the Ballers off while bending his fingers down one-by-one. "Linc, Christopoulos, Ivy, and Irving, too."

"Dad, they're not—"

"No, it's okay," Jacquin says. "This will work for all of them." He turns toward me. "If you take Shooting Guard MVP, O'Brien has to leave you alone for all of next year."

I tilt my head at him. I search their gazes to make sure they're serious. "That's great." I smile briefly, but it washes off my face in the next instant. "I've tried to get Lake to make sure this is handled on the court. That's why I was willing to ride the bench until I proved myself, but we, apparently, all know how that worked out."

"He won't be able to resist this offer. He thinks he can't lose."

"Yet, he'll say that it's rigged. If I win, he'll just say my dad gave it to me. He'll never follow through. He won't even take the bet. Trust me."

Dad leans forward. "Tess, Pumpkin, this is a way out. Trust me as a basketball player when I say that we all take bets, especially if it's one we think we can't lose. Once he takes it, all you have to do is win MVP. You've done it before. I know you can do it again. When you win, they have to leave you alone next ball season. They can't use any of their influence to have you ride the bench. It'll be fair this year."

I hate to see the hopeful look on his face when I know there's no way this is going to happen. "That doesn't mean the girls will stop, Dad," I tell him, reminding him of the fact that the problem wasn't just the Ballers. It was their bitches, too. If *my* plan works, and I walk into RHS with all of the Ballers, minus Lake, at the start of the school year, there's no way those bitches are going to let me get off easy. They'll hate me even more, for sure. They thought they won, and if I come out on top again, all bets are off. I can just see it now.

"But we can talk to the school about that. You know I handled that badly last year. I won't again. The school will need to step up and make sure the bullying doesn't happen."

I want nothing more than to be as hopeful as he is, but I don't think it will work. I mean, it could, but I highly doubt Lake will take the bet. He thinks that everything I have has been given to me by my dad. He won't risk it. I've tried to tell him to keep it on the court before, and he didn't listen then either.

Jacquin shrugs. "I'm with your dad. My friends and I are always betting one another. In fact, one of them owes me big for getting into the draft this year."

He smirks, and he's so sure of himself in that moment. I find the Ballers' confidence hot as sin. In him, it's just a turnoff.

"I'll think about it," I tell them. "But Lake and I are far from friends. He doesn't trust me, and I don't trust him."

My dad shakes his head. "It's just a shame. The six of you on that team could be something. Even Ryan says so."

I almost choke on a bite of chicken. My gaze lifts to my dad, but he's not even looking at me anymore. *Ryan actually thinks that? Why does that make my heart beat faster?*

I know the answer; I just don't want to admit it to myself. Ever since that year at camp, I've been searching for his approval one way or another. I didn't want to believe he'd use me and leave me. Maybe that's why everyone assumes I like Ryan the most. I just have the most to prove to him.

"Some people just can't get out of their own way," Jacquin says. "It's sad when you think about it."

The door to the cafeteria opens, and we all look up. Ryan Linc walks in, rubbing his eyes. When he sees just the three of us there, he's taken aback for a moment before he catches my eye, then quickly moves on to my dad who sits up straighter. "I'm glad you two are here. Go get your food, Ryan, then come sit with us."

I stare back at my chicken, only I feel the heat of someone's gaze on me. Glancing up, I find Jacquin's stare glued to mine. I look away immediately, an uneasiness taking hold in my stomach. When Ryan sits down beside Jacquin, Jacquin excuses himself, saying he has to call his grandma. My dad's the only one to tell him goodbye. Ryan and I are just staring at one another.

If I keep this up, my food is going to get cold.

"Alright, so," my dad starts. "Ryan, your mom's coming up tomorrow. The two of us thought it would be a good idea to all go out to dinner tomorrow night."

Ryan and I still haven't talked much about what happened between my parents and how it directly affects his mom. He's the first one to say it sounds good to him, so my dad turns toward me now. He looks hopeful, and there's really no way I can get out of going anyway. "Sounds good, Dad." Maybe it won't be as bad as I think it will be.

"Excellent. I hope the storms have passed. I wouldn't want your mom driving up in that."

"Yeah, it was intense," Ryan agrees.

He picks at his macaroni and cheese the same way I'm picking at my chicken. My dad doesn't stick around too long. He tells us he'll text us both later with more information on the dinner. When he leaves, I look at Ryan. "I don't think my dad even remembers the year I liked you at camp."

"Liked?" he asks. He raises an eyebrow in a challenge.

"You know what I mean."

"I'm kind of glad he doesn't, to be honest."

"Really?" I ask doubtfully. "I thought you didn't like this whole situation either."

He sighs. "It's not ideal. But my mom deserves someone like your dad."

I can't help but narrow my gaze at him. He just freaking cheated on her yesterday for crying out loud.

"He said it was all a misunderstanding."

"I'm not saying it wasn't," I tell him. "He explained everything to me, and my mom pretty much said the same thing. She kissed him. She kissed him because she misses him."

Ryan winces. "That's the only part I don't like. Your mom's a nice person."

"My mom's great," I tell him, finally pushing the tray away.

"Not many women would let me into their home after what happened." He pushes my tray back at me.

"You should eat. You're pushing it too much on those runs. I think you're losing weight."

My mouth drops. I had actually noticed that there was extra room around the waistband of my shorts earlier, but how the hell could he tell?

"If you're going to run like that, you have to eat more. Remember, fit doesn't mean skinny."

"Are you seriously giving me a talk about diet and exercise? I grew up with the king of diet and exercise." I'm not exaggerating either. My dad went to school for nutrition. Not only does he have the sports related experience, but he actually knows what he's talking about academically too.

"I guess he's rubbing off on me." He looks back to his plate again with an almost bashful grin. "I hope you didn't give him too much of a hard time earlier."

I make an annoyed noise in the back of my throat. "And I hope you did."

He smirks. "I'm sure my mom gave him enough hell."

We're just joking, but I can't help but be affected by what he's said. My dad being with anyone else is going to take some serious getting used to. Then there's the whole issue of when my mom starts dating. From what Ryan's saying, it seems like his life is just starting to turn out right while mine had to crumble for his to get that way.

"I don't know if I've said it before, but I'm really sorry about what happened between your parents, Tessa. Mine divorced when I was little, so I get it."

I groan inwardly. Why does he have to be so nice sometimes? It does crazy things to my insides.

I don't respond because what do you even say to that? I don't really want to bond with him over the fact that we have broken families. Instead, I pick my fork up and start eating again. At his request, I even go back up and get some more chicken. It's another fifteen minutes or so before anyone else shows up. Sloan walks in, dropping a kiss on my temple before heading into the line. Alec, Hayes, Lake, and River are behind him.

I know I should probably leave to give them some time alone, but I can't help but stare at Lake and wonder if the plan Jacquin came up with would work. I have to admit that it's better than any plan I have because I don't have one. I only have two paths to take. Either take Lake down, which I guess could be construed as making this bet with him or let it all go.

I'm not usually one for letting things go though. Once I set my mind on something, I follow through.

When Lake sits, I'm still staring at him. Finally, he looks up. "Take a picture, Dale."

My cheeks burn.

"It's okay, sweetie," Sloan says. "You can stare at me all you want."

Ryan leans over and says something to Lake who nods. Whatever it was he said, Lake doesn't say much throughout the rest of the meal. When we're finished, I happily go back to my room all by myself. Sometimes being around all of them is exhausting, and on top of all that, they make me nervous.

Being with them is like stepping up to the foul line and waiting for the ball to drop.

26

Like one big happy family, my dad wants us to drive to the restaurant together. I get out of it by telling him I need to do some stuff in town before going back to camp, so I delay the inevitable awkwardness for at least another fifteen minutes. The only thing I didn't plan on happening is Ryan standing next to my car as I'm walking up to it to leave. He has sunglasses on. Aviators, of course, that make my knees wobble as I walk up to him.

"They said you were driving by yourself, so I thought I could hitch a ride with you."

It's suddenly a lot hotter outside than the eighty-degree weather would imply. "You're putting it off, too?"

He cocks his head at me. "No, I just thought they

might like some alone time considering what happened."

I forgot. He's used to being with my dad and his mom. This is just another day for him. Actually, for all of them, I'm the only extra factor in this whole equation. *Damn. Why does this suck so much?*

I unlock the car and we both get in. It's like an oven inside, so I put the top down quickly and blast the AC. It's been so long since I've driven my car that the interior has that stale, stagnant air feel. Ryan looks comfortable already though. He's got his arm outside the door as I reverse from the parking space and drive toward the small town.

When I'm alone with Ryan, sometimes it feels like it's three years ago all over again. I can almost forget other things have happened between he and I since then. "How come you don't let me drive your car?" Ryan asks. "Alec said you let him drive it."

"Maybe because Alec was nice to me." I look over and give him a teasing smile. I mean, it's totally true, but I guess I'm in a forgiving mood right now not to give him shit for it.

"I can be nice." His hand reaches out to drag the backs of his fingers down my cheek.

Flames scorch my skin in their wake. I brush him off though. "Nine times out of ten you're not nice."

He's staring at me now. I peek over to see if I can get a grasp on what he's thinking, but all I can see is my own reflection through his mirror-like glasses. I turn away quickly, pulling my hair to the side of my shoulder and holding onto it, so the wind doesn't whip through it too much. Otherwise, it'll look like I haven't even bothered to brush it by the time we get to the restaurant.

"I like your hair down," he says softly.

"You're just saying that because you want to drive my car."

"I don't want to drive your stupid car, Tessa."

I swallow. *Okay...*

A few minutes later, I pull into the parking lot of the restaurant, and we both get out. It doesn't look like it's going to rain anytime soon, so I leave the top down and just make sure there's nothing visible in the car for someone to reach in and steal. I highly doubt this small town is rampant with theft, but you never know.

My dad's car is already in the lot, so I take a deep breath and head for the front entrance. Ryan beats me to it, opening the door for me and holding it, so I can walk in first. He's taken his sunglasses off now, so I can finally see the look on his face. It's intense to say the least. It makes a shiver start at the base of my spine and stay there. Oddly, this feels like a date right now. If it was just Ryan and I going out, I think it would be exactly like this. Instead, my dad and his mom are waiting for us at a table in the middle of the room.

They both get to their feet when they see us. His mom is the closest to the door. When I walk up, she actually holds her arms out to give me a hug. I go into them like a tiptoeing cat. The slightest movement might make me want to bolt in the other direction. Doing this, acting like this is okay, seems like I'm betraying my mom. Realistically, I know that's not the case, but it isn't as if I can forget about the fact that my parents were together for years, and that if my mom had it her way, they'd still be together now. Quickly, I move on and raise to my tiptoes to give my dad a kiss on the cheek before sitting in the chair to his right.

The waitress comes over. She's a girl mine and Ryan's age who's more than likely waitressing during the summer for some extra cash. She's all eyes for Ryan, but he barely looks up at her, which is so different than I imagined. We order right away, and Ryan's mom, Leslie, launches right into asking us questions about basketball camp. I can tell she's so proud of Ryan for his accomplishments, and she's also doing the best she can to include me in the conversation. "So," she says, her pinky tapping on her water glass. "What are your chances for overall MVP this year?" she asks him.

My dad chuckles, but the questions only make my skin grow warm in embarrassment.

Ryan squirms in his seat. He peeks over at me. "I have a good shot, I think. Top two, definitely."

I tilt my head at him, surprised he said that. "Top two? Who do you think could beat you?"

He takes a sip of his water. My dad leans back in his chair, crossing his arms over his chest with a smile. "Um, you?"

I recoil, my mouth dropping slightly. "Seriously?"

He shrugs.

"Huh."

"Come on, Tess," my dad says. "You're not one to act so modest."

"Oh, I'm not trying to," I assure him. "I think I have a good shot, I'm just surprised Ryan thinks so."

It's Leslie's turn to look taken aback. "Ryan always says how good you are."

"Mom," Ryan says, a pink spot blooming on his cheeks.

"Well, it's true."

"I think Ryan's my worst critic," I tell them honestly. "Otherwise, I don't understand why I didn't get any playing time this past year."

"Can we not do this?" Ryan asks no one in particular. He'd lifted his water glass to take a sip, but he places it right back down on the table and twists it in his hands.

"Well, Ryan wouldn't have anything to do with that," Leslie says, laughter in her voice.

She looks at me inquisitively, and I just shrug. She's so out of the loop when it comes to her son. She probably thinks he walks on water, too. Why not? Everyone else at school does.

Thankfully, we're saved by the waitress delivering our dinners. Dad and Leslie start small talk again with Dad asking about her job, and she, in turn, asking about how running the camp is going. I pay attention only because it seems like there's a brick wall to my right. The tension coming off Ryan is so thick that if I punched the air between us, the universe would probably crack right down the middle.

By the time we've eaten dessert and Dad and Leslie are each having a glass of wine, the tension seems to take over the whole table. I instantly know something is up because Dad and Leslie keep having silent conversations with their eyes. Ryan notices, too. He sits up straighter until both of us are just staring at them, hoping whatever they have to say will come out soon. My mouth is dry. I hope this isn't some major bomb. I can't deal with a detonated bomb right now.

"So," my dad starts. "You guys know Leslie and I have been together for more than a few months." He grabs her hand on the table, and my stomach lurches. Suddenly, I'm praying the word baby or marriage don't slip off his tongue. God, no. "We've decided we're moving in together."

I can't help the gasp that escapes my lips. I peek over at Ryan, and his surprise mimics mine. I can tell he didn't know about this ahead of time either. "Wow," he says. "That's...great."

That's something alright. I wouldn't use the word great, however.

Leslie's beaming. I take a sip of my water as casually as can be and match my dad stare for stare. "We actually already bought a place," he says.

My stomach sinks even further.

"Wow," Ryan says again. It's the only word he knows right now. He glances over at me. I cross my arms over my lap, digging my nails into my skin to keep from overtly reacting. If they stayed together any longer, I knew something like this was going to happen, but there's something to be said for knowing something is going to happen and actually having to live through that something happening.

Dad nods. "You actually know the place, Tessa."

I clear my throat. "Oh yeah?" The sound of my voice sounds so fake to me. It's like I'm an actress reading lines.

"It's just a couple of blocks away from our—your mom's house. The place the Harris's used to live."

I blink at him. They're buying a house near mine? Let's face it, *he's* buying another house near our old house. There's no way Leslie could afford anything like that on her own.

"I wanted to get a place near you," he says, clearly proud of himself. I know he thinks he's doing a good thing. Living up to his end of the bargain about not pushing me out of his life, but this is terrible.

"That's great, Dad," I say through a forced smile.

"It's got a pool, Ry," Leslie says, smiling at her son with glassy eyes. It almost makes me feel bad for not being happy about all this. Clearly, this is a big deal for the Linc's.

"Awesome," Ryan says.

Dad and Leslie look at one another. I can tell we're not giving them the reactions they wanted, but come on, it hasn't been that long since they've been in high school. They're blending two families with same aged kids. What the hell did they think was going to happen? That we'd all hug and kiss, skip from the table holding hands?

I peek at Ryan. I want to kiss Ryan, but not in the brotherly way. Far, far from it. Maybe that's why this seems so much worse than it should.

Leslie takes a deep breath. Her gaze switches from Ryan to me. "I know everything hasn't been perfect, but this is what Tim and I want. And, I want you to know, Tessa, that I don't blame your mother at all for kissing your father the other day. Mistakes happen."

My jaw clenches. The fucking nerve of her. "Well, that's good," I say, my voice high. I definitely don't even sound like myself anymore. Electricity shoots up my veins. I try to tell myself to let it drop, but I just can't. Not anymore. "I guess I don't blame you, either. You know, for kissing my dad before my parents were even separated."

"Quintessa," my dad snaps.

I turn my glare on him. "Or for moving in together before you're even divorced, too."

"Your mother and I are working on it. Not that it's any of your business."

"And like I told you yesterday, you keep bringing me into your business. You want me to be happy about this? You tell us at dinner like it's some sort of special occasion? Come on," I plead, looking around the table.

I can't be the only one who's thinking this. Or maybe I'm just the only one that's not a hundred percent behind their pairing.

Leslie's face is beet red. She's looking into her lap. My dad puts his arm around her shoulders to comfort her. "You, young lady," my dad starts.

"Tessa's right," Ryan says, interrupting him.

All eyes move to him.

He looks over at me. My brows are in my hairline. I didn't expect him to agree with me at all. Especially since I just insinuated his mother's a whore. I didn't quite mean it like that, but they really shouldn't be expecting me to be happy about all this so soon.

"I think you guys forget what all this means for her."

His mom's eyes are pleading. "Ryan, we're not forgetting. I feel for Tessa. I do."

He shakes his head. "Obviously it's not coming across that way. I've never known Tessa to be mean-spirited, but yet, this is driving her to be."

Holy shit. Ryan fucking Linc just stood up for me.

My dad leans back in his chair. His gaze darts from Ryan to me. Leslie sits forward, her forearms resting on the ivory tablecloth. "Okay," she says, nodding her head. "What do you two want us to do then? You don't want us to live together? You don't want us to be together? What?"

Ryan looks over at me. His gray eyes dull. I can tell he wants me to take this question. I run my hands down my face. "I don't care if you're together. I don't even care that you're moving in together. I understand that my parents aren't going to be a couple anymore. All I ask is that you please, please, don't try to make me feel like I should be excited about something that I don't even know how to process yet. I'm glad you're happy. I'm glad my dad's happy. That's all you're going to get out of me though."

"And what you said about Mrs. Dale was insensitive, Mom."

Leslie balks, like the air is taken out of her. In the next second though, she snaps her mouth shut and nods. "I didn't realize it was going to come out like that. I apologize."

I swallow. My skin crawls. I've about had it with this dinner. I don't know how the hell I'm going to deal with all this, but I at least have the rest of camp to process it before I'm thrust into a world my father is moving in with Ryan's mother. I pick my napkin up from my lap and place it on my plate in front of me. "Thanks for dinner, Dad. I'm going to head out now."

My father's gaze follows me, and then Ryan when he stands after me. "I'm going with Tessa."

He and I turn from the table. We leave two very confused parents there, but it serves them right. When we get outside, Ryan intertwines his fingers with mine. He holds them so tightly wrapped in his that when he lets go so we can both get in the car, my hand feels like it's lost something.

"Do you know somewhere where we can be alone?" Ryan asks.

I start the car up and reverse out of the parking space. I know the perfect place.

27

Up the road from where my dad and I parked to eat our doughnuts the other day, there's another boat launch, but it's not as maintained. It's basically a rut-filled drive down a small dirt path that leads right to the lakeside. The Mustang jostles us as we make our way down, and I put the car in park facing toward the water. Across from this spot, I can see the small square that's my cabin at Camp Holly.

"My mom was out-of-line," Ryan says. "I swear she doesn't think."

I unbuckle my seatbelt and turn toward him in the car. The sun is low in the sky. Wispy oranges and pinks mix with the twilight that's rolling in. Soon, this place will be buzzing with mosquitoes, but right now, it's kind of perfect.

"She probably didn't mean it like that. I'm just sensitive about it, I guess."

Ryan takes a deep breath, leans his head back against the headrest, and stares up into the darkening sky. "I never thought in a million years this would be happening."

I crack a smile. "Of all things," I say. It's not all that funny, but I've always preferred smiling over crying.

"I'll tell my mom she needs to respect your mom more."

"Oh God," I groan. "You don't think we're going to have awkward family meetings and Christmases, do you?"

He grins. "Definitely. It's inevitable."

I wipe a black thread off my knee. "I can't leave my mom on holidays. I'm all she has now."

Ryan reaches over and places his hand on my shoulder. "You shouldn't have to."

The weight of his hand feels like the only thing grounding me right now. "My parents still fight, you know. It's all still raw and bitter at my house. Don't tell me what goes on at yours. I don't want to know. But I'm sure it's nothing like mine."

I peek up to see Ryan look away and swallow. That tells me everything I need to know. It's exactly as I thought. They're all playing house while my own is exploding from the inside out. Ryan and Dad probably sit and watch sports every night. They probably talk about the draft and who's playing baseball on TV that evening. Or golf. Or track. Or whatever sport happens to be on that night.

His fingers dig into me. "I'm sorry, Tessa."

I place my hand on his, and he intertwines our fingers again. He brings our clasped hands to the center console between us. "I wish I hadn't pretended not to like you now. Maybe I would've introduced my mom to your parents as my girlfriend's parents and then we could have avoided this whole mess."

My stomach twists and turns and flops over like it doesn't know how to feel about that statement. "Or it could have been worse," I suggest. "Maybe the same thing would've happened only under more scandalous circumstances."

One side of his lip pulls up. "I guess. We'll never know now."

"No, I guess we won't."

My throat feels so clogged with emotion that I swallow it down. It takes several times before I feel like I have myself under control.

"Tessa..."

I look over at Ryan. His gray eyes suck me in, and before I know it, I'm moving toward him and he's tugging me over the console. I land on his legs and he grunts. "Sorry," I say, right before he silences me with a searing kiss.

He lets my hand go, then pushes my knees to the sides of his hips before pulling on the underside of my thighs, moving me closer to him. He wraps his hand in my hair, tugging me closer until I moan into his mouth. He breaks away from me. "I'm an idiot."

"I know."

He captures my lips again, this time a steady and fierce possessiveness that's just the right amount of push and pull. He gives as much as he takes.

Nighttime wakes up around us. The colder air breezes in. The night owl insects wake up. They chirp and buzz, and it sounds like they're all cheering us on with a long sigh of "It's about time." I slow the kiss, burning the memory of it into my brain before I pull away. I lean back on his thighs and reach up to brush a hand over his cheeks. He's flushed with want. With a small smile, I say, "I can't do this right now, Ryan."

His jaw ticks, and I think that's the last thing he thought I'd say.

"I'm sorry," I tell him while extracting myself from him. I manage to flop back behind the wheel not so delicately.

Ryan runs a hand through his hair. "There's

nothing to be sorry for. This is all my fault. I'm the one who keeps pushing you away."

We both just sit there, staring outside the car as the moon begins its reflection over the lake. Once the mosquitoes show up, I push the button so the top comes back up, enclosing us in the car. "Did you mean what you said about me having a shot at overall MVP?"

"You're just as good as any one of us, Tessa."

It's crazy, but the fact that Ryan Linc is acknowledging that makes pride seep into my pores. It shouldn't matter what he thinks, but for some reason, it always has to me. I lean on the seat facing him. "Can I ask you something?"

He nods, finally looking over at me.

"My dad thinks I should make a bet with Lake. He says I should bet him that if I win Shooting Guard MVP, he has to leave me alone from now on."

His eyes widen. "What if he wins?"

I shrug. "I don't know. I guess that would be up to him." When he doesn't say anything else, I ask, "What do you think? You made an agreement with him before. Do you think he would do it with me?"

"I think he'd take that bet," Ryan says. "But I also think you should be worried about what he'd want you to do if he won."

"I figure he'll probably ask me to leave you guys alone. That's what he wants."

"Are you willing to take that bet?"

I bite down on my lip. "I would if I thought I could win."

Ryan scratches his jaw then wipes the back of his hand over his mouth. "I can ask him about it if you want."

"Maybe," I tell him. I just don't know that I'm ready to decide yet. "Can I ask you something else? I just really have to know, Ryan. I've heard it from the others, but...why do you guys put up with him?"

"He's my best friend."

The same old answer time and time again. "It's just insane," I say, my fists clenching in front of me.

His gaze narrows. "We all have a history, right, Tessa? A secret? Like it being hell in your house right now without your dad. Something you haven't come right out and told everyone. What if Lake had the same thing?"

"I'm not sure whatever it is could excuse everything he's done."

"I guess that's for outsiders to judge."

I rub a hand down my arm. "Well, are you going to tell me what it is?"

He shakes his head right away. "No. It's not for me to say."

"I don't think I can ever forgive him."

Ryan looks away. "I'll never ask you to."

I dribble my fingers over the steering wheel. "Right. Well, I suppose we should head back." I put the car in reverse, and back all the way out of the short path until I hit the main road again. My dad brought me fishing here once, before I was even invited to camp. It was probably the only time we ever went fishing period, and I have no idea why he even thought it was a good idea. Fishermen we are not. It's the whole waiting for something to happen aspect that blows. Kind of like my entire season where I rode the bench. Not fun.

My headlights light up the road as we drive back to camp. Ryan and I must be stuck in our own little worlds because neither one of us speaks. Maybe it's because we don't really know what to say to one another. I basically just told him I wasn't ready to start something with him again. Trust me, my body is ready. As he's pointed out in the past, I'm always ready for him, but my body and my mind aren't reconciled. They're on completely different pages at the moment, especially since our parents are a thing now, which makes it almost taboo to think of Ryan like that, even though I've been thinking about him like that longer than my dad has even noticed Leslie is alive.

I remember a time when my dad only had eyes for my mom. She was the first one he wanted when he got off the court. The first one he would call after an away game. He used to send her postcards when he was gone of every single city he played in. My mom still has them stashed somewhere. That is, if she hasn't thrown them all away yet. Maybe she won't want the mementos after what her relationship with him turned out to be.

Ryan's phone ringing breaks into my internal thoughts. He pulls it out of his pocket and answers it. "Yeah?" After a pause, he says, "You let him drink!?"

I glance over at him. Ryan's profile is all taut muscle. He's squeezing the life out of his cell phone. I barely hear the other voice on the line, but it's raised now, too.

"Christ, Sloan."

"Sloan?" I ask, unable to help myself.

Ryan sighs. Then, he says into the phone, "Yes, it's Tessa." There's another pause, and he says, "I don't know why you couldn't get a hold of her."

"What's going on?"

Ryan drops his hand to his lap. "The guys are at a bar in town. They borrowed a car from one of the other players, but they've all been drinking. They need a ride back to camp."

I stare unbelievingly in front of me. Ryan and I are almost back to camp ourselves, but I certainly can't let them stay at the bar like that. If my dad, or any of the other coaches found out that they went and got drunk, they'd probably get kicked out of camp. Not to mention that they're all underage. I take a left down the next turn, and then do a U-turn to bring us back to the main road.

"We're on our way," Ryan says after he pulls the phone back to his ear. "What bar are you at?" Ryan ends the call a few moments later without saying good-bye. "Fucking idiots," he fumes.

"The drinking?"

He shoves his phone back into his pocket. "Not just the drinking," he says. "I go away for one night. Not even for a night. For one evening."

He seems a little too upset about them drinking than I would've imagined. I know they do that. Never on a game night or anything, but I've heard stories about parties that I was never invited to during practice on Monday afternoons. It's not like the Ballers are saints. At least I can say they never let it interfere with basketball.

Ryan seems super agitated now. His knee is

bobbing up and down. He keeps checking his phone like he's going to get another message, or a phone call any minute. He's so nervous it's making me nervous, and I can't help but think there's something far more serious going on.

"What is it, Ryan?"

"Just drive," he says. "Okay? Just drive."

Because of the urgency in his voice, I push the pedal down a little harder. Despite the fact that he seems so pissed that they're at the bar, he still knows exactly where the place is. I pull into the parking lot and park around the side of the building in case my dad and Leslie are still around town. My car is unmistakable in this small place.

Ryan practically leaps from the car, slams the door behind him, and is at a jog when he hits the front door of the bar named Charlie's. I have to run to catch up with him. When we get in there, all hell is about to break loose.

Holy shit...

28

The first thing I see when we barge inside like we own the place is an older man gripping the collar on Alec's shirt. He has it in a white-knuckle grip, his face a sneer of rage that makes my stomach bottom out. Sloan is behind Alec's body, trying to edge his way through. The other locals aren't far behind the angry man holding Alec.

The air whooshes out of me as Ryan rushes forward. I grab at air trying to stop him, but his fist pulls back and slams into the cheek of the guy holding Alec.

The rest is a tangle of limbs as I gasp at the scene ahead of me. There were never fights at Broadwell. It sounds ridiculous to even say, but the rich boys and girls don't fight with fists. They have other means. This expression of power and anger is new to me. Sure, I've wanted to pummel Lake—along with the rest of the guys—but this is beyond anything I've ever imagined myself doing. It's like a pure display of testosterone and dick measuring that turns my stomach. Insults and crass curses fly in between the thuds of contact. The Ballers give as good as they get, which is almost shocking to me. The crowd in here is mostly middle-aged. We're fucking teenagers for crying out loud.

"Stop!" I yell.

But it's fruitless. No one's listening. I step forward, my knees wobbling. A fist lands on Ryan's brow, and his skin splits open. Sloan's lip is bleeding. Alec, I can't even see right now.

My gaze searches the bar for Hayes. He's propping Lake up, one arm slung over his shoulders. Lake looks completely out of it. His eyes are rolled back into his head, his head bobbing to the side. Hayes looks up and meets my eyes. "Get out of here," he grits out.

I move forward. I don't know what to do next. Help Hayes with Lake, so he can help his other friends or try to talk some sense into these Neanderthals. All my life, it's been basketball first. Nothing came between me and it, but it's clear the Ballers don't have the same hang-ups I do.

"Get the fuck out of here, Tessa," Hayes growls.

My lips form a thin line. I walk up to Lake and put his hand over my shoulder to help Hayes carry him out. "I got him," I tell Hayes. I silently plead with him to help Alec, Sloan, and Ryan.

Lake's head swivels around. His eyes are hooded, but he blinks when he sees me. Despite his drunken state, he somehow manages to pull away from me. "Get the fuck off me, Dale. I fucking hate you."

His breath is all alcohol. "Feeling's mutual, prick." I tug his arm back around my shoulder. "I've got him," I tell Hayes. "Help the others."

Again, Lake must gather some sort of strength from somewhere. He can hardly keep himself upright, but he manages to push me. Because I'm not ready for it, I fall to the ground. My hip hits the wooden floor of the bar hard.

"Get the fuck away from me, bitch," Lake slurs. "I don't know how many times I have to tell you." He bends over to get in my face, but he trips over his feet and ends up falling. We're too close for comfort, and he immediately backs away. "I loathe you."

Behind him, I see Sloan shove one of the guys he was tousling with to the ground. He looks over, his gaze meeting mine. Concern etches his features, a stark contrast to the streaks of blood over his face.

In front of me, Lake falls fully to the ground. He's

passed the fuck out for good this time. I rise to my feet, ignoring the jab of pain from my hip, and pull at Lake's wrists. I slide him across the floor. He didn't want me to help him on his feet, so he can suffer through me dragging him to the car. I yank hard once, getting his body moving. Hayes assesses the situation and must think I have everything handled because he turns, but the look in his eyes terrifies me.

A quick check of the bar tells me the police have already been called. The bartender is standing with his arms crossed over his chest as he glares at the commotion in front of him. Maybe this is a typical Saturday for him. But what's not typical is the fact that the Ballers are all underage with fake ID's. If they get found out, they're fucked. This thought spurs me on. I'd be just as happy leaving Lake here, but the Ballers won't go without him. In order to get them to leave, I drag his drunk ass out to the car. He grunts when I drag him over a large stone that was used to designate the parking area.

Maybe I enjoy ruthlessness too because a sick smirk of satisfaction crosses my lips.

"Get the fuck out," someone yells. I look up as I round the corner of the building to find Alec stumbling out of the bar. Sloan and Ryan follow while Hayes stalks forward without a bruise or telltale sign of a fight on him. An overweight man with a scraggly mustache fills the door frame. "Don't ever come back."

Sloan waves his middle finger behind his head, and I shake my head at his audacity. Is this what the Ballers do for fun? What the fuck is wrong with them?

"Here," Alec says, moving forward. He reaches around in his pocket and brings out a fob. He pushes a button down and, the car I'm just about to pass beeps to life. This must be the car they borrowed to come here.

I drop Lake's hands. They fall freely to the ground and bounce once they hit the dirt of the parking lot. I can still see the venom in his eyes from the bar. The way he stared at me and said he hated me makes a shiver of fear skirt up my spine. To my knowledge, I've never done anything to incur someone's hate like that.

"We need to get the fuck out of here," Ryan says, dragging his hands through his blond hair as he checks the road.

I'm already walking toward my car. If they think I'm going to go down with them if they get caught, they have another thing coming. I haven't worked so hard at this camp to go down like this.

"I'll drive Lake," Ryan says. Alec and Sloan are already sliding him into the backseat of the borrowed car. If he's as drunk as I think he is, there's no way that car is getting out of this unscathed. The contents of Lake's stomach will probably be all over the upholstery by the time they get back to camp. "You guys go with Tessa."

"Tessa's leaving," I snap back, holding my keys over my head. "Now. So, if anyone wants a ride, they better get in the fucking car."

I whip the driver's side door open and get in. The engine starts underneath me with a push of a button, and even though it sounds like it's normal growly self, I kind of wish I had the power to make it sound angrier. I start backing out of the space, but the passenger door opens and Sloan shouts, "Hey."

I slam on the brakes. "Get in the fucking car."

Sloan pushes the front seat forward and lunges for the backseat, Alec following him. The seat snaps back into position and Hayes gets in, his expression stoic. As soon as he shuts the door, I gun the engine. I whip the steering wheel to the left just as Ryan's about to back up. My tires catch in the dirt as I maneuver around him. At the end of the parking lot, I squeal my tires as I leave the neon lights of the bar behind me. I'm seething on the way back. Sloan attempts to put his hands on my shoulder, but I shrug him off.

"Aw, come on," Sloan says. "You didn't find any of that hot?"

"Am I an animal?"

He kneads my shoulders.

"I mean it, Sloan. Get the fuck off me."

Hayes twists in his seat and sends Sloan a menacing look. Sloan immediately pulls his hands away.

I nod toward the glove compartment. "There are probably napkins in there for the idiots in the backseat."

I close my eyes briefly at the thought of them getting blood all over my car. It would be one thing if they were injured through no fault of their own. If the guys in the bar just started beating them for no reason, I'd want blood myself. I probably would've thrown my ass right in the middle of it, but what the hell were they doing there in the first place? Giving up their careers, obviously.

I glance at Alec in the backseat. He catches my eye, and I shake my head at him. He could've thrown two careers out the window tonight. All he needs is a broken wrist. A broken hand. Or worse. As soon as we get back from basketball camp, his pre-season baseball games start. The ones he won't give up because he refuses to abandon the dream of playing baseball, but he'll give it up by getting into a bar fight with a bunch of townies. That's so smart.

I thought these boys were as driven as me. Maybe I was wrong the whole time. They're used to getting things thrown into their lap, so they'll take all the risks they can get.

"I see that look," Sloan says. "Trust me, I don't need anyone else looking at me with so much disappointment. I've seen and heard it all before."

I nibble on my lip. I know his parents are a sore subject, and no matter how much I want to tell him I wouldn't have to look at him like that if he didn't do this one stupid thing, I imagine he has heard it all before and then some. Keeping silent only makes me more furious though. Maybe I expected more out of these boys than they deserve.

Headlights follow me all the way back to camp. When I pull into the same parking spot I vacated hours ago with Ryan, I feel like I can finally breathe. Hopefully the guys at the bar won't be able to trace us back here. If we're lucky—what am I saying? If they're lucky—they kept their mouths shut about basketball while they were there.

The borrowed car pulls to a stop beside us. I turn the Mustang's engine off and stand from the car. Ryan whisks his door open and the telltale noises of someone vomiting erupts from the car. I was right. Whoever they borrowed this car from is going to be so pissed, and rightfully so.

"Give me a hand guys," Ryan says. He shuts his own door and opens up the back. He pulls Lake out by the shoulders. His legs drop to the ground. He's still vomiting. He's shaking, too. His skin is pale white and there's fierce red streaks over his cheeks.

"Jesus," I sigh. "What the hell's wrong with him? How much did he drink?"

Ryan glances up at me. His face is demure even though everything he's feeling is hiding in his gray eyes. "It's the alcohol mixed with the pills," he says. He glares at the other Ballers. "I can't believe you let him do this."

"Pills?"

Everyone ignores me. Sloan and Alec fidget on their feet. Alec's wadded up, blood-soaked napkin is pressed to his nose. The only one who looks on the scene impassively is Hayes. Ice Man strikes again. By the look of him, I have no idea what he's thinking and feeling.

"We were just trying to have some fun," Sloan says. He sways a little. I bite the inside of my cheek to keep from going off on him.

Ryan doesn't have that problem though. He discards Lake's arms and spins on the Ballers. His face is snarling, and he looks every bit the Point Guard in that moment trying to rally them when there's five seconds left on the clock and they're down by two. "You knew what would happen."

"He said it would be fine."

"Yeah, because he's in the right fucking head space," Ryan snaps back.

"None of us are in the right fucking head space," Alec growls.

Sloan steps in, his hands raised in the air. I perk up, not expecting Sloan to play the peacemaker. "Everything was fine until those guys started with us."

"How's that?" I can't help myself from asking. "Did they bust you for underage drinking?"

Sloan turns on me, and for the first time tonight, I can tell he's in pain. Suffering. Emotionally and physically. "No." His words are clipped and hang in the air.

"We'll talk about this later," Ryan says. "Let's get Lake into his bed."

Ryan takes Lake by the shoulders, and Alec grabs his feet. They carry him, and I watch how lifeless his body is as they manhandle him through the shadows as we sneak down to the cabins. Thankfully, no one else is out tonight. Despite myself, and the harsh words Lake just spoke to me, a niggle of worry wiggles its way inside me. "Is he going to be okay?" I ask

Hayes, who's still keeping close to me in his calm, cool way.

Hayes glances down at me, his blue eyes calculating when he says, "The pills and alcohol don't mix well."

"He said he wasn't taking them," Sloan says, his fingers curling around his own arms.

I'm almost astonished that the guys are freely talking about this in front of me. "Pain pills?" I ask. I had no idea Lake was injured. If he is, he's doing a damn good job of hiding it. We're still equals in many ways on the court. It's only in being a general good human being that I far surpass him.

Hayes nods. Ryan's back goes ramrod straight. There's still a singular light on in the cabin Lake, River, and Ryan share. Luckily, they left Baby O'Brien at home for their little stunt at the bar. Probably only because he doesn't have a fake ID, even though I'd like to think they'd draw the line somewhere. The kid's only like fifteen. He doesn't need to be drinking and getting into bar fights. I don't think he should be holding girls down on a track either, but what the fuck do I know anymore?

"Oxy," Alec says.

I almost choke. "Oxycodone?"

My stomach squeezes. I feel like they're trying to

tell me something without telling me. None of them deny my question, so I take it that I've guessed correctly.

"How long has he been taking them?" I ask. A memory erupts in my mind of Coach Bradley telling me there was something wrong with my drug test and Miss Lyons having to watch me pee in a cup. Did he do that?

"On and off. For a while," Ryan grits out.

Ryan goes up the small porch first. Sloan runs ahead of him and opens the cabin door. "What the...?" River says. Then he's right there, hovering over his brother as Alec and Ryan lay him on the bed. "Jesus. How much did he drink?"

"A lot," Ryan says, rubbing the back of his head. The guys all share looks. I watch from outside, and I get a sinking feeling that River doesn't know Lake's hooked on Oxy. He probably has no clue.

I turn toward Hayes, the only other Baller who hasn't entered the cabin. The door closes behind the others as I say, "Answers, Hayes. I need them."

He shrugs like he hasn't another care in the world, but the slight sideways glance he gives me only makes me think what comes out of his mouth next is a half-truth. "He's hooked on painkillers. What more is there to know?"

My eyes practically bulge out of my head. I point toward the cabin. "Is he going to be alright?" I'm not a doctor, but I've also heard tragic stories about people who mix the two.

"He's thrown up already, so that's good. Ryan will stay with him tonight, and if he has to make him throw up again, he will."

I shake my head. "This is all kinds of fucked up." Just the fact that he's talking about this so nonchalantly makes an eerie shiver tiptoe up my spine. It's like they've been fighting with this for a while, so it's already second nature. "How can he even function normally? He's addicted?" I ask again, needing him to make it plainly clear to me.

Hayes turns toward me fully. He grabs my shoulders and leans over. His presence makes my heart skip a beat. I'm suddenly not so agitated anymore. My pulse screams through me as he licks his lips. "He's off and on, but yes, he keeps going back, so I say addicted. Some of us would argue that point, but I've about had it with him, Tessa. I don't want to talk about Lake."

There are shadows in his deep blue eyes. He tucks me into his side, and we walk the short distance to his, Alec, and Sloan's cabin. He turns the lights on when we enter. I look him over now that we're in the light. There's only one speck of blood on his cheek. I go to the bathroom and get a washcloth. After wetting it in the bathroom sink, I come back out and wipe the red droplet away. Then, I pull his fists up and examine them one at a time. They don't look cut at all.

"I didn't hit anybody," he says.

I twist my head. I'm almost surprised. "I just forcefully moved the guys so we could all leave."

"I wish the others would've been as smart as you."

The corner of his lip tugs up. "I don't think anyone's called me smart before."

"They must not know you."

His arms move around me. They work up my spine, then he drags his fingers down my back. I have to completely hold my neck back to look him in the eyes, but it isn't awkward. I love that he's a force that looms over me. I've needed him to be that way ever since the Ballers abandoned me. "I don't care if no one else knows me. I just want you to." His hand moves up and tangles in my hair. Carefully, he tugs until he leans over to kiss me. The air sucks from my lungs as his lips pass over mine in such a gentle way that belies everything about him. After several soft caresses, he pulls just a hair's breadth away. "I'm sorry you had to see that tonight. It wasn't one of our finer moments."

I cup his cheeks and bring him down again. To bridge the distance quicker, I lift onto my tiptoes until we're kissing again. This feels so right. Like two people comforting one another, not like two people sneaking around or two people kissing one another who know they shouldn't. It makes me want to stay here.

That is, until the door opens, and a gust of wind accompanies Sloan and Alec as they walk into the room. "Don't mind us," Sloan says.

"I won't," I say.

Hayes steps away from me, but I follow him. I pull on his collar, bringing him back to me again, finishing our kiss the right way. When we pull away this time, it's not because we were interrupted. His left arm slides around me, tucking me into his side.

Sloan moves forward, raising his hand toward Hayes. He waggles his eyebrows. "Come on. Knuckles."

Reluctantly, Hayes gives in and presses his knuckles into Sloan's. He doesn't seem very thrilled with his friends right now either, and I wonder if this is Sloan's way of saying he's sorry.

Noticing the state the other two are in, I go back into the bathroom with my washcloth and come back out. Alec looks like he's in worse shape, so I start with him. I remove the napkin from his nose. He's swollen there, but the blood has stopped. I gently wipe the washcloth over his face, removing all traces of blood on him. Like with Hayes, I bring his hands up and inspect his knuckles. Unlike Hayes, though, his are all red and the skin is broken. I tsk and wipe away the dried blood. Alec winces. I don't let that stop me. "If you behaved like a gentleman, I wouldn't have to be doing this right now."

"It's not me," Alec says. "Talk to Sloan."

I turn, my gaze flicking down the length of Sloan Ivy. He has a cut on his forehead and lip, and his knuckles are also cut and bleeding, though they're dry now. I go into the bathroom and wet another washcloth before coming back out. Alec enters after me and soon, I hear the shower going.

"What did he mean by that?" I ask Sloan.

"Thanks a lot, bro," Sloan calls out, even though I'm sure Alec can't hear him right now.

"It means," Hayes starts, "someone started to say shit about his family. Ivy doesn't like people who say shit about his family."

My brows pinch together as I work on Sloan's fists, wiping crusted blood away to reveal the damage underneath. Luckily, it doesn't look as if any one of them are too badly off. When I glance up, Sloan is pulling a Hayes. His face is a mask as he looks down at my work without a sign on his face one way or the other. "Care to elaborate?" I ask, keeping my voice even.

Sloan's tongue darts out and licks his lips as he locks gazes with me. "Someone recognized me. I don't think they agreed with my father's politics."

"They called his dad a manwhore," Hayes supplies.

Sloan's faces changes in an instant. The death glare he's sending his friend right now makes a lump form in my throat. "Isn't someone talkative all of a sudden?"

Hayes lifts his hand, giving Sloan the middle finger. Luckily, Sloan just laughs it off.

"So, you went ape shit?" Part of the scene I witnessed earlier makes sense. Sloan egged the fight on, but Alec was right there when his friend needed help. He is the bigger of the two, even though I'm sure Sloan can hold his own.

Sloan takes the washcloth from me and sets it on the table, dismissing my attention. He falls back on his bed and crosses his feet and his hands behind his head. "I don't know why I care. It's true."

I know exactly why he cares. I'm not exactly happy with my father at the moment, but that doesn't mean I don't still love him. "It's natural," I tell him.

His gaze slides over to me. He truly looks at me, probably wondering if I'm just placating him or if I'm being serious.

I give him a small smile, and then walk back into

Hayes's grip. He sits on his bed, dragging me with him, and I settle myself in his lap. A quick check of the clock tells me it's almost midnight. I should go back to my cabin, but at the same time, I'm too wrapped up in these guys. I don't want to have to worry about them all night. I turn in Hayes's grip. "Can I stay here?"

His jaw tenses. The steady rise and fall of his chest hiccups for a moment before he leans back, wordlessly. With little effort, I fall right into place next to him. I kick off my shoes and let them drop off the side of the bed.

Sloan sighs. "If any more funny business happens with Tessa tonight, I can't promise I won't jackoff to it."

Hayes actually smirks. He kisses the corner of my lips, and I'm so comfortable right next to him that I close my eyes, letting myself drift off immediately. So many things went down today. Ryan...Lake...but somehow, none of that seems to matter when I'm sleeping curled up next to Hayes.

29

What I don't expect when I wake up is the massive hard-on pressing into my back. I blink awake. Hayes doesn't stir, so I know he's not even aware of it, which makes me smile into the pillow. I lift my head carefully. Sloan and Alec are still asleep, too. Both of them look peaceful, the bruising that's starting to appear on their handsome faces a juxtaposition to their cherub-like forms as they're lost in a dream world. I'm glad it's Sunday. I don't have to worry about basketball today, but more than that, neither do they. Their fists need to heal, and maybe some of their cuts and bruises will go down, so that they don't have to explain anything to anyone. The fact that the cops didn't show up last night is promising. It means they probably won't be, so at least the Ballers are out of the woods on that front.

Now, the guy's car they borrowed? That's another story. I flip on the bed until I'm staring at the ceiling.

Lake's addicted to pain killers.

I can't even remember him being injured recently, not that I would've heard when I was at Broadwell. No, this has to be at least a year old or more. No wonder why he's such a fucking prick all the time. Isn't that one of the side effects of drug usage? Massive assholery.

Regardless of that, when he said he hated me yesterday, it wasn't the drugs or the alcohol talking. No, that came from his core. Something that still baffles me, but I know my guys won't ever give me the answers I want. Some of what they've done makes sense now. They were trying to help Lake. They probably didn't want him to go back to the pills if he was, in fact, staying off them recently.

Hayes stirs. His hand lifts and rests on my stomach. I slept in my jeans, something that didn't prove to be very comfortable. Right now, however, the shirt I have on is halfway up my stomach. Hayes's palm glides over my bare skin.

I turn my head to look at him. His eyes are bright this morning, like sapphire chips glistening in the noon sunlight. "What are you thinking about?" he whispers.

Reaching out, I trace my fingertips over his sculpted cheeks. I don't want to bring Lake up this early in the morning, and honestly, I'm not sure if I should. He's dealing with his own demons. And just when I had myself convinced I should make that bet with him. Then again, if I made a bet with him about MVP, maybe he'd get off the drugs. He'd have to if he wanted to beat me.

Hayes's fingers press into my lower lip. "You're not going to tell me?"

I smile. "Nothing important."

"I know that's a lie. You have that fierce look on your face, and I know Tessa Dale doesn't think about trivial things."

His hand traces lower, across my chest and over my stomach, dipping just under the tops of my jeans. His touch makes my heart stagger inside my chest.

"Is this okay?"

I gulp and nod. As soon as I do so, the part of his fingers I can't see any more traces the top of my panties. My breath comes to a grinding halt. His other hand deftly maneuvers the button on my jeans through the buttonhole. Still keeping his gaze locked on mine, he lowers the zipper.

I bite my lip.

"That's so sexy," he breathes. He leans over and captures my swollen lips in his, all the while sneaking his hand lower and lower until they scoop under the lace of my underwear and he cups me. I moan into his mouth, but he swallows it up.

He keeps his lips on me, kissing me in a languid rhythm that matches his finger strokes once he pushes inside. My hips come off the bed, but his kiss doesn't let up. Any moans or whispers my body is begging me to make are all caught up inside Hayes now as he works his finger in and out. Of all the things I've done with any one of them, this moment feels the most intimate. Hayes is trying. I think if I asked him to stop being friends with Lake, he would. I won't. I don't ever want to give them an ultimatum like Lake gave them. Maybe if Lake gets off the Oxy, we can coexist.

Hayes curls his finger inside me, and I gasp into his mouth. His tongue glides over mine, and he presses his dick into my thigh. I reach down to cup him and his kiss falters for a moment before he continues ravaging me.

Hayes is fucking huge. I wrap my fingers around him and wonder at the logistics of fitting him inside me eventually. *Maybe not now...*

His thumb presses on my nub.

Or now.

I try to turn toward him, but Hayes holds me in place. His finger moves faster. I'm so caught up in his movements that all I can do is clasp his dick in a tight fist and continue to kiss him back. My high builds and builds. I know I'm going to come soon. Hayes must realize it too because he deepens the kiss. I cling to his shoulders with my free hand, my nails sinking into his skin as I ride his finger. Sparks fly in front of my eyes as I constrict over his finger, my body sending me blissfully over the edge.

His finger slows as my body rides a slowly decreasing high. He finally lets me break away, and I almost gasp as I try to rake in air that my chest so desperately needs. "That was evil," I tell him.

He pushes hair back from my face. "I didn't want an audience." When I raise my eyebrows at him, he says, "I didn't want to wait either."

I give him a smile. He pulls his fingers out of me, rearranges my pants back as they should be, and leaves his hand on my stomach like he had it when we started. A sleep-mussed Hayes is a gorgeous Hayes. His dirty blond hair is wild about him and the blue in his eyes, either excited from what we just did or from just waking up, is intoxicating. Seeing as I still have my hand on his hard cock, I start to stroke him. Immediately, he entwines our fingers and pulls me away. "I won't be able to keep quiet, Tessa." He leans over and kisses me on the nose.

"Not fair," I tell him. "You tortured me."

A smile plays over his lips. "You call that torture?"

"I call that one hell of a way to wake up."

His gaze burns into mine. The way he looks at me leaves me with no uncertainty of his feelings for me. "If only they weren't here," Hayes says, raking his gaze down my body.

Wherever he looks, heat pricks start. It makes my mind go there, and I guess Hayes is thinking the same thing because he asks, "Have you had sex before, Tessa?"

I nod. I'm watching him the entire time to try to gauge his reaction, but like usual, I can't tell. "My ex," I tell him, thinking about Andrew and how quickly he forgot about me. The only part that hurts about any of that is the fact that Tiff didn't waste any time after I'd left to shack up with him. It's like I never belonged at Broadwell to begin with. Maybe I was always meant to be at RHS. "Not extensive knowledge, and it wasn't even that good," I admit.

My cheeks bloom red. I remember Andrew fumbling and after too short of a time dropping on top of me when he'd finished. He'd asked me if I'd enjoyed it, and I'd lied. That was the first time, but it didn't get much better from there either. So much so that by the end of our dwindling relationship, I'd been avoiding him and definitely any advances of that nature. I felt like there should be something more. With Alec, Sloan, and now Hayes, I know I was right. If I let my guard down with Ryan, I know it'll be the same way.

I don't need to ask Hayes if he has experience because clearly, he does. In fact, I don't think I want to know how much experience all the guys have. They have reputations and have told me themselves that they shared girls. They even have that game of theirs where they can only go as far as the others have with the same girl. They want to toy with them, so that's what they do.

I shake that thought away because I think it's different with me, and not because they've told me so. I'm actually starting to believe them.

Which only brings another round of problems. Not only do I like four separate guys, but they all like me. How much longer will they be willing to share me? Sloan gave Hayes knuckles after they walked in on us kissing. Is that a show?

"Don't worry," Hayes says, misconstruing what must be plainly written all over my face. "We'll go easy on you."

"We'll?" I ask.

"You belong to us."

My body should automatically resist that remark, but instead, it gives in and lets the full force of his words flow through me. I swim with feelings, letting goosebumps prick my skin and revel in how much that one sentence makes me feel wanted. It makes me feel everything I've ever wanted to feel when it came to the Ballers.

I glance down. He's still straining in his boxers. I lick my lips. "I think you need to practice your quiet voice." I push him down on the bed, wrap my fingers around his boxers, and peel them down. I think he's in shock because he doesn't move.

"Tessa..." It's a warning mixed with excitement. He can't lie. I know he wants this. He wants me.

I lean over, and he turns on the bed. I almost gasp at the size of him. His silky head is erect, calling to me. He shivers when I get closer, and I'm just about to wrap my lips around him when footsteps on the small porch outside stop me.

Oh fuck.

Hayes quickly pulls his boxers up, picks me up, and trades places with me on the bed until I'm pressed against the wall. My heart thuds in my chest. I squeeze my eyes shut, praying it's not my dad. It's Sunday morning. I don't know why it would be, but stranger things have happened.

Hayes stretches out, completely blocking me from view while arranging the covers over me. He leans over, and I hear him open the book I saw on his bed the other day and prop it in front of him. A knock comes on the door. I have to clamp my jaw shut. This isn't good. If it was Ryan out on the porch, he probably would've just walked right in.

"Come in," Hayes says tersely.

On the other side of the room, I hear someone stirring. When the door opens, a mattress creaks and Sloan says, "The fuck..." It's laced in sleep, but the next time he talks, he says, "What the fuck are you doing here?" It's more cautious, strained. He's probably wondering where I am, and if I've been caught by whoever walked in.

"Calm down, Ivy," Jacquin says.

My eyes widen underneath the sheet. Jesus. He's a coach, and I'm sure if he found me in here, he'd turn me in despite the fact that he's basically our age.

Another body stirs, and this time, I hear Alec groan.

"What the fuck's wrong with your face?" Jacquin asks. I'm not sure whether he's asking Alec or Sloan. It could be directed toward either one...or both.

No one answers.

"Whatever," Jacquin says. "That's not what I'm here for."

Hayes shifts, propping his body up more. Footsteps creak the floorboards near us. Hayes is doing his best to angle his body in front of me. Thankfully, I'm so small compared to Hayes that I really don't think I'll be found out as long as I can stay quiet.

"What are you here for?" Sloan asks, every bit the part of his senator father coming out now. He's direct and upfront. His voice is almost laced with this cold, bored indifference that sends shivers up my spine. I was once on the receiving end of that voice, and I hated every minute of it.

The floorboards stop creaking. "I want to make it clear that I know O'Brien's dirty secret. It's obvious if anyone is paying attention, so I'm going to explain one small thing to you guys. I'll gladly spill. There's only one thing stopping me."

"And what the fuck is that?" Sloan sneers.

Hayes hand moves back and wraps around my thigh, holding me tightly.

"My good will, but that'll end soon if he doesn't leave Dale alone."

What the fuck? Me? Hayes's fingertips curl into my flesh.

"I don't care that you guys are content to sit back and let all this play out. I'm not, so here's the deal. If Tessa wins Shooting Guard MVP, O'Brien leaves her alone until you guys graduate. He doesn't mess with her chance to play for the team. He doesn't terrorize her. Basically, he doesn't say shit to her."

I'm so confused. This is the bet idea he came up with. Why does he want to make it for me?

"And if she loses?" Alec asks.

"If she loses, I won't say a thing about Lake's pill problem."

Sloan chuckles. "How does this help Lake? Either way, you won't say a thing."

Jacquin gives it right back to him. "Trust me, I'll talk if he decides he won't do this. And he has to leave her alone from here on out, too, until the MVP is decided, or I'll make a phone call to your coach back at Rockport."

"What do you care about all this?" Sloan snaps. "Why are you trying to help Tessa?"

Here's Sloan's possessiveness that he hid away yesterday when he saw Hayes and I kissing. Maybe Hayes is right. I belong to them, so they don't care about each other. Only the outsiders. I perk my ears up because I'm interested in Jacquin's answer, too. Why does he care so much?

"Unlike you guys, I guess I don't like to see innocent people being fucked with."

After a pregnant pause, Sloan says, "We'll talk to him."

"Talk fast," Jacquin says. "Either way, I'd get your buddy some help if I were you. Opioid addiction is no joke."

Footsteps cross the floor and then I hear the telltale squeak of the door as it opens and then slams closed. I wait a few beats before I emerge from the mound of covers. When I come out of my hiding place, both Sloan and Alec are looking toward us. They visibly relax.

Hayes sits up. He eyes me, half looking away. "What's up with that?"

I shrug. "Your guess is as good as mine."

It sucks that I automatically don't trust people. There's just this vibe I get off Jacquin that I don't like. He's actually trying to do something nice for me, something I didn't want to instigate myself, but I don't want his help. What he's doing sounds a lot like a bribe and that's not really my thing.

Jacquin knew I probably would never take the initiative, so he pulled the strings his way.

How he found out about Lake, though, I have no idea.

30

After returning to my cabin shortly after that, I don't see any of the guys until lunch. Alec texted me that they were already there if I wanted to meet them, so when I stroll in, I'm not surprised to see all of them in the cafeteria already, without Lake. River is there though. Without his brother, he isn't as terrifying. He just looks like a little boy trying to be an adult. I almost feel bad for him. He probably looks up to his brother so much and has no idea what's really going on with him. I'll have to make a note to ask the guys if they should be getting Lake professional help.

Then again, none of this is actually my problem.

A few of the lacrosse guys wave at me while I step away from the line with a full try of food. I wave and smile at them while Chase looks over his shoulder at me. He smiles back, but it's not a full-lipped smile. It's soft and small, almost sad. Before I can think any more about it, a hand closes around my wrist. I look down to find Hayes's eyes locked onto mine. I go to sit, but he moves his thigh in my way, so I end up sitting in his lap. He's already done with his food, so he pushes his own tray out of the way and moves mine in front of him.

Alec smirks. "I never pictured you as a PDA type of guy."

I almost laugh at that. That's what the Ballers all do. Even Hayes. I've seen it with my own eyes. Though, I suppose when it came to Hayes it was that the girls were always hanging off of him. He never reciprocated. They were just like an extension of his body, like an awkward growth or something.

Though River leers at me, he keeps his mouth shut. Even though I'm dying to ask how Lake is, I don't bother. I know I won't get straight answers right now anyway. If anything bad happened, I'm sure I would've heard about it by now. He's probably just sleeping away a massive hangover.

I hope someone compensated for the puke-filled borrowed car though.

At River's request, the guys regale them with stories about their bar fight, leaving out every detail regarding his brother. In fact, I can tell that Sloan and

Alec at least are a little paler today than normal. Alec is downing water like the well's going to dry up, and Sloan keeps rubbing his head. It serves them right. Hayes drank, too, I think, but he must not have had as much as the others. Then again, his drunk state might be similar to his everyday state. The only time I really feel anything from him is when his eyes are zeroed in on my own, and I'm captured by his sight. Then, it's like being in a warm embrace.

Ryan keeps checking the watch on his wrist, so I'm sure he intends on sticking close to Lake today. I wonder if Alec, Sloan, and Hayes told him—or even Lake—Jacquin's proposition yet. He looks up at me after checking the time again. I smile. "Is your mom still in town, or did she head back yet?"

"Speaking of," Sloan says, twisting his head toward me. His hazel eyes are dull today, like muddy brown. I can tell he doesn't feel good, even though he's trying to act like his normal self. "How come you didn't tell us you and Ryan are going to be house buddies?"

Ryan shakes his head. "Fuck you, Ivy."

Sloan laughs. For the first time today he actually sounds more like his normal self.

Ryan smirks. "I don't know why you're laughing. That just means I'm right down the hall from her. At all times of the night. Barely clothed."

I gape at him. "I don't think I'll be sleeping over much. I thought I made that clear yesterday during dinner."

Leaning back, Ryan smoothes his hands down his shorts.

"I think that was a denial," Sloan singsongs. I can tell he's loving every second of this.

"Trust me, she'll be wanting to sleep over."

Why does all this just sound so wrong?

Hayes's arm tightens around me. There's a glint of amusement in his eyes, but it's Alec who speaks next. "I'm down with having sleepovers again. We can pretend we're in middle school."

Oh God. My whole face burns red. It was one thing to have them all in my house for a pool party, but for a sleepover? I'm not sure I'd live through it, though I can tell they'd have a fun time torturing me.

Sloan pats Ryan on the head and then ruffles his hair. "My poor RyRy, moving up on the hill with the big timers."

I roll my eyes. We're nothing special up there. Ryan catches my eye though, and I don't think he's thinking about moving up with the big timers. I think his mind is otherwise engaged judging by the way his gaze rakes over me. Hayes can probably feel the flames that flare off me. I'm engulfed.

Ryan bats Sloan's hand away. "To answer your question, she's still here. She's going to come by to see me before she goes."

I smile tightly. "Tell her hi for me."

He nods once, and for a fleeting moment, I think I detect relief in his eyes. I don't know why. I said I would try. As long as they don't keep trying to shove their relationship down my throat, I'll try.

A hand touches me on the shoulder, and Hayes stiffens. When I turn, Chase is standing there. He isn't getting that nice of a reaction from the Ballers, so I make sure to smile at him. Quickly, he takes his hand off my shoulder. Hayes's laser-like stare probably burned it off. He sweeps his hand through his hair. "We're leaving. I just wanted to say goodbye to you."

I stand, Hayes's arm brushing over my hip and then down. "You're leaving? I don't know why I thought you were staying this next week."

One of his teammates comes up behind him. "We were getting restless, Tessa. We all decided we like girls too much to stick around this sausage fest."

I chuckle, shaking my head at him. He gives me a small salute. I watch as the rest of the team files by. Some of the guys give me a hug, which I'm sure is killing the Ballers. But really, these guys were there for me when we first got here. I'm actually going to miss them. Chase made me feel wanted here when no one else did. That's twice he's done that for me. When he stands there awkwardly, I tell him I'll walk him out.

He seems relieved. He opens the door to the main building for me, and I sneak through, not looking back. Trust me, I can feel the heat of their gazes enough on me as it is. I don't need to see their faces to know they hate what I'm doing right now. Oh well. The possessive fucks should learn a lesson.

We take the trail all the way up the small hill to the parking lot. A few cars are already backing up. They blow their horns, and Chase and I wave at them. He turns toward me. "My sister wants me to tell you that she hopes you kick ass the rest of camp. She said something about girl power and all that. I don't know. I stopped listening after a while."

I laugh at that, thinking that when I get back from camp, I should actually try to hang out with Christie. I think we could be good friends.

He jams his hands in his pockets. I can tell he's nervous, and I don't know how to calm him down. The way he glances over at me, I think he wishes there was more between us. "So you and the big guy?"

I smirk. Me and *all* of them, but he doesn't need to know that. "Something like that," I say.

"I just hope you're giving it back to them, Tessa. They don't deserve you."

Apprehension crawls over my skin. There's a ring of truth to what he's saying, but I'm not going to let that deter me. "Friends?" I ask.

"That depends," he says, finally cracking a real smile. "Are you actually going to text me?"

"I think I will," I tell him honestly. The Ballers will just have to get over themselves. I'm certainly not going to stop talking to other guys just because it makes their jealousy freak flag fly.

I step forward and give him a short, awkward hug. "Take care of yourself, Chase. Find one of those college girls your friends like so much."

His smile isn't as wide as it was a second ago. He nods. "Call me if you need me. I mean it. No matter what. I'm staying with a teammate in his apartment next to the college for a couple more weeks before going back home. I can be here if you need me to be."

"I will," I tell him. Who knows, if this all blows up in my face like before, I might need a friend like him. But no, I don't see it going down like that again. I really don't.

He steps away, and I give him a wave as he walks to his friend's car. They back out, and his friend beeps the horn as they start down the road away from Camp Holly.

Strong arms surround me. It's Sloan who nuzzles my neck from behind. "Thank God that fucker's gone."

I look over my shoulder. Ryan and River are already walking away. It's just Hayes, Alec, Sloan, and I. There's still a lot of hours left to Sunday, so I smile. "Who's up for a swim?"

Alec is the first to take off running. The rest of us catch on quick after that. I start laughing, giggling even as I chase after them as we race to the water. Hayes sprints, his long legs taking him away fast. He's almost caught up with Alec. I laugh as they both race into the lake at the same time Sloan and I hit the sand. Sloan reaches out and grabs me, swinging me through the air before running with me into the water. I scream as the water splashes up my body. There's a chill in the water today, and it takes my breath away. It also might be the fact that Sloan's as hard as a rock against my back.

To feel this carefree with them is a weight off my shoulders. We play in the water, splashing one another and laughing, drenched through in our regular clothes without a care in the world. The only thing is, I know it's just a facade. If Lake were here, things would be different. Hell, if Ryan were here, things would be different, too. I told him I couldn't handle the idea of him yet. There are still too many things up in the air, and no matter how much I try to drown out these thoughts while I'm with the others, they keep popping back up until I'm left wondering when everything might go back to some semblance of normality.

There's hope on the horizon. If I win Shooting Guard MVP, I could regain control of my life for this next school year. I can fight for a spot on the team and only my skills will decide if I get minutes or not. Not some stupid, misplaced faux-royalty hierarchy system. Just me and my basketball skills. The way it should be.

31

No one overtly says anything to me, but Lake must've taken the deal Jacquin presented him with. I know this for two reasons. One, Jacquin doesn't call him out on the pill popping thing. And two, for a few days, Lake looks seriously sick. I don't ask, and they don't offer up an explanation, but the only thing I can guess is that Lake stopped using for now. I guess he wants to make sure he's on top of his game, so he can beat me.

Too bad for him, I'm not going to let that happen. I want that coveted, peaceful existence more than anything. Don't get me wrong, I want to beat him when he's one hundred percent the basketball player I know he can be, but I'll take it either way. As long as I win my freedom, that's all that matters.

I don't know if it's Jacquin's idea or not, but for the next couple of weeks, the coaches display who's on top of the MVP leaderboard. I actually don't think it's such a bad idea. We get ranked in our basketball conferences. We're ranked and seeded in Championships. This is no different. It also lets me know where I stand, and also lets me know that Lake is being the best basketball player he can be. I won the week that he felt like shit. But the week after that, I came in second.

Jacquin keeps gently nudging me, telling me it's close. It's so close. Dad hasn't said anything like that to me because he can't, but I can tell by the way he studies us when we're in practices that he's thinking the same thing. I know he won't be judging my position, but I like to see what he thinks overall.

Across the board, the Ballers are winning their MVP positions so far. It's not surprising. This is the reason why I wanted to go to RHS. No other school can compare. I don't know how these five guys found each other, but it was like some cosmic ball players dream. Coach Bradley is so lucky to have not only one amazing player on his team, but five.

Since Lake is feeling better, I've made myself scarce around the Ballers for the most part. I'm fine with it because once again, it gives me time to do some extra training. I do laps in the lake at night. Sometimes,

Sloan will come down and do them with me. Other times, one of them might come watch, but I think they can tell that I'm taking this very seriously. I don't want to even think about what might happen if I don't win MVP. As I said before, he'll probably want me to leave the Ballers alone. Now that I've crossed the line with them, I don't think I'll be able to do that. Then again, they might be the ones to force my hand again.

They better not force my fucking hand again.

Because the lacrosse team is gone, I still eat with the Ballers. I just usually sit off to the side a little. One of the guys usually keeps me company while the rest of them talk. Don't get me wrong, I intervene sometimes. When I do, Lake doesn't bat an eye. He's keeping his end of the bargain up so far. He hasn't said or done anything to me since he agreed to the deal.

One night on the phone, I tell Dawn the agreement Jacquin fixed for me. "Oh shit," she says. "Seriously? Tessa, that's great. This is what you wanted."

"Well, I haven't won yet."

"Are you kidding me? You're going to mop the floor with him. You're going to do just exactly what you did to make the team last year. You're going to keep your head down and your eyes on the prize."

She pretty much uses every bad one-liner a coach could use, but she's adorable when she says it, so I light up when she's done. What she finds most interesting about our conversation is when I tell her that my dad and Ryan's mom are moving in together.

"Are you shitting me?" she practically screams.

I have to hold the phone away from my ear to keep my hearing ability intact. "Nope."

"What are you going to do?"

I chuckle at that. "Not much I can do, I guess." I don't tell her that my mom came down to camp and tried to get my dad back. Next time she sees her, I don't want her to look at my mother any differently. As far as she knows, she's recuperating from her husband leaving her out of nowhere.

"You seem way too blasé about this," Dawn quips. "This is Ryan fucking Linc we're talking about here. He's like sex on a stick. Holy fuck." She pauses. "Do you think you're actually going to end up step-brother and step-sister."

My stomach twists until I feel queasy. "That better not fucking happen. If my dad thinks I flipped out over them moving in together, he hasn't seen anything yet."

Dawn chuckles freely into the phone. "I can imagine Godzilla Tessa coming out. No one wants that hot of a stepbrother. Damn. You can barely even function around him now, what about then?"

"Thanks for the vote of confidence," I tease.

"You know what I'm saying," she says, brushing my thoughts aside. "Ryan fucking Linc."

Exactly. She really doesn't even need to say anything else. His name is enough. It evokes more than enough responses in me.

Looking back on that night in the car, I wish I hadn't stopped us from kissing. Yes, I know his mother and my father, but...I saw him first. It sounds so middle school, but I'm going with it.

A knock sounds on my door while I'm talking to her. I check the clock. It's not quite curfew yet, so I yell out, "Come in."

"Who's that?" Dawn asks.

Sloan walks in. I smile at him. He takes in my lazy sprawl over the bed and then glances at the phone to my ear. "Dawn?" he mouths. When I nod, he says out loud, "Hey, Dawn."

"Which one is that?" she asks, her voice only a tinge of uneasiness. She definitely doesn't agree with the fact that I've let them all back into my life.

"Sloan," I tell her.

"Shit," she says. "Tell him not to turn on the TV."

My brows pull together. "Why?"

"Another scandal involving his parents."

I fret over my lip, looking up at Sloan's carefree smile. I doubt he knows anything about it yet. Maybe it's not even on the national news. Maybe it's just local. "I got to go, Dawn. I'll call in another couple of days."

"Be safe," she calls out just as I hang up the phone.

Sloan must've heard because a smirk graces his beautiful face. He crawls over me on the bed. I don't know how I'm going to be able to go back home and not have the ability to have one of them less than a hundred yards away from me at any given time. Now that we're all on pretty solid terms, having them around has been nice. It's like before when they actually wanted to spend time with me. "Are you telling all our secrets to your bestie?"

I toss my phone to the small table by my bed. "No," I say, drawing the word out. "She barely likes you guys."

His mouth pinches. "No? Wasn't she hot for Christopoulos not too long ago?"

"Yeah, then you guys ripped away my dreams and stomped on my heart."

"Oh that," he says, a small smile coming to his face before it washes away instantly. "I wish I could go back, Daddy's Girl. I'd change my own mind."

"Aren't those lyrics to a Taylor Swift song?"

He shrugs. "You got me."

I hit him playfully on the shoulder. "Come up with your own material, Ivy."

"Fine. How about I'm really sorry, Dale. Next time I stomp on your heart you have my permission to kick me in the balls."

I hold my hand out and make him shake on it. If that happens, I'm holding him to it.

Once the levity fades, I peek up at him. He's still hovering over me on the bed. I have to tell him what Dawn just confessed. I can't let him be blindsided about it if he doesn't know yet. "So," I start, trying to come up with the right words. It would be easier if I knew exactly what the scandal was. I should've asked before I hung up the phone.

"Out with it, Tessa," Sloan says.

He looks at me carefully, and I sigh. "Dawn told me she saw your parents on the news."

He blinks at me. Then, he sighs and falls back on the bed next to me. He runs his hands through his dark brown hair. "Did she say for what?"

I shake my head. "I can ask if you want," I tell him, automatically reaching for my phone.

He pins my arm with a look, so I stop. "Don't bother. I'm sure I'll hear about it sooner or later."

Seeing Sloan upset makes me feel uneasy. He's usually the light-hearted one. Even when he's not, he's playing at being the light-hearted one. "I'm really sorry." I sit up and place myself in front of him with crossed legs.

An unfeeling smile passes over his lips like a discarded memory. "Did you ever think the Rock Ballers were this fucked up? One's hooked on Oxy, one's parents are complete pieces of shit," he says, talking about himself. "One's scared of his own temper, one—."

"Who's scared of their own temper?" I ask.

"Hayes. You haven't figured that out yet?"

I look down at my lap. "No. I didn't know I needed to."

"You do remember when he walked away from the playful lacrosse game we were having that turned out to be not so playful, right?"

"Well, yeah, I just thought..." I trail off. I don't know what I thought. "Why?" I ask.

"If he wants you to know, he'll tell you."

I agree with the sentiment, but it's super fucking annoying that it seems like every Baller has a secret hidden away. I grab Sloan's hand. "You're not your parents, Ivy. This will blow over."

"The only thing I'm happy about is the fact that I'm not home right now, so I don't have to live through the fucking turmoil of it all. The phone ringing off the hook from the media. The fucking cameras outside the door. It's ridiculous."

"A price to pay for fame," I say, looking away and remembering my dad's own little shit starters that kicked up over the years. Sloan and I can relate to one another on that front.

He reaches out and entwines our fingers. His pressure is steady, unlike the mixed emotions stirring around him right now. I'm sure he wants to know what the hell is going on. We could Google it on our phones if he wanted, but it doesn't look as if he wants to do that right now.

"Now that you've soured the mood, I won't ask you what I came here to ask you."

I playfully gasp. "Well, what's that, Ivy?"

"I was just lying in bed, you know, in the room full of cocks, and thought to myself that I'd really like to see some boobies."

I crack up laughing. "Boobies?"

His face turns serious. "Do you want to go skinny-dipping?"

"Sloan Ivy, are you insane? You know my dad walks around this camp."

He blows my excuse off. "Are you kidding? He's probably talking to Ryan's mom on the phone right now."

"What about the other coaches?"

He glances at the clock. "There's still five minutes left before curfew."

"So anyone could be around outside? Are you trying to talk me out of this or into this?"

He slides off the bed and grabs my hand. "Come on, Dale." He waggles his eyebrows at my cleavage. "You wouldn't turn me down, would you? Not when you've decided to ruin my good night with rumors of my parents' selfishness."

"Sloan," I start to argue.

He hauls me to my feet and winds his arms around me. "I was just joking. Come on." He gives my ass a quick squeeze before grabbing my hand and pulling me outside.

We cross the small porch, then the beach until our toes are dipped in the water. We shuck our shoes off, and Sloan squeezes my hand. "We can wait to undress until we're out there. No one will be the wiser. It'll just be the two of us taking an evening dip."

"You're crazy," I tell him, but I follow him out into the water anyway. I'm not going to lie and say that this thought hadn't crossed my mind. I mean, the camp is set up for this scenario, isn't it? It's freaking summer camp. Things like this happen.

The water swallows my calves and then reaches

my thighs before slipping over my hips. I still have a little soreness there from Lake pushing me to the bar floor a couple weeks ago, but it's not anything I can't handle. It's just a reminder of why I need to continue to work hard.

He drags me further and further out until the water reaches our collarbones. Turning toward me, I don't think I've ever seen such a devilish grin on his face before. I feel his hands at my hips. They come around to my button and zipper and he starts undoing them. My heart is stuck in my throat. Somehow, this seems so much more sensual than just two kids skinny dipping. He's going all in right now, isn't he?

With the help of the water, his hands glide over me as he pulls my shorts down. They rise to the surface and hover near us. I look up at the sky, finally seeing how dark it is out. This really is the perfect night for this.

"My turn," I breathe.

I reach out, my fingers wrapping around the waistband of his basketball shorts. His are easier to discard. I bring them to the surface after he steps out of them and place them right next to my own shorts.

"Shirt," he says next. His voice is thick. Those hazel eyes of his that love to turn colors are awash with arousing green flecks. I reach my hands over my head as he tugs the bottom of my shirt up. The lake water drips over me as he drops the shirt next to our bottoms.

I've seen Sloan without his shirt off before, but I've never actually taken it off myself. I run my fingertips up his chiseled stomach, taking the hem of his shirt along for the ride. The planes of his abs dip and even out several times until I reach his chest and then haul the shirt over his head.

"This isn't fair," I say, noticing our predicament. I have two items left on while he only has one.

His hands slide around my ribs and down, his pinkies teasing the tops of my panties. He and I have had our fair share of problems with lace panties, but not this time. He cups my ass as he moves the soaked fabric down. Eventually, I have to help him, stepping out of my undergarment before he has them in his possession again, just like the blue ones. It feels so freeing to be almost naked in the middle of a lake. It's like Sloan and I have a secret now. He was right. No one can tell that we're undressing out here.

He takes my hands and sets them on his hips. I can tell by the thick band that he has boxers on. I move forward, gliding my palms down his hips and thighs. He has to pull the band of his boxers out and around his erection, but soon enough, the boxers are floating on the surface of the lake now, too.

There's just one more clothing item left.

Sloan's fingers cup my cheek. He moves in, placing a soft, tender kiss to my lips as he unclasps my bra with one hand. If it wasn't so water-logged, it would spring open, but it just floats on the surface, still clinging to me. When he backs away, he looks so proud of himself for his one-handed trick that I can't help but smile back at him. His hands trail up my arms, his fingers hook under the strap of my bra and then slowly pull it down until my arms are free.

We just stand there, hidden away in the water if only for a little while. Neither of us can see any of our important parts, but my mouth is dry like this is a big deal. I can feel the current of his hand moving through the water first before he cups my breast. My mouth drops at the touch, and then my eyes feel heavy as he cups the other, too. His thumbs pass over my nipples as he kneeds and plucks until my nipples are hard, practically begging him not to stop.

"I've thought about this more than a few times," he admits, his voice breathy.

My breaths are coming out raspier and raspier the more his fingers play over me. I guess he really did just want to see boobies, but I'm not going to let that stop me from having my fun either. I reach out, bridging the distance between us through the water until I clasp his dick in my hand. He stills, then lets out a groan that echoes far and wide with the help of the water. I run my thumb over his tip until he's sucking his lower lip through his teeth. "Not fair, Dale."

"Completely fair," I exhale.

"I really just wanted to go skinny dipping and yet here you are violating me."

I work on him harder. He throws his head back, but his jaw locks tight, keeping whatever sound that was begging to come out at bay. One hand leaves my breast and drops to my ass. He pulls me up his thigh until I'm straddling his hip. My breasts just peek out of the water. He takes in their roundness and kisses me softly. "Fuck, Sloan."

I maneuver around to his front, so I can grab him again. I stroke him as he takes my nipple into his mouth, thrashing it with his tongue until I'm squirming over him, looking for relief. He gives it to me happily.

After locking me down with one arm, he spreads my knees and then follows my inner thigh until his finger pushes inside me. I cry out, then bite down on my lip. I don't want to call attention to ourselves, especially now that I'm arching my back to give him better access to my breasts.

"Fuck me, Tessa," he says. He's not asking for it, he's only voicing his approval of our hidden touches right under everyone's nose. He pulls one finger out, then pushes two inside. I gasp at the feeling, having to steady myself on him with one hand. "So fucking tight," he grits out.

We stroke one another in unison. With his mouth, he drops kisses to the curve of my breast and my cleavage, groaning when we reach a crescendo of touch. I know I'm so close to slamming head on into a rush of euphoria, and I don't think he's that far behind me.

"Hold on," he says.

My free hand digs into his back as he pulls his other around. While he's still moving his fingers inside me, he uses his other hand to swirl around my nub. "Oh, Sloan," I cry out.

He pitches his hips forward, and then it's a mad frenzy until both of us release our contentment to the wind. For a brief moment, I wonder how far our expression of ecstasy travel, but then Sloan is pulling me close, dropping a kiss to my lips as he holds me to him. My legs automatically tighten around his hips and we just stand there and hold one another.

I'd tell him I really like his idea of skinny dipping, but I have a feeling he already knows.

32

It turns out there's a video of Sloan's dad going into a hotel room with his now former secretary. Sloan assures me that his father's team will hush it up, so it won't impact his senatorial career, however it's probably World War Three in his house right now. When things like this get out, the offended party in his family makes the whole house miserable—in this case, his mom. Even though he knows his mom just got back from a weekend trip with one of her many boyfriends.

Honestly, all of it sounds terrible. I know my parents are separating, but at least it's not like Sloan's parents, where image is everything and nothing else matters. For me, I'd rather be with someone who cares about me for me, not because of some job I hold or how good I look on their arm. It brings me back to Mrs. Ivy dismissing me from their house the one and only time I ate dinner there, and how no one asked me how well basketball was going for me.

Sloan's mother doesn't like me, that much I can tell. I'm sure she doesn't like the fact that I play basketball, that I wear shorts instead of dresses, that I sweat instead of glow, or that I get up and move when I really should be sitting with perfect posture with my legs crossed at the ankles.

So not me. It's so unlike me that the image of me doing that makes me laugh.

Tension's high at camp as the next week passes. On Friday evening, the coaches reveal that I've taken the number one spot in the shooting guard MVP ranking. A thrill shoots through me. I have to bite my lip to keep from celebrating. Hayes squeezes my shoulders. Alec and Sloan smile my way. Ryan nods at me, but I can tell most of them are torn. If I'm number one right now, that means Lake is number two.

River has always been number three. He's good, and he'll be amazing when he grows a little more, but this is really just a two-person race for the top spot.

Everyone files out of the largest room in the main

building to go to dinner, but I stay behind. I sneak a picture of the rankings and send it to my mom and Dawn. My mom, of course, has no clue what's at stake, but she's rooting for me anyway. Even if I win, I'll have to talk her out of sending me to Springs, but Dad will be on my side. Dawn, however, knows everything. She sends me a bunch of cartwheel emojis and a few middle fingers I'm guessing are directed toward Lake.

My sentiments exactly.

"You earned it," Jacquin says.

I start. I hadn't realized anyone else was still in the room with me. "Thanks," I tell him. I shift from foot to foot, watching as he walks up to the corrugated board they've put all our rankings on. He runs a finger under the piece of paper with my name on it. "I hope I can keep it that way," I say.

"I want the best person to win." He swings his gaze my way with a playful smirk. "But I'm pulling for you."

My jaw hardens. I hate situations like these because it's so easy for someone to think I'm getting things handed to me. "I want the best person to win, too."

He cocks his head. "I know, Tessa. You don't have to go on the offensive. Not with me. Lake needs to realize that hard work gets people things. It's not always pure talent, not that you both don't have plenty of that."

"Is that why you orchestrated this whole thing? To teach Lake a lesson?"

He bites his bottom lip and smiles. "No. Nothing like that." He stops in front of me. "I hate to see anyone who deserves to be on top taken down by jealous, ignorant haters. Our world has too much of that."

His voice is soft, dropping several notches in the span of a few seconds. It makes me think he's had to deal with things like this. Maybe this is a him 'paying it forward' type of deal. "I should say thank you for doing this."

"Don't thank me until you beat him out for the spot on your own merit, then you can finally flourish at Rockport instead of getting stuck on the sidelines."

He keeps moving closer to me. I shift back on my feet. My dad's words are penetrating my brain. He thinks Jacquin likes me. I hope he doesn't. I'm already juggling the guys I want right now.

The tips of his shoes touch the tips of mine. He reaches up to run a hand down the flyaways that have escaped my ponytail. I slip out of his grasp, and he frowns. "You remind me of my girlfriend."

Oh shit. No, no, no.

"She was so good at ball, you know?" he asks no one in particular. I'm not sure he even sees me in front of him right now. "She did everything right. Played for our school's girls' team, of course, but she was captain and had stats as good as mine." His eyes are far away. He flinches, and a wave of grief crosses his face. My stomach bottoms out as he says, "She died in a car accident two years ago."

"Oh, God. I'm so sorry, Jacquin." I reach out to run a comforting hand down his upper arm. "What was her name?"

"Kelley," he says, a small lilt to his voice, like he wants to talk about her, but doesn't want to at the same time. "She played shooting guard, too."

I swallow hard. He lifts the tank he's wearing. There's a number nine tattooed right over his heart.

"Her number," he says.

"Mine, too," I breathe.

He drops his shirt, covering his sculpted torso back up. "I know."

"It sounds like we would've had a lot in common," I tell him, but I don't even know if he's listening to me anymore. He's looking at me, but he's staring right through me like I'm not even there, or as if he sees someone other than me. I'm not quite sure what it is, but it's making my skin prick and warning hairs rise on my neck.

"God, I miss her."

I sidestep him, trying to create space. "That's understandable. I bet she'd be so proud of you."

My lips feel almost numb as I try to bring him back to the present. He's too lost in his own head. He grabs my wrist and pulls me to him.

"Jacquin," I say, my voice wavering a little. He's so distraught. His whole face has morphed into sadness. His eyes are dull, almost dead looking.

"You remind me so much of her," he repeats again.

I try to struggle out of his grip, but he's holding on to me so tightly. He lowers his face to mine. I turn at the last second, so he kisses my cheek, his lips open like he'd expected a welcome.

"Please," he begs, his lips moving against my cheek. "Just give me this."

His huge hand clasps onto my neck, holding me in place. He leans down, and I press my lips together. He's like a guy gone mad. His eyes are shut so tight, matching the rest of his strained face as he lowers his face to mine.

"Stop," I tell him. "Jacquin." I twist my wrist this way and that, trying to break free from his grasp. If I do that, maybe he'll break out of whatever spell he's under. I can't imagine what it's like to lose a close loved one like that, but I'm not her.

"Let her go!"

I turn quickly. Jacquin and I bump faces, which creates space. It's a good thing, too, because Alec rips him away from me after that.

Alec pulls his fist back.

"No!" I shout.

He doesn't listen. His fist slams forward, catching Jacquin in the jaw who stumbles back. I move in between them. Alec's usually beautiful green eyes are alive with fury. He sucks in ragged breaths, his shoulders hunched and tight. His gaze clashes with mine, and I see betrayal there. "You told him no."

I step forward. "I did." I look behind me. Jacquin has his hand on his jaw. The sound Alec's fist made when it connected with it still echoes in my mind. *He did that for me.* My gut wrenches. Alec is a beast. "It's not his fault." I don't even know what the fuck I'm saying, really. Is it his fault? I just don't want Alec to get in trouble. Fighting is strictly prohibited. He can't do that here. He shouldn't want to do that here. Baseball is only a couple of weeks away now.

"Not his fault?"

Jacquin comes up behind me. He pushes me out of

the way with a quick movement of his arm. "Calm down, Christopoulos."

The words could've worked if he hadn't laid a hand on me. "I said don't fucking touch her." Alec launches himself at Jacquin Sellers again. I'm so surprised I jump back.

They fall to the ground, a mass of limbs. I reach down to try to pull Alec off, but all I do is allow Jacquin to get a shot in at him.

"What the...?"

Ryan runs in. He's able to do what I couldn't. He pulls Alec up, and I immediately intervene in front of Jacquin. There's no way he's going to get me out of his way this time. "What do you even care?" Jacquin shouts. "She's not even your girlfriend." He wipes blood away from his lips.

"The hell she isn't," Alec snaps.

If there wasn't so much tension in the room, I'd swoon over that.

There's so much commotion now that others swarm the room, including my dad and the other coaches. I sigh, there's no way we're going to cover this up now. Jacquin is bleeding. What excuse are we going to use? He tripped? He's a phenomenal athlete. He doesn't just trip.

No, there's no denying it. Alec isn't even in the

right place to try and downplay his anger.

"What the hell's going on in here?" my dad barks.

I'm a little relieved. Only because there's no way it's going to escalate again. I finally turn my back on Jacquin and move toward Alec. Ryan still has his hands on his shoulders. I sneak past him and put my hand on his cheek. "It's okay. I'm okay."

"You did tell him not to touch you, didn't you?"

I nod.

Relief floods his eyes. He pulls me into an embrace, and I let him.

Right there in front of everybody, his fingers sink into my skin, pulling me that much closer to him.

"What's going on here, Sellers?" my dad asks, moving forward.

Alec finally lets me go, and I spin to look at Jacquin. There's really no getting around the fact that these two got in a fight. My heart constricts. "Dad," I say. "Can I speak to you privately?" Maybe if I can just explain what happened, but there's no sense in embarrassing either one of them.

Alec pulls back on my arm. "It's okay," he whispers. Louder, he says, "I punched him, Mr. Dale."

My father's eyes widen a fraction. I knew he suspected something happened, but the fact that Alec isn't trying to hide it is surprising. It's more than surprising to me. It's infuriating. "Don't, Alec."

Alec turns, his jaw clamped together.

"You're going to get kicked out," I say under my breath, hoping he's the only one who catches it.

"I don't care," he says. "You know I don't care."

Ryan's head snaps up. "You don't care? What the hell does that mean?"

He's livid. His whole body is vibrating from head-to-toe. He knows what's about to happen as well as me. The other Ballers surround us now. They sense shit's about to go down. Guilt swarms me. If only I'd been able to put a stop to Jacquin's advances before Alec walked in.

"I don't care, alright?" Alec says. His voice rises after his eyes bore into mine. "I don't want to play basketball." He shrugs. "I want to play baseball."

Everything happening in that room at that same exact point in time, stops. It feels like the world outside the room crashes to a halt, too. It isn't news to me, but the rest of the Ballers' reaction makes my stomach twist. They look hurt, shocked. A couple of them outright deny it.

"Sellers, Christopoulos, my cabin now," Dad says.

"Dad," I say, moving forward.

He looks back at me over his shoulder. "Don't go anywhere. I'll talk to you after."

Alec walks by me, trailing his fingers over my arm. I watch all three of them walk out the door. The only one with his head down is Jacquin.

Alec's chin is lifted. He's looking straight ahead like he's going to accept his fate no matter what.

"What the fuck?" Lake grits out. He gets in my face. "You did this."

Hayes is right by my side as I turn away from Lake. I go to the side of the room and sit on one of the wooden benches with the plain orange cushions, dropping my head in my hands. I can't believe Alec just dropped that bomb in front of everyone, and I really can't fucking believe he punched Jacquin Sellers for trying to kiss me. He's fucking insane.

"What happened?" I hear Ryan ask.

I look up to find all the Ballers lined up in front of me. Hayes's shoulder is in front of Lake's like he's trying to box him out. The rest of the guys, who'd walked in to see what was going on, all walk back into the mess hall whispering to one another.

"I don't want to talk about it," I say, glancing at Ryan's gray eyes, trying to beg him to let it drop.

"Bullshit," Lake says. "You were the only one out here with them. What happened?"

I glare at the boy who's given me so much trouble. I see fear in his eyes and at least I can see that it's worry for his friend. He's entitled to know what Alec tells him, but he doesn't get to know my shit. "Fuck off, O'Brien. Sellers is still here, so unless you want to forfeit the arrangement we have, I suggest you shut your mouth now."

His already balled-up hands shake with anger at his sides. The skin around his knuckles is white as he glowers at me. "I look forward to kicking your ass, Dale."

"Bring it on," I tell him half-heartedly. I don't have the energy to fight with Lake right now. My mind's on what's going on in my father's cabin right now.

Alec.

Sloan comes forward and sits next to me. He puts his hand around my shoulders, rubbing circles over my shirt. Lake's gaze darts around to the other Ballers. With each set of eyes he stops on, the more light seeps out. I think he realizes they're all on my side, at least to a degree. He's not running the show anymore.

"Did he hurt you?" Sloan whispers in my ear.

I shake my head. My fingers absentmindedly trace my wrist he clamped down on though. With Jacquin, all I saw was a scared, grieving boy with misplaced affections. No, he shouldn't have done that, but my heart aches for his loss. To be so young and to have felt that much pain already, what a terrible burden.

Shortly after that, Lake and River leave. Surprisingly, Ryan doesn't follow. He stays there, and when my father calls me in to give him my side of the story, Ryan goes with me. It's under the pretense that he walked in on things, too, but he stays so close to me that I also know he's there for my support as much as he is to tell his side of the story.

At the end of the day, both Alec and Jacquin are leaving camp. I fight hard for both of them. I try telling my father it's all a misunderstanding. However, my father is steadfast. The look he gives Sellers tells me he wants to take him down himself.

I didn't have to retell that part of the night. Jacquin told him the whole thing. He copped to it right away. From what Alec told me afterward, Jacquin feels terrible.

The only one who has no remorse about anything is Alec. He's glad he stood up for me. He's glad everything is out in the open about baseball now. Seeing the Ballers take this in is almost as if they've lost one of their appendages though. It's hitting them hard.

When Alec's mother and sister show up to take him home, I help him take his things to their car. I know she's spoken with my father already, but I don't want her to be mad at Alec for this. "I'm so sorry," I tell her as soon as we get there, ignoring Roberta's frantic waves from the backseat.

She tilts her head, and a soft smile plays on her lips. "I've spoken to my son and to your father, no one blames you, and they shouldn't. I don't condone violence, and I'm not mad at your dad for sticking to his policy on this." She reaches up and puts her hand on the back of Alec's neck, smiling fondly at him. "But he's a good boy. I'm proud of him."

Emotion crawls up my throat. It's then I realize I didn't even thank him. Everything settles over my shoulders in that moment. Alec's leaving. I won't see him for at least another two weeks, and when I get back, he'll only have a few short days until he's busy with baseball. His mom seems to sense we need to say goodbye because she takes the bag I carried up here and turns to put it in the trunk. I turn to Alec. "I'm so sorry."

He pulls his fingers through my hair. "Stop saying that. I'm only sorry to not be living so close to you for the next two weeks."

"You should rest," I tell him, my voice rising. "Before baseball. Let your body relax. You don't need the strain."

He nods. "Look out for the guys, okay? Call me if

anything happens?"

I can tell he's worried about their relationship, too. He's happy to have his secret out, but he didn't tell everyone right away for this very same reason. What would it mean for their friendship if they all weren't defined as basketball players anymore?

His fingers trace over the line of my jaw. "Bye, Tessa."

He leans down, his lips a whisper over mine that makes my heart melt. The kiss is parent appropriate, but also so deliciously teasing that I know I'll be thinking about it from now until the time I get to see him again.

A loud cry of surprise erupts from the backseat. "Are you my brother's girlfriend?"

"Roberta," Mrs. Christopoulos chastises.

"They just kissed!"

Alec and I laugh. He rests his forehead on mine. "Bye, Babe."

As if I could swoon anymore. "Bye, Alec. See you soon."

He steps away, opening the passenger side door. "Work hard. Do your best. Let me know what happens."

I step back and nod. I finally wave to Roberta who's going crazy in the backseat. Alec's mom waves at me after she shuts the trunk. "Goodbye, Tessa." She looks so pleased it makes my cheeks warm.

As she backs out of the parking space and drives away, I can still hear Roberta demanding to know what's going on. Their car disappears, and I turn around, heading straight back to my cabin for the night. I think I've had enough excitement for one day.

33

Dawn finally gets the opportunity to come visit me, so that next Saturday, we spend the day in the nearest town doing everything the small town offers, which isn't much. We get ice cream, swim at a local beach, and just walk the streets until she has to leave.

I'm glad I've gotten to spend time with her and talk everything out that's been happening in person instead of on the phone. The guys wanted to come with us, but I told them no. I don't think Dawn is ready to just accept the fact that the guys, who were so mean to me, are now wanting to be with me. Of course, if they keep doing things like Alec did, she's more likely to come around. Even she looked impressed when I told her that he got kicked out of camp for intervening on my behalf.

Another coach takes over our morning runs from now on since Sellers is gone. My dad doesn't talk about it much, only to make sure that I'm doing okay. I think it's guilt for liking the idea of Jacquin and I together. My dad takes over the Shooting Guard training. It's probably the only thing that keeps me safe from the O'Brien bastards for the rest of camp.

It feels natural to have my dad coaching me from the sidelines. He can't vote in the Shooting Guard MVP race, so this feels like it's the next best thing, having him coach us. At least now no one can say he's not doing the same for Lake and River as he is for me. He gets on them as much as he gets on me. By the time we leave our position specific trainings, all three of us are dead.

Other coaches come by to observe. They switch off between coaching and observing, so they can give us our ranks. Lake and I are still neck and neck. In fact, the last week before we're about to leave, they rank us the same. We both occupy the same spot at the top of the Shooting Guard leaderboard. One of the other coaches explains that this is going to be the toughest decision for them as we're both high-caliber players.

I don't like it.

I don't want to be on the same line as Lake O'Brien. I want to be kicking his ass. So, for that next week leading to the reveal, I throw myself into training even more. I'm up at night shooting. I talk Hayes into playing defense on me as I try to make shots around his large body. He takes his job as seriously as I want him to. If I would've asked Sloan, he would've tried to turn it into a makeout session, but Hayes doesn't. He plays hard with me, making sure I know he doesn't give the shot up to me. I have to earn it. With our size difference, he's one of the most difficult guys I've had to play against, but that's exactly the way I want it.

Ryan is distant for the last week. I think he's blaming himself for not realizing that Alec wasn't happy with basketball. He's still their ringleader after all. He believes he should've noticed. He's also watching Lake like he might just suddenly throw pills back at all times. Lake's more agitated than he's been lately, but he seems to be putting it to good use on the court instead of outside the court.

For the last week of camp, the coaches break us into three separate teams, and we all play one another in a competition type format. One of the coaches takes Alec's spot, and for someone who's aged, no one would even know it. He's really good. The teams are all really good. I just happen to end up on Sloan's team, which allows him to be a little more friendly than I would like when we're doing basketball related things.

Every time I turn around, my dad is eyeing us, and I know he must have questions about how he's seen me with Hayes, how Alec punched someone for me, and now Sloan, who keeps touching my lower back in between plays, letting his hand linger there. Even though we're in the middle of something important, my focus is on his hand and the sparks he ignites in me. He knows how much it gets to me, so when I turn toward him with a look, he just smiles and winks.

Like he promised, nothing else has come out about his father's affair. Hayes hasn't blown up and stalked off since that night with the lacrosse players. Alec, I talk to on the phone every couple of nights when I'm not too busy with basketball. It sounds like he's loving the time off he's getting. He hasn't had a summer off in years. Ryan, apart from eyeing Lake and catching my eye, is quiet. He's so damn good, though. I'm trying my best, and I have no idea if I'm going to be able to take him for Overall MVP. It would be a dream come true if I did.

This being our last year eligible to go to camp here, it's getting crunch time, and by the end of the week, we're all feeling it. The guys in the Power Forward position even have a shot at the MVP award now with

Alec gone. Everyone is on edge. It's always like this at the end of every camp. There are so many hopes and dreams up in the air. So many attainable goals, but no one knows what will happen. The scholarship funds are dangled in front of our faces, and everyone has their own love for competing and winning to want to win it for themselves. Even River, who has to know he doesn't have a shot in hell, has stepped up his game the last week. It's encouraging, and it's exactly what I like most about coming to camp every year. Everyone who's invited here is good, but you elevate yourself to play among those better than you. I don't think the Ballers—or myself—would be half as good as we are now if it weren't for my dad and this camp.

On the night before the last day, I take a card for my dad around to everyone and have them sign it. The messages the players have left in there are beautiful. It fills me with pride to know that my dad has affected so many people in such a positive way.

No, he's not perfect. Far from it. But in this one sliver of his life, he truly is great. He's pushed boundaries, he's helped those less fortunate than him, and he's always giving back. My father really cares about all the players at this camp, so when I present him with the card and make a speech, he's humbled.

My dad's not the crying type, but his eyes get

glassy as he stands up to give a speech of his own. "No matter what happens tomorrow, you're all winners. The amount of growth I've seen over the past weeks is astounding. For some of you, this is your last year." His voice breaks then, and heat swims in the back of my eyes. "I wish I could have you all stay. Some of you have been with me for years. But I also know that there are a lot of players just like you out there that also need our help. The end of camp is always bittersweet. It's saying goodbye to the players moving on to the next part of their lives, and it's thinking ahead to the young ones we'll be inviting next year. That new, fresh potential. There's one thing that I see in everyone's eyes no matter if it's their last year or their first though. It's hunger. I promise you if you keep that hunger, that drive, you will go far. Never lose it. All the coaches in this room can attest to that."

As he's talking, I'm dreaming about making him proud tomorrow. I want this more than anything. Lake and I happen to look at one another at the same time as my dad sits. His cold eyes seem to reach out and clasp ahold of me. He doesn't let me go for the longest time, and when he does, it's almost as if he's dismissing me.

I've had a long time to think about Lake O'Brien this year at camp. I'm sorry for the troubles he's had to face, but that doesn't mean he gets to have free reign over me and everyone else. It's just such a shame that someone with so much talent is a prick.

Hayes leans over. "I have faith in you tomorrow."

I shrug. "I've pretty much done all I can do. It's up to how everyone sees it now." I gave it my all, and I know Lake has given it his all, too. I honestly can't say how I think it's going to go down. Like the coaches said last week when they put us on the same top spot, it's anyone's for the taking. The only thing I hope they don't decide is that we should share the top spot. I would rather come in second than share anything with him.

The last dinner breaks up. Sloan stands from his seat on the other side of Hayes and waltzes over to put his hands on my shoulders. He kneads my skin, and I bite down on my lip as he presses into my sore muscles. I hope Mom will take me on a trip to the spa after I get home. "It's time for our annual bonfire," he says.

I look behind me. "Annual bonfire?" I've never been invited to any annual bonfire before.

He shrugs. "It's a tradition."

I turn right back around. It sucks that I've been excluded from these things in the past. A piece of me doesn't want to take part in it this year either, but the look Lake is leveling at me right now pushes me over the edge. "Sounds great," I say, smiling at him. At least if I don't win tomorrow, I can make his life miserable tonight.

By the time I meet them an hour later on the beach, I'm so hyped up for tomorrow I don't know if I'll even be able to sleep tonight. I tried so many different hairstyles in my hair just to pass the time, but eventually, I just wear it straight down. I have my hoodie around my waist as I walk out in a pair of capris and an RHS shirt.

The situation before me is pretty much identical to the bonfire the lacrosse players had except for I know these guys more. I know why Ryan is sitting next to Lake. I know why Sloan is checking his phone, and I know why Hayes is the first to get to his feet and meet me where the grass turns to sand.

When he pulls me down to the ground, sandwiched between him and Sloan, we easily break into a conversation about camp over the years. The guys dig each other about things that happened in the past that I wasn't privy to. That is, until Lake brings up Ryan pretending to like me. His words don't sting anymore though. I know the truth. Ryan did like me. Ryan *does* like me. And I know that Lake saying that is just trying to hold onto the past when I'm the Ballers' future.

I let his words roll off my back and not caring who's

there to hear it, I say, "At least he was my first kiss though."

Lake almost gags. If he wasn't trying to be an asshole to me all the time, I honestly think we could get along. It's not possible. He's made it clear he hates my guts for reasons unknown to me, but when he's just talking with his friends, I think he can be a decent guy with a funny sense of humor.

"I was your first kiss?" Ryan asks.

When I look over at him, the small smile on my face fades. He swallows, waiting for my answer. I shrug in response. "I was just coming out of eighth grade." Should I have been kissing by then? I don't know. All the guys at the private school that fed into Broadwell were obnoxious. Ryan was nothing like them.

Lake elbows his friend in the ribs, and I know what he's thinking. He's thinking Ryan gave me a fake first kiss. He didn't. It was real, just like the feelings pulsing between us all these years later. No matter how hard Lake tries, he can't take that away.

Thankfully, Sloan diverts the conversation after that, but the way Ryan stares at me for the rest of the night, I think he's still stuck on the idea of him giving me my first kiss. Eventually, the time for curfew comes, and none of us want to test the boundaries of camp and have our top rankings stripped just because we wanted to stay out a little while longer.

Ryan looks at everyone around the fire, locking gazes with us each individually. That's when I miss Alec the most. He's supposed to be there. "May the best man win tomorrow," he says.

"Or woman," I say with a smile.

He nods. "May the best person win."

Right there in that moment, even Lake doesn't balk. That feeling of being a part of something drenches me in a warmth I hold close. I don't know what tomorrow will bring, but as of right now, it feels like I'm accepted, and that's all I've ever wanted.

34

Something's not right.

The morning went as normal. I stayed in my room packing everything that I've used over the past few weeks, getting everything ready for the presentation of the awards. The only thing is, instead of being herded into the main building one last time, we're being led out to the outdoor courts.

The weather is beautiful today. There's a slight breeze that keeps the heat at bay and tickles the tiny hairs at the base of my neck.

When we get there, my father is standing in the middle of the court, his hand around a ball. He's smiling, but it's not a full-on smile. It just kind of lingers there. "Thanks for coming, everyone. I'm going to hand out the awards we have ready here, but then I'm going to need your assistance in handling one small thing."

I shift from foot to foot, my shoulder bumping into Hayes who's looking on at the scene with a perplexed expression.

"As you guys have seen, there's been one position that the coaches have been having a difficult time deciding who should take the top spot. As it concerns my daughter, I haven't been involved." I take in a deep breath that fills my chest and then release it slowly as my father keeps talking. "The coaches and I have discussed that the only true way to pick a winner for the Shooting Guard position is to have a head-to-head match between Lake O'Brien and Quintessa Dale. I want to reiterate that this was the other coaches' decision and that as long as Lake and Tessa agree, the player who scores five points first will take home the award and the scholarship money of one thousand dollars. Tessa?"

My dad looks at me expectantly, but I'm still trying to sort through everything. I didn't win. At least not yet. I look toward Lake whose face is glowing red. He looks indignant, like he thinks he should've won outright. "Sounds good to me," I say, keeping my eyes peeled on my opponent.

"Lake?" my dad asks, moving his stare toward him.

My dad's jaw ticks. He's mad I didn't win outright either. He knew all about the agreement we made, minus the drug part. He knows what's at stake for me here.

"Fine," Lake shrugs. "I've beaten her before."

My lips thin. He has beaten me before, but I've also beaten him. And, he's forgetting that the last time he beat me, he cheated like a little bitch. This time, I won't let that happen.

I quickly check to see what bra I put on this morning. When I see it's a sports bra, I walk forward and take my shirt off, throwing it to the side. Sloan intercepts it and folds it, throwing it over his shoulder with a wink. I'd smile, but I'm both excited and pissed that we have to go through this. As far as I know, this hasn't happened before.

The other coaches clap. I start to limber up on the sidelines while the other MVP awards are given out. Ryan, Hayes, and Sloan all win for their respective positions. I clap for each of them, trying to ignore Lake on the other side of the court prepping just like me. His brother is in his ear, and even now, it hits me hard that I'm all by myself.

A split second after I think that, my father comes over after having given away all the certificates. He puts his arm around me. "This is it, Tess. Take him down. Don't let him bully you out there."

I nod. This is how I've always wanted to solve this with Lake anyway. Maybe my dad suggested it for that reason. If I'd won outright, Lake could say, even though it's never happened, that the award was given to me because of who I am. On the flip side, if Lake won, I could say the coaches just don't like girls, even though I would never be that petty. I know sexism exists. Hell, I live it, but not here. Outsiders opinions are none of my concern.

"Play hard. Play smart," my dad says, his words settling over me in a kind of soothing way. Ever since I played for the kids' teams back home, he's been saying the same things to me. I know I can beat Lake at this game, I've done it before. I just need to do it now when it matters the most.

It's all come down to this. If I win this game, I win Shooting Guard MVP. Shooting Guard MVP will give me a quiet senior year at RHS. Lake can't do anything to me. If he does, I'll turn him in for pill popping myself. I'll turn him in under the suspicion that he probably tried to mess with my drug test results last year. If he values his character at all, he'll follow through now that I've got something on him.

One of the coaches that's been with my dad for a

while stands in the center. He gestures both Lake and I forward with his hands. "First to five wins. Play fair." He slips a coin from his pocket. "Call it, O'Brien."

The coach flips the coin in the air as Lake says, "Tails."

It lands on Tails, so he gets the decision. Obviously, he wants the ball first. This game will be close, so he wants every advantage he can get. "Shake hands," the coach says.

Lake glares at me, but he reaches across the distance between us anyway. His hold is firm, almost bone-crushingly so. The look in his eyes sends a shiver down my spine. The scene at the bar spins through my head. He said he hated me, and now more than ever, I know he means it. He really does hate me. He *loathes* me, just like he said.

"Come on, Tessa," Hayes calls out, clapping.

If he could hate me any more, he would. Lake's gaze twists toward Hayes and it's as if I see a knife sinking into his back right then and there.

"Check," the coach says, then stands back and blows his whistle.

I'm on D first. With my heart pounding in my ears, I watch Lake's every movement. I move when he does, trying to anticipate, but not wanting to anticipate too much so that he fakes me out of my shoes. All the players stay for our game. They clap and shout our names. It's been apparent to everyone from the beginning that there was no love lost between the two of us. They all know it, shouting for the one they think deserves this the most. I try not to focus on them, but I do hear my name being said, and I don't think it's just Hayes the whole time.

Lake tries to spin, but I've seen him start to advance. I make my move, reaching for the ball. Slapping it out of his hand, it bounces to the sidelines right into Ryan Linc's hands.

I smile but hide it right away. This game has a long way to go yet. We're just getting started. Ryan glances at me as he throws the ball back to the coach. His gray eyes are swirling, laced with a worry I don't comprehend.

I shake my head and turn away, lining up at the top of the key. "Check," the coach tells us.

I bounce the ball to Lake, and he bounces it right back. He's low in his stance, arms stretched out wide. I try to fake him out. I try to move him back. He's brought his A game tonight when I don't see a way around him. Since he won't let me pass, I pull up for the jumper, only I don't have my feet set. It clangs off the rim. I grit my teeth when the ball falls to the court.

Sloan grabs the rebound this time, tossing it back to

the coach. I look away after making eye contact with him. There's too much going on right now that I can't focus on him, on any of them.

Lake takes position and checks the ball to me. The next several times either one of us has the ball, we can't complete a shot. Tension streaks through my body, firing up my nerve endings. I try to shake my hands out in between possessions. Finally—finally—I get past Lake on a fake, dribble around him, and then jump for the layup. The ball swishes through the net, and I pull a Tiger Woods after he's made a great put.

"Fuck," Lake curses under his breath.

Now that it's his turn with the ball, he comes out right away with reckless abandon. He pushes and pushes me back until he hits me with enough force that I fall on my ass. During a regular game, it would be a foul, but I scramble to my feet and jump in the air to try to block the shot. Only, I'm too late. All I can do is turn and watch as the ball hits the backboard but bounces right down into the hoop.

We're tied. All the other guys cheer. I'm tense as I make my way to the top of the key now. I hear my dad in the background telling me to "Take it easy." It must be apparent to everyone that I want to kick Lake's ass about now. I need to keep my head in the game though, so when I start to move, I pull the same thing back on him. He may be bigger than me and playing rough has never been my thing, but I do the same move back to him. I move him back and move him back until a well-placed hip check creates space for me. That's when I pull up with enough time to make my shot perfectly. The ball arcs through the air and falls right into the net.

Two to one.

The more we play, the more the atmosphere crackles with electricity. I want to take him out so badly. We're so evenly matched though. We're not playing for who's a good person. If we were, I'd win every single time. No, this is about basketball, and in basketball, Lake and I are almost the same.

We match each other shot for shot until it's four to four. There's only one point separating me from having my freedom next year. I let that feeling envelop me. Not everyone else out there knows what's on the line. Sloan and Hayes are practically bouncing on their feet. Ryan is the only one who looks conflicted. I'm pretty sure I've heard him celebrate for the both of us.

My gaze switches to Lake, who looks much less cocky now than he did when we started this. I'm about to win. I can feel it.

Maybe he can feel it too.

He gives up some space the next time I have the

ball. I'm too eager to take what I see as a gift. What I don't understand in that moment is that Lake is and always will be an unfeeling psycho.

When I jump for the shot, he anticipates it. He's up before I am. He brings his hand down to block the ball, only he doesn't slap it away like we've been trained to do. No, he drives his hand down hard on top of the ball. My wrist bends back. Tendons pop and tear. A snap sounds.

I scream.

When we both land, he's still there pressing down on the ball in between us. My wrist yells in protest until his eyes cloud over and he just steps back. No one moves. No one speaks. The sound of the basketball bouncing away is the only thing I hear until chaos ensues.

Ryan runs out into the middle of the court. Lake's body goes flying until he skids on the unforgiving pavement. I bring my wrist to my chest and stare down at the awkward angle, tears in my eyes.

Oh no.

Everything I fought for in this camp, I see drain away from me with one look at my wrist.

My wrist. My *shooting* wrist.

I can't help the tears that come. I don't even hide

them as I look for my father through fractured vision. He runs toward me, holding me to his side.

Pain ricochets through me. I grit my teeth and bear down, so I don't cry out.

There's yelling behind us. I hear the coach who refereed the game shouting angry orders. My dad holds my head to his chest as he leads me away. Up ahead, his car looms into view. He hurries me there and places me in the passenger seat.

I throw my head back and cry then. My dad tries to peel my hand away from me, but it only makes me cry harder. "Please, Pumpkin," he says. "I have to put your seatbelt on."

I let my hand go for a split second while he pulls the belt around me. Then, I clutch it to me again, keeping pressure on it as it throbs. The pain is pulsing, and with each sharp jolt, I wrestle with what I know about wrist injuries. What's the recovery time? Is it bad like an ACL? What if I can't play anymore? Goddamnit!

When my dad gets into the driver's side, my head falls to the seat as I look over at him. Tears puddle and spill over. "Dad."

"I know, I know," he says, every bit as frustrated as I am. He starts the car and then throws it into reverse. The tires kick up tiny stones as he peels out of the camp. I hear him speak into his phone, "Nearest hospital to Holly Lake."

I look over just as we're passing the path to the outdoor courts. My Ballers are emerging. They watch me leave, faces like stone. I'll never forget those looks. I'll never forget the determination, the feelings conveyed, and the love in all three hard gazes.

This is it. I played with fire, and it's gotten me again. Only this time, I'm not walking away with nothing.

I close my eyes and replay the scene. The fury on Ryan's face as he threw himself at Lake.

Lake's taken it too far. There's no coming back from this.

It may have just been one-on-one out there, but it won't be for long. Welcome to five on one, Lake. I hope you enjoy getting a taste of your own medicine.

EPILOGUE

My eyes feel like sandpaper a couple of hours later. I've done enough crying for a lifetime in the span of a few hours. I have no answers about my wrist. Nothing concrete, yet. My dad's going to fly us to L.A., so we can go to a specialist he knows out there. He's supposedly the best of the best.

A hand touches my shoulder. I start, but it's just my dad. He's breaking me from the merry-go-round of my thoughts. "Ryan's here, honey. He wants to see you."

I swallow. "Yeah. Okay."

My dad's gaze moves to my bandaged wrist again, the sorrow evident in his eyes. "He drove your car here. I asked him to," he says quickly, like he expected me to get upset.

I shrug. It's not like I can do anything about my car right now.

Footsteps sound in the hallway. My dad steps back, excusing himself from the room as Ryan and the rest of the Ballers, minus fucking Lake O'Brien, of course, step in.

Hayes pushes past everyone first. "Are you okay?" He reaches for me, but then his hand falls to the bed when he can't decide where to touch me so it won't hurt.

Instead, I reach up to trace his cheekbones. "I'm okay. They have me on some good pain meds."

I've had x-rays here. It's just that this hospital is so small, there's no one around to read them yet. My dad won't trust their opinions anyway, which is why he's already been on the phone with the doctor's office in L.A.

My brain is hazy due to the meds. I'm thankful for it because it's not letting me feel the pain right now, but it's also not letting me think clearly either. "So, what happened? Did I win?"

The Ballers all exchange a look. Ryan comes forward then, even though Hayes doesn't give up his spot right next to me. "Coach Tanner disqualified him from the game. He declared you the winner."

A smile passes over my face. "That's good," I say. "That's what I wanted. MVP."

My stomach twists though. I know I didn't actually win it. Lake made sure of that.

Sloan comes around the other side of the bed and sits near my feet. He reaches his hand out and rests it on my calf. His eyes are heavy and sad. Every one of them refuse to look at my bandaged wrist.

"But overall?" I ask, looking at Ryan. "You won that, right?"

He looks away, his gray eyes shimmering in the corners. "I don't know. I think you're the only one who deserves it though."

I shake my head at that. "Nonsense. You've won it how many times in a row?"

"It doesn't matter, Tessa," he says, his voice like ice. He leans over my bed. "I'm a terrible fucking human being. I don't deserve awards."

I cock my head at him. "Don't say that. Let's ask my dad." I look around him, but Ryan shifts until he takes up my entire view again. My vision is getting fuzzy around the edges. Whatever pain relievers they gave me, they're working wonders. It's muting everything.

"Tessa," Ryan says, and it sounds as if my name is

ripped from his chest. "I should've seen what he was about to do. I don't know if you can ever forgive me."

I see the whole scene again. Me, jumping up for the basket. Lake bringing his hand down at that odd angle. I feel my wrist and the snapping again, but it's as if I'm an outside observer this time around.

I look around the small hospital room. None of the guys are looking at me. Their gazes are shifted away, shame heavy in their eyes. For the first time, I notice Alec is there. My heartrate speeds up. "You're here," I say. "Did your mom drive you?"

He turns his full attention toward me. Veins pop out of his arms, his face is sharp, angular, not bothering to hide his anger. When he doesn't say anything, I reach out for him. Immediately, he pushes past Ryan and moves toward me. He doesn't stop there, he stoops down, his fingers moving behind my head until he brings my face to his.

His heated lips envelop mine. The physical distance between us lately hasn't diminished our feelings for one another. He seals them into one hot kiss, delivering them to me with a passion that makes a noise catch in my throat.

"Alec," a voice says.

He pulls away, his gaze saying everything his mouth can't. "I'm so fucking sorry I left you."

"I'm fine," I tell him.

Realistically, I know that's not true. I just think I've been telling everyone that so much lately that I've started to believe it myself.

I'm not fucking fine. My wrist is fucked up, and I have no idea what the outcome of that will be.

"It's not your fucking fault. We were there."

My eyes dart to Sloan. He's biting down on his lower lip so hard I'm surprised he's not drawing blood. On instinct, I try to reach out to him with my closest hand, but it's my fucked-up hand. I hiss in a breath at the surge of pain.

Sloan looks at me like I'm killing him. He moves forward. I have enough time as he approaches to know he intends on kissing me, too. I let him take his time, his hazel eyes raking over me before he captures my lips in his. He kisses me tenderly, and I'm reminded of the boy who told me he's never said sorry in his life until me. He's saying it again with the caress of his lips against my own. I wait until he pulls away to tell him he doesn't have to apologize.

"I'll never not need to apologize," he says, his voice full of sorrow.

Hayes leans over me, dropping a kiss to my forehead. My gaze flicks to his. That quiet beast of anger in him is sitting close to the surface. When I look down, I see his knuckles are split again. I reach out with my good hand and take one of his in mine, careful not to touch the bruised skin. "Lake?" I ask.

"Don't say his fucking name."

"Hayes," Ryan snaps.

They exchange a look, and Hayes backs down, not before I bring his hand to my lips and kiss his broken skin. I close my eyes as I do so, willing with everything in me that he doesn't ever have to do that again. It's not him.

"Your mom will be here soon," Ryan says.

I've already spoken to her on the phone. I don't know what my dad told her happened, but she was a wreck. "You guys probably shouldn't be here when she comes. She doesn't like you guys very much."

Ryan nods quietly.

"You should drive my car back home. I don't think I'll be able to."

"If you want," Ryan says.

"Just be good to her," I smirk.

He doesn't fall into an easy smile himself. He still looks like a cross between sad and pissed.

"Where's Lake?" I ask.

All four of them at once look like they're going to explode. "He's none of your concern, Tessa," Ryan says. "We'll take care of him."

I've waited ages to hear those words in some form or another. I would've even settled for an agreement to ignore one another, but it's progressed far past that. Not even the strength of these pain meds can make what he did to me go away.

"I want him to suffer."

Ryan peeks at Hayes's fist.

"More," I say.

"He will," Alec promises.

"He won't go away quietly," Ryan says, as if he's noting an opinion he's long had.

"Neither will we," Hayes says.

I feel the intensity of all their stares on me. I'm going into senior year more or less how I wanted. The Ballers are with me. I've gotten them back. But for the life of me, I can't find it in me to care. I may have traded in my entire career just for the chance to have one in the first place.

I see red.

They all reach for me. Their hands touching whatever they can grasp onto. In the brush of their fingertips, I feel the inclusion I always wanted. My heart hardens around them, keeping this moment inside me forever. I'm no longer worried they'll turn their backs on me. They won't.

"He'll pay, Tessa."

I'm not sure which one utters it because the pain meds have finally taken their toll on me. I blink rapidly, trying to stay awake, trying to stay conscious in every moment I have with them, but it's a losing battle.

"Shh, baby. Go to sleep. We'll be here when you wake up."

The End

If you enjoy a badass female main character, UPPERCUT PRINCESS will be right up your alley!

About the Author

E. M. Moore is a USA Today Bestselling author of Contemporary and Paranormal Romance. She's drawn to write within the teen and college-aged years where her characters get knocked on their asses, torn inside out, and put back together again by their first loves. Whether it's in a fantastical setting where human guards protect the creatures of the night or a realistic high school backdrop where social cliques rule the halls, the emotions are the same. Dark. Twisty. Angsty. Raw.

When Erin's not writing, you can find her dreaming up vacations for her family, watching murder mystery shows, or dancing in her kitchen while she pretends to cook.

Printed in Great Britain
by Amazon

24424478R00229